Blue Water

Manette Ansay

headline
review

First published in Great Britain in 2006 by Headline REVIEW
An imprint of Headline Book Publishing

First published in paperback in 2006 by HEADLINE REVIEW

A HEADLINE REVIEW paperback

1

Cataloguing in Publication Data is available from the British Library

ISBN 0 7553 2989 9

Typeset in Perpetua and Din by Avon DataSet Ltd,
Bidford-on-Avon, Warwickshire

Printed and bound in Great Britain by Clays Ltd, St Ives plc

Headline's policy is to use papers that are natural, renewable and recyclable
products and made from wood grown in sustainable forests. The logging and
manufacturing processes are expected to conform to the environmental
regulations of the country of origin.

Headline Book Publishing
A division of Hodder Headline
338 Euston Road
London NW1 3BH

www.reviewbooks.co.uk
www.hodderheadline.com

For Jake Smith;

for Genevieve;

for the cruisers we met along the way;

for my longtime editor, Claire Wachtel, who waited for this one so patiently; and with thanks to the people involved in making my new life possible and whole: Arya Nielsen, Surendra Patel, Deborah Schneider, Dr Erika Schwartz, and Oprah Winfrey, whose kindness set in motion the experiences that launched Blue Water.

Thanks to Ted Doran for Top Billing, to David Hartmann for the table saw, and to KD for a story that affected me deeply. I'm indebted to Scott Rost for his legal expertise and to Diane Goodman for a swift final read. Extra special thanks to 'no rules, no fear' Sylvia J. Ansay for hundreds of hours of last-minute babysitting.

And enduring love and gratitude to Ann Patchett and Karl VanDevender.

You can spend a year at sea waiting, but one day it becomes impossible to endure even another hour.

Gabriel García Márquez, *The Story of a Shipwrecked Sailor*

Part One | Chelone

Chapter One

Forget what you've read about the ocean. Forget white sails on a blue horizon, the romance of it, the beauty. A picnic basket in a quiet anchorage, the black-tipped flash of gulls. The sound of the wind like a pleasant song, the curved spine of the coast—

—no.

Such images belong to shore. They have nothing whatsoever to do with the sea.

Imagine a place of infinite absence. An empty ballroom, the colors muted, the edges lost in haze. The sort of dream you have when you've gone beyond exhaustion to a strange, otherworldly country, a place I'd visited once before in the months that followed the birth of my son, when days and nights blurred into a single lost cry, when I'd find myself standing over the crib, or rocking him, breathing the musk of his hair, or lying in bed beside Rex's dark shape, unable to recall how I'd gotten there. As if I'd been plucked out of one life and dropped, wriggling and whole, into another. Day after day, week after week, the lack of sleep takes its toll. You begin to see things that may or may not be there. You understand how the sailors of old so willingly met their deaths on the rocks, believing in visions of beautiful women, sirens, mermaids with long, sparkling hair.

The crest of a wave becomes a human face, open-mouthed, white-eyed, astonished. The spark of a headlight appears in the sky, edges closer, fades, edges closer still. There's a motion off the bow, and I clutch at the helm, catch myself thinking, *Turn!*

But, eventually, I learn to let my eyes fall out of focus. Blink, look again. Wipe my sweating face. There is nothing out there but gray waves, gray waves.

Clouds. A translucent slice of moon.

Space.

We alternated watches, Rex and I: four hours on, four hours off. We had a ship's clock that rang out the hours. We had charts and a sextant, a handheld GPS. We had an outdated radar system; we had a small refrigerator, a water maker, clothing and books sealed in plastic wrap. We had five hundred pounds of canned goods, nuts, dried fruit and beans, powdered milk.

We had a ship's log, where we jotted down notes: latitude and longitude, course and speed, wind direction, weather, unusual observations.

We had a float plan, which we left with my brother, Toby;

he posted it in the fish store, on the bulletin board behind the cash register. People stopped by with farewell gifts: cookies sealed in Tupperware, a book of crossword puzzles, religious cards, funny cards, cards simply wishing us well. Everyone in Fox Harbor knew why we were leaving, of course, and this was another reason why I'd agreed to rent our house and move onto the sailboat Rex had bought in Portland, Maine. Our first destination was Bermuda, our ETA three to five weeks. From Bermuda, we'd continue southeast to the Bahamas, island-hop down to the Caicos. Perhaps we'd winter over in Puerto Rico. Or perhaps we'd cross the ocean to Portugal — who could say? We might even head to Panama, pass through the canal, find our way north along the coast to the Mexican Bajas. So much depended on weather, on wind. On our own day-to-day inclinations.

The plan, Rex liked to tell people, is not to have a plan.

It had always been Rex's dream to live aboard a sailboat, and *Chelone* was exactly the boat that he had wanted. A blue water boat, he called her. A boat built to sail around the world. He'd grown up on Cape Cod, sailing with his father; at twenty, he was captain of his college sailing team, and before heading west to Madison for law school, he'd worked as a mate aboard a private schooner, cruising the Virgin Islands. On cold winter nights as we lay in bed, listening to the east wind screaming off Lake Michigan, he'd tell me about the islands he'd seen, casuarina trees and pink sand beaches, sailboats at anchor outside each rustic harbor. Passing these boats, you'd see dogs racing from bow to stern, bicycles lashed to the safety lines, laundry fluttering from the rigging. Entire families spent their whole lives just cruising from place to place, dropping anchor wherever they chose. No bills to pay, no responsibilities. You didn't like your neighbor, no problem, you sailed away.

Maybe, he'd whisper, his breath warm against my neck, we could do the same thing someday.

I like our neighbors fine, Rex.

Seriously.

I am serious.

At the time, I couldn't imagine saying good-bye to Toby, to my friends at the accounting firm where I worked, to our fieldstone house overlooking the lake, to the small Wisconsin town where I'd been raised. Still, after years spent trying to conceive a child, after the shots and surgeries, the herbal teas, the special masses; after trying to adopt the infant of a teenage girl who changed her mind, I started to pay more attention whenever Rex talked about heading to sea. I leafed through his copies of *Practical Sailor*, his scrapbook of sail plans and hull designs. I studied the glossy brochures he received from boat builders around the world. I'd always enjoyed sailing, and though I'd only sailed on the Great Lakes, I figured that the ocean couldn't be all that different. Water was water, after all. You wore a life jacket. You learned to hang on.

Then, one week before my fortieth birthday, I discovered I was pregnant with Evan. After eleven years of marriage, we were finally — unexpectedly — about to have a child. Our plans no longer belonged to us, and the truth was that we gave them up eagerly. We wanted to make sacrifices. We wanted to shake our heads ruefully, saying, *But then we had the baby so we couldn't . . .*

Six years later, our lives changed again, when Evan was killed in a car accident involving someone I'd known since grade school. Someone whose birthday parties I'd attended. Someone who, the summer I turned sixteen, became my closest friend before our lives diverged, abruptly, the way the lives of young girls do. Someone who'd left her family's farm to marry a man much older than herself and build a magnificent house on the lake that was featured in magazines. Someone who, twenty years after that, was driving her own three daughters to school when her life intersected with my own once more, this time irrevocably, permanently.

It was 7:55 in the morning. It was three weeks before Christmas, 1999. Crows rose out of a hawthorn bush as I slowed for the right turn onto County C, glossy feathers like fingertips, stroking the milky air. The thin black swoop of telephone wires. The smell of Evan's cough drops, eucalyptus flavored, sweet. He'd been out of school since Thanksgiving, confined by a stubborn case of bronchitis, and I still had my doubts about whether or not he was quite ready to go back.

But he'd begged, cajoled, pleaded, not wanting to miss any more school, and the truth was that I was just as eager to return to work. My cubicle, across from my good friend Lindsey Steinke. My files, my favorite coffee mug, my ergonomic chair. Though I'd worked from home when Evan was younger, I never got as much done in the breakfast nook we referred to, generously, as my *office*, as I did when surrounded by colleagues, friends, everybody red-eyed and commiserating over the end-of-the-year crunch.

'If your cough starts acting up,' I said, 'ask Mrs Hochman to let you see the nurse.'

Evan said, 'Do you know what they call a group of crows?'

'Promise me,' I said, accelerating onto the straightaway, and he said, pieces of cough drop clicking against his teeth, 'A *murder* of crows.'

'Is that right?' I said.

He said, 'Do you know what they call a group of buzzards?'

We lived just a few miles from the elementary school, which was new; beside it, the middle school was still under construction. In a matter of just a few years, County C – which ran east and west – had evolved from a sleepy back road into a busy rural highway. At the remains of the old brick schoolhouse, where my grandparents learned their ABCs, a second highway, known as the Point Road, ran to the north and south. This intersection had always been dangerous, County C yielding the right of way, which meant you had to slow just as the slope of the hill pulled you forward. But with the schools coming in, C had gained, at last, the upper hand. Now you could ride the curve, down and down, passing beneath the flashing yellow light, until you reached the foot of the hill. Weekday mornings, cars lined up a quarter mile to turn into the school yard, everybody dropping their kids off at the flagpole in front of the principal's office.

That morning, we were running late, Evan and I. The roads were strangely empty. The power had gone off during the night – nothing much, just a blip – but enough to disable our bedside clock and, with it, the alarm.

'Let me drop Evan on my way to work,' Rex said, watching me fly around the kitchen like a madwoman, but it wasn't on his way. Rex's law firm was in Milwaukee, while Lakeview Accounting was right in Fox Harbor, three doors from the fish store, five minutes from Evan's school.

'It's okay,' I said. 'We'll get there.'

We'll get there. Looking back, it strikes me as an odd thing to have said. Because, of course, we didn't.

I was coming up on the intersection when the old brick schoolhouse caught my eye and, just beyond it, headlights. People tended to forget that the Point Road, now, had the posted yield. That's why I observed those lights, noted them, tucked them away in my head. That's why I made absolutely certain that the vehicle, an SUV, was slowing deliberately, significantly, before I let myself glance away.

'A group of buzzards is a wake,' Evan said, and I grinned at him in the rearview.

'I used to know that one,' I said.

'What about a group of magpies?'

He'd been born, so it seemed to us, loving words. He'd been reading since the age of two. For the past few weeks, he'd been writing little stories as he lay on the couch, his smooth, narrow chest slick with Vicks. *How do you spell marsupial?* he'd asked me one morning, and I'd had to call Rex at work, smothering my laughter, whispering into the phone so that Evan wouldn't hear.

'How *do* you spell it?' Rex had said.

'What the hell is it, anyway? A monkey, right?'

'No, a kangaroo.'

'I thought a kangaroo was a kind of rat.'

There I was in the kitchen, doubled over with laughter and pride. Above the sink, the cuckoo clock chimed. Already, the gods had closed their eyes.

More crows rising, wheeling. The blinking yellow light ahead absorbed as if by cotton. My mind busy with the day to come, the work that was waiting for me, Christmas shopping. Would we visit my parents in Florida this year? Rex still didn't know if he'd be able to take the time. Already, it was the third of December. We hadn't reserved our flight.

'A ponder of magpies?' I guessed, and Evan said, 'A gulp,' and I was lying under bright lights, my neck immobilized, naked from the waist up. I do not remember the moment we were struck. I do not remember Cindy Ann Kreisler – I'd known her as Cindy Ann Donaldson – continuing to accelerate after hitting Evan and me, pushing our Taurus twenty feet along the Point Road before we spun free, flipped 180 degrees, plunged down into the gulley. Evan's neck was broken. I broke my right ankle and the bridge of my nose, cracked several ribs, bit through my tongue. Cindy Ann's three daughters were treated for minor bumps and bruises, while Cindy Ann herself complained of a stiff neck, a headache that – she told a triage nurse – was probably *just a hangover*. Her blood alcohol level, determined two hours after the crash, was barely within Wisconsin's legal limit.

Why hadn't any of the officers at the scene administered a Breathalyzer promptly? Why had it taken a nudge from that triage nurse to get it done? We would learn, Rex and I, that Cindy Ann had been argumentative, angry, cursing the paramedics who examined her daughters as they crouched by the roadside, stunned, hugging their school backpacks. Eventually, one of the officers, Randy Metz, had confined her to his squad car. He was a slow-eyed, heavyset, awkward-looking man, someone who, like Cindy Ann, I'd known since childhood. In court, he would say that no one had tested Cindy Ann because, well, they'd been busy with the injured.

And after the paramedics arrived?

'To be truthful,' Randy said, looking directly at me, 'it

never did cross my mind. You just don't guess a person like that has anything to drink about so early in the morning.'

I took a leave of absence from Lakeview Accounting, then extended it, extended it again. Even after the swelling in my face had subsided. Even after I could sleep lying down, hobble around the house. The live-in nurse we'd hired went home. Rex went back to work. My father returned for my mother, who'd stayed on after the funeral to help. She did not fly — refused to even consider it — so the two of them drove all the way back to Miami, to the planned community where they'd retired: identical townhomes with red tile rooftops, sidewalks spooling around a series of landscaped preserves. Three times a week, then twice, then once, Toby drove me to physical therapy in Horton while his girlfriend, Mallory Donaldson, filled in for him at the fish store, manning the register, answering the phone. We did not talk about Mallory, who just happened to be Cindy Ann's youngest sister. We did not talk about the accident, or Evan, or anything else, for that matter. At the time, I was not yet angry. Shame had lodged itself in my throat, a lump that could not be swallowed. How could I have survived, and with relatively minor injuries, while my six-year-old child, in his top-rated booster seat, died after reaching the hospital?

I didn't want to see anyone. I didn't pick up the phone. Neighbors stopped by with casseroles, but I did not let them in. Even when Lindsey circled the house, calling at the windows, I kept silent. I couldn't imagine facing people, accepting, with grace, all their genuine sorrow for Rex and me. And when I finally did venture out again, I was careful to avoid the lakefront park, the Cup and Cruller Café, the bicycle path that wound along the bluff, places where, holding Evan's warm hand, I'd occasionally encountered Cindy Ann.

Hey, you, she'd always say, as if she'd been expecting me, and she'd give her long, blond ponytail a flip. She'd ask after Toby and my parents: I'd ask after her mom, her sisters. By then, the older man was long dead; Cindy Ann had remarried and divorced, married, divorced again. Through it all, however, she'd kept his name, as well as the house, which stood less than a mile from our own: a mansion, a showplace, the sort of home that people, even strangers from Milwaukee, drove to Fox Harbor to see. After I could drive again, I always took the southern route into town, so I wouldn't have to pass it, but Rex made a point of driving that way as he went to work in the morning and, again, as he came home at night. He reported that the shades were always up, the lights always on, as if Cindy Ann were inviting anybody to look inside and see how *her* life hadn't changed since the accident. A fat Angora cat snoozed in the bay window; roses bloomed in the greenhouse; an American flag fluttered from a mount at the side of the garage. Evenings, you could see the blue light of the TV, and the bent, blond head of Cindy Ann as she dished out the evening meal. And, too — more than once — the outline of a wine bottle, a slender long-necked glass. Rex was certain that Cindy Ann was still drinking. Still getting into her car in the morning, regardless of how much she'd had the night before, what time she'd gone to bed.

'I hope she chokes on it,' he said, sitting down to our own empty table. 'Christ.' He pushed his plate away.

'Stop driving past her house,' I said, 'if it bothers you so much.'

But I didn't mean it, not really. The truth was that I, too, savored each detail Rex excised from Cindy Ann's life with a surgeon's care: the new pink bicycle that appeared in the driveway; a second cat, another Angora, napping on top of the newly repaired Suburban; the small, pale face in an upstairs window, looking out at Rex until he drove away. Just as he'd feared, the delayed Breathalyzer had worked in Cindy Ann's favor. At the arraignment, Cindy Ann pleaded guilty to involuntary manslaughter; jail time was suspended in exchange for community service, driving school, and twelve months of counseling for substance abuse. As far as Rex and I were concerned, she'd gotten away with murder. And, judging from letters to the editor that ran in the parish bulletin, in the *Harbor Pilot*, in the county paper published in Sheboygan, nearly everyone in Fox Harbor agreed.

Excepting Cindy Ann's two sisters, of course. They were quick to counter with letters of their own; this was to be expected. What we did not expect was that the worst of these letters, the most hurtful, would come from Mallory herself. It could hardly be supposed, Mallory wrote, that Cindy Ann set out to harm anybody. Yes, she'd had too much to drink the night before, but who hasn't woken up with a hangover, taken two aspirin, jumped in the car? Who, after all, hasn't made a mistake?

> *I've known Rex and Megan Van Dorn a long time, and while I feel for the tragedy they have experienced, I don't see how they can possibly believe that destroying my sister's life — not to mention the lives of her children — will make up for the loss of their son. What happened was an accident. It wasn't deliberate. It wasn't personal.*

And then—

> *The only deliberate, personal attack was the one that took place in court.*

Sallow-faced Mallory Donaldson, with her animal rights petitions, her aggressive vegetarianism — the result, we all supposed, of growing up on a farm that raised veal. Summers, she traveled around the Midwest, selling handmade jewelry at flea markets and craft fairs. Winters, she washed dishes at the Cup and Cruller, dressed in flannel shirts and shit-kicker boots, a man's synthetic cap pulled low over her forehead. Yet, Toby had fallen in love with her. They'd been together for almost two years. Every now and then, they'd even babysat for Evan.

'I can't take sides on this,' Toby said, after the letter appeared. 'Not against her. Not against you.'

Everything, now, seemed poisoned. Pointless. Mornings, I'd wake up, stare out the window at the naked, gray shoreline, littered with fat chunks of ice.

What, I thought, do I do next?

The sun coming up and going down again. The clock tick-ticking on the wall.

Shortly after Cindy Ann's sentencing, I wrote my letter of resignation to Lakeview Accounting. 'Take a little more time to decide,' Lindsey pleaded, filling all the tape on our answering machine. 'Let's talk over lunch, okay? C'mon, I'll meet you at the Shanty, my treat.'

But I didn't want to have lunch with Lindsey. And I'd already made up my mind. I was going to do something else, something different, though I didn't know what that might be. I thought about starting a business. I thought about going back to school. I even thought about working for Toby at the fish store, the way I'd done in high school: keeping his books, doing his taxes, helping him with the charter fishing trips he ran on summer weekends aboard his boat, the *Michigan Jack*.

But since Mallory's letter, I'd kept my distance – from the fish store and, now that I was driving again, from Toby, too – and, at any rate, I wanted to move forward in my life, not step back into the past.

My mother invited me to Florida. 'A change of scene,' she said. She'd stopped asking if I'd seen Toby lately; like my father, she'd decided to ignore the rupture between us. After years spent building Hauskindler Stone and Brick, they'd sold out to a Chicago-based firm. Now they devoted the same fierce attention to retirement that, once, they'd devoted to the family business. Throughout my childhood, they'd worked twelve-hour days, leaving Toby – ten years my senior – to fix my supper, help with homework, read to me, tuck me into bed. He'd been more like a parent to me than a brother. More like a parent than my parents had been. Until recently, I'd never felt this as a loss.

'Rex could come, too,' my mother said. 'We'd take good care of you.'

I told her I'd think it over.

But Rex was a partner at his firm; he couldn't take time now, after all he'd already missed. And I was afraid to leave him on his own, picking at frozen dinners, flipping through channel after channel on TV. Shortly after the criminal verdict, we'd filed a civil suit against Cindy Ann, as well as the city of Fox Harbor, the police department, Officer Randy Metz. This triggered a new round of letters to the editor, fresh arguments at the Cup and Cruller, where everyone, Rex said, fell silent now when he stopped in for his usual to-go. Because this time, he'd hired Arnie Babcock, a friend of a friend, an attorney who was known far and wide for exacting extraordinary damages. In the past, Rex and I had both referred to attorneys like Arnie as ambulance chasers, opportunists who lined their pockets with other people's grief. Now, Rex called Arnie a genius, and the first time I'd looked into his broad, handsome face, I, too, found myself feeling as if we'd finally found someone who cared about us, who'd fight for us, someone who understood.

Cindy Ann Kreisler, Arnie said, had robbed our home like the worst kind of thief. We couldn't ask an eye for an eye, but we could demand her assets, teach her to regret what she'd done. Of course, Arnie understood this wasn't about money; still, why should Cindy Ann continue to enjoy a comfortable life while we, the innocent party, were left suffering, uncompensated, forgotten? We could donate any funds we received to charity. Or, perhaps, start a scholarship in Evan's name. Only then would we find some kind of closure. We'd finally begin to let go. We'd come to accept what had happened at the intersection of the Point Road and County C, where Evan's teachers and classmates had erected a small, white cross.

At last, I thought, we were getting somewhere. We had a plan in place. There would finally be justice, resolution, just the way Arnie promised.

And yet, instead of feeling better, Rex and I only felt worse. Night after night, he muttered, twisted, unable to fall asleep, while I sat reading the same page of the same book over and over again. That none of Cindy Ann's three girls had been injured! It was just so unbelievable, Rex said, so ironic, so goddamn unfair. Even if she lost her house — and she would, Arnie had promised us that — she'd have those girls long after she'd forgotten about us, and she would forget, Rex was sure of this, he dealt with people like Cindy Ann all the time. She was a drunk, she'd had those girls by different fathers, she probably hadn't even wanted the last one anyway. On and on he went, rising to pace between the bed and the big bay window overlooking the lake. Rex, who was so gentle, so elegantly soft-spoken. Rex, who'd worked as a public defender for his first five years out of law school, protecting the rights of murderers and rapists, drug dealers and thieves. Not that I didn't understand. In fact, I agreed with everything he said. Mornings, I woke with an ache in my throat, a sourness in my stomach, that had nothing to do with Evan. The truth was that, with each passing month, he was harder to remember, harder to see. I felt as if I were grasping at the color of water, the color of the wind or the sky.

And this only made me angrier. My mind returned, again and again, to Cindy Ann, to what she'd done. When I passed Evan's room, the closed door like a fist, I thought about how Cindy Ann had destroyed us. When I saw other people's children, I promised myself that someday, Cindy Ann would pay. When I managed to get myself to mass, I always lit a candle for Evan, but as I knelt before the flickering light, my prayers were for vengeance, my words red with blood. I imagined choking Cindy Ann, beating her with my fists. I had dreams in which I walked up to her front door with a gun. I constructed scenes in which she begged my forgiveness, even as I turned my face away.

I would never have guessed myself capable of hating another human being the way I hated Cindy Ann Kreisler: virulently, violently. How can I explain the sheer cathartic power of such rage? Whenever I gave myself over to its spell, I felt nothing but that one, pure thing. The nuances of sorrow, of guilt, of grief, burned away like so much kindling. I was terrible in my anger: strong, and fierce, and righteous. I could have led an army. I could have marched for days without food, bootless, euphoric, mile after mile.

'Maybe you could get some kind of counseling,' Lindsey said, when, at last, I joined her at the Shanty, sliding into my usual seat at our usual table overlooking the harbor. My fish fry had arrived, but I couldn't touch a bite of it. Until then, Lindsey had been doing her best to hold up both ends of the conversation, chattering about her husband, Barton, the golfing lessons he'd gotten her for Christmas. Bart was an avid golfer, and he was always trying to interest Lindsey in the sport. Usually this amused me, but today I just stared out the dirty windows, wishing I hadn't agreed to come, wishing Lindsey would do something about the gray, puffy coat and piano keyboard scarf she'd been wearing for the past ten years.

'Why should *I* get counseling?' I snapped. 'I haven't done anything wrong.'

'It's *counseling*,' Lindsey said. 'Not punishment. I just think it might help you feel better—'

'Feel *better*?' I said. 'When the person who murdered my child is walking around, free as air? When *we* have to face the rest of our lives in this *prison*, this—'

I was too angry to finish.

'I'm sorry,' Lindsey said, quietly. 'It was just a suggestion.' She began looking for her keys, digging around in her oversize purse. 'I hate to see you suffering, that's all.'

Early in May, on our first warm day of the year, I saw Cindy Ann and her oldest girl, Amy, in the grocery store. Five months had passed since the accident. There they were, standing in front of the dairy case, picking out a carton of ice cream. *Ice cream*. It seemed inexcusable, unbearable, that they should indulge themselves in such pleasures, that they should enjoy themselves, in any way, ever again. I took a step toward them, and with that, Cindy Ann saw me. There was nothing in her face, not sorrow, not guilt or fear. She simply stared at me, hands at her sides, waiting for whatever it was I might say.

'You—' I began, the word squeezed from my throat, and then I was running out of the store, into the parking lot, the asphalt spinning beneath me. I got into my car, another Taurus – it still smelled of its awful newness – and sat for a moment, gasping, gripping the steering wheel with both hands. I could see the double doors leading in and out of the store; Cindy Ann would emerge at any minute now, Amy beside her, the ice cream carton swinging in its plastic bag. All I'd have to do was wait until she entered the crosswalk, and then—

I blinked. I was sweating hard. There was still no sign of Cindy Ann. I pulled out of the parking space slowly, cautiously, making sure to signal when I reached the end of the row.

That night, I did not tell Rex that I'd fantasized about running Cindy Ann Kreisler down with my car. Instead, I told him about the ice cream, about the way Cindy Ann had looked at me: without remorse, blankly, indifferently.

'Oh, she'll be remorseful all right,' Rex said. 'Her days are numbered, believe me.'

Arnie had hired a private investigator to find out if she was, in fact, still drinking; if she ever raised her voice to her kids; if she drove within the speed limit. This guy was the best, Arnie'd worked with him before, and if Cindy Ann so much as sneezed, we were going to find out about it. By the time Arnie was done with her, Rex promised, she'd wish that *she'd* died in the crash.

And I said: 'That isn't good enough.'

And Rex said, 'Nothing could be.'

The ugliness of those words. I stared down at my hands, horrified, as if they were not my own. At that moment, I began to suspect the truth: we would never be satisfied. We might tear the flesh from Cindy Ann's limbs with our teeth, strip by bloody strip, and still, it would be insufficient. In the end, we'd be animals, worse than animals. I thought about how I'd felt, sitting in the parking lot of the grocery store, my hands gripping the wheel like talons. I thought about how, whenever I tried to remember my son, I wound up thinking of Cindy Ann's daughters instead, hating them simply for drawing breath. I thought about Randy Metz, the way he'd looked at me in court.

'I can't live like this,' I said.

The following morning, I told Rex that I wanted to let the civil suits go.

'You don't mean it,' he said, scraping butter onto his toast. 'You're tired. So am I. But it's important that we follow this through.'

There were lilacs in water on the table, bunches of red and yellow tulips on the counter. In the window, the last of my hyacinths were just past their peak, releasing their sweet, sweet smell.

'Since when,' I said, 'are you the sort of person who tells other people what they do and do not mean?'

He got to his feet, drained his coffee in a gulp. 'We'll talk about this later.'

I got up, too. 'Call Arnie,' I said. 'I mean it, Rex. I'm finished.'

'And what should I tell him? That we're letting a murderer off the hook? That we're sorry for wasting his time?'

'Tell him I won't participate. Tell him I'll refuse to testify.'

Rex stared at me. 'You'd sabotage the case. You know that.'

'I do.'

He pushed past me into the hall, grabbed his briefcase from the stand, stood before the mirror to adjust his tie. On the opposite wall hung a framed photo of Evan, bundled into a red snowsuit, laughing. I thought of my father's belief that the dead were always with us, always watching, and I hoped with all my heart that he was wrong.

'Fine,' Rex said, abruptly. A pale blue vein divided his forehead.

'What does that mean?' I said.

'It means *fine*.' He pounded his fists against his thighs, hips, chest; it took me a moment to realize he was looking for his keys. 'It means that I don't want to argue with you right now, okay? It means that I don't fucking want to argue.'

'They're on the stand,' I said.

He snatched them up in a clatter. 'Only think about what you're saying,' he said. 'I'm pleading with you. Because we're going to have to live with this for the rest of our lives.'

'We're going to have to live with it anyway,' I said.

'Not if we win.'

'It doesn't change anything.'

'Of course it does,' Rex said. 'We live here, Meg. In this town. With people who know everything about us, who will always be looking at us and saying, Remember when their kid got killed?'

I laughed, bitterly, bitingly. 'Right. And remember how they sued us because of it?'

'Remember,' Rex said, landing hard on each word, 'how they just lay down and took it? How they didn't have the stomach to make certain the same thing wouldn't happen to somebody else?'

For a moment, neither of us said anything.

'I don't want to live here anymore,' I said.

I hadn't known I was going to say it.

Rex looked at me. 'You mean it?'

I nodded.

He nodded, too. 'Okay, then,' he said. 'Okay.'

We studied each other in the mirror, a middle-aged man and woman, each sallow-skinned with exhaustion. Shadows like bruises beneath the man's eyes. Abruptly, he reached for the woman. The woman's hands rose to rest lightly, uncertainly, on his broad, shaking back.

'Okay.'

Later, I put on a pair of old jeans and a T-shirt and went out into the garden. The cool mud rose between my bare toes; I bent to clean out the choked iris beds, the daffodils and peonies. But I felt nothing, cared for nothing. I could not concentrate. Inside the house, on the answering machine, there were messages from Lindsey, from Toby, from St Clare's – would I chair the festival committee again this year? – and I knew that I needed to call people back, get out of the house, make a life for myself. Instead, I sat back on my heels, staring out across the bluff at the water. My ankle ached, but I didn't change position. It seemed right to me that it should hurt. A single sailboat tacked to and fro, following the outline of the coast, and suddenly, I wished with all my heart that Rex and I were on it, far away from everyone and everything we knew.

Evan was gone. Living with that knowledge was like living with the sound of someone screaming inside my head. By the time we left Fox Harbor, seven months after the accident, I couldn't imagine silence anymore. It was as if the screaming sound had always been there.

Chapter Two

We left Portland harbor on the Fourth of July, entering the Gulf of Maine in fog so thick that Rex sent me up to *Chelone*'s bow to watch for channel markers. The markers were equipped with bells, in addition to flashing lights, and whenever I heard something, I'd turn my head, shout back to Rex's gray shape at the helm, and he'd slow us down and down until, at last, the marker materialized. Hunched as a demon. Blinking red eye. The fog warped every sound, transformed the tolling bells into distinctly human cries. As the day passed into evening, we heard the muted thump of fireworks, but we saw nothing, just the gradual seal of dusk, the visible world dwindling close, closer still.

Chelone. Rex had found the name in a book of Greek mythology: Chelone had been one of Zeus's many nymphs. When she refused to attend his wedding – out of jealousy, out of grief – Zeus punished her by turning her into a giant turtle. From then on she was homeless, forced to roam the world without rest, carrying everything she owned upon her back.

'Isn't it unlucky?' I'd asked. 'Naming a boat after someone who was cursed?'

By then, we'd found someone to rent our house. We'd sold Rex's car and put mine on blocks, cashed in our mutual funds. We'd hired Lindsey Steinke to deposit checks, pay bills, keep an eye on our finances. Our personal items sat boxed in the attic, the flotsam and jetsam of twenty years of marriage: photo albums and clothing, a celedon vase from our trip to Korea, the tumbleweed that Rex had carried all the way home from New Mexico. Evan's baby toys, folders of drawings. The story he'd been writing on the day he'd asked me to spell *marsupial*.

'Maybe it was a curse in the beginning,' Rex said. 'But, think about it, Meg. Suddenly she's free to do whatever she wants.'

Tears stung my eyes. We were on our way to the bank. In the morning, we'd carry the certified check to the airport, get on a plane, taxi to the marina where our new life waited for us.

'I don't want to be free,' I said.

It took us hours to creep through the channel. By the time the fog finally lifted, the lights of the coast were out of sight. It was dark now, and cold. Rex was on watch. I opened my sleeping bag and lay down in the cockpit, too queasy to go below. The stars came out in misty sheets. Long, thin clouds trapped the moon's narrow eye. With each tall swell, its pointed chin bobbled, nodded, until it seemed close enough to touch. Suddenly, I was a child again, staring up at my mother, who was bending over me. And then, I was a mother myself, looking down at Evan as he slept. The fine, downy hairs on his cheeks. The coffee-colored birthmark inside his elbow. A pane of clear glass stood between us; I reached out to push it aside—

—and there were Cindy Ann Kreisler's girls, sitting by the highway in the frost-covered weeds. In the distance, Cindy Ann was screaming, telling the officers she'd done nothing, I was the one at fault. The sky filled with purple clouds, arranging and rearranging themselves, spectacular and strange. I thought it must be a message, but when I tried to understand, something seemed to press down on my chest, and then there was the lurch of being lifted into the ambulance.

My baby, I said.

Don't worry, the paramedic said. Jesus loves us all.

I blinked up at him: had I heard him right? Black bits of razor stubble peppered his chin. A gold cross ticked at his throat.

I awoke to see Rex's dark shape at the helm. For a moment, I didn't remember where I was. Then a wave splashed up against the bulwark, misting my forehead and cheeks. *Oh*, I thought. *This.*

'What is it?' I said, wriggling out of my sleeping bag.

A clean, white light shimmered on the horizon.

'Tanker,' Rex said. 'It'll pass off our port side. Were you able to sleep?'

'A little,' I said. The light seemed to be getting closer, but it was difficult to say. Above us, clouds hung in a loosely woven net, backlit by the waxing moon. 'Do you think they can see us?'

'Doubt it. We're too low in the water to show up on their radar.'

'I was dreaming about Evan,' I said.

He looked at me. 'A good dream?'

I tried to decide. 'Better than nothing,' I said.

Lying in bed shortly after his death, flipping through channel after channel on TV, I'd discovered a cable show in which a man communicated messages from the dead to members of an audience. *Is somebody here in this section*, he'd say, *who has a relative, an uncle? A father? Yes? I'm getting something about Andrea, Amelia . . . Angela? Are you Angela? Yes? Your father wants you to know about the kitchen door — does this make sense? Yes? He's telling you everything's all right now, you shouldn't worry. Do you understand this message?*

I'd been raised on stories about the saints, visions of angels, the literal voice of God. After the funeral, after my injuries healed, after my parents returned to Florida and Rex went back to work, I'd been stunned by the mounting silence that followed, day after day, in which I saw nothing, sensed nothing; in which even my dreams were meaningless, gray. One moment, I was a mother, driving her son to school. *A gulp,* he'd said, and I was stripped to the waist, unable to turn my head. Somewhere else, someone else. Completely.

Do you understand this message?

Rex was squinting through the binoculars again. 'Would you take a look at this thing?' he said. 'Now it doesn't seem to be moving at all.'

I took the binoculars, forced myself to concentrate. It took me a moment to find the light, which was not a single light at all, but two lights, one red, one green. The green light shimmered on my right. Which meant—

'Start the engine,' Rex said, in a strange, calm voice. 'They're heading right toward us.'

Everything seemed to be happening very slowly. I climbed down the companionway, fumbled the key into the ignition. The motor coughed, caught. Even before I got back into the cockpit, *Chelone* was moving faster, sails snapping in the artificial breeze. By now we both could see the tanker clearly; it was cutting through the waves with remarkable speed. Moments later, it passed less than a hundred feet in our wake, its own wake rocking us violently. Then, it was behind us, a dwindling pair of lights. A single light growing smaller and smaller. A blip on the horizon.

Gone.

I turned to Rex, and he put his arms around me; I buried

my nose in his neck. We stood that way for a long time, not speaking. His body against mine was both familiar and strange; he smelled of the ocean and, inexplicably, warm bread.

'Kiss me?' I asked Rex, and then his mouth was on mine, salty, his chin stubbled and rough. We reset the autohelm and lay down together on my wet sleeping bag, carefully, trying to move with the waves, but it was a clumsy business, and we knocked elbows and foreheads and knees before finding a soft, slow rhythm all our own. Looking up into Rex's face, I was struck by his beauty, his high cheekbones and almond eyes, as if I were seeing him for the first time. It wasn't that we hadn't made love since Evan's death, but we'd done so perfunctorily, efficiently. It was like the meals we cooked and ate together, night after night, without appetite. The body had its needs and you met them. You put one foot in front of the other. You kept going, out of dumb, animal habit.

Afterward, Rex pressed his lips to my nose and cheeks, my forehead, my eyelids, one by one. 'What are the chances,' he said, 'that two vessels should cross paths like that in the middle of all this space?'

I shook my head to silence him.

'I mean, if we'd started the engine even thirty seconds after we did—'

'You can't think that way,' I said.

But of course, that wasn't true. I knew it, and Rex knew it, too. The mind is built to think exactly that way, to move, serpentine, through every shadow of what might or might not have been.

If only we'd charted a course one mile to the east, or to the west.

If only Cindy Ann Kreisler had gone to bed early, if she hadn't stayed up hour after hour, drinking wine.

If only I'd kept Evan home from school one more day. If the power hadn't gone out. If we'd left the house on time. If only I'd let Rex take him to school, for Christ's sake, he'd even offered to! If only I'd kept my eye on the Suburban for just a few seconds longer.

Or else, if I'd awakened five minutes sooner. One minute sooner. Even thirty seconds. You simply can't bear not to think about it. Because the truth is this: it could have been enough.

The days passed. The first week. The next. Twice a day, at dusk and dawn, we walked to the bow and back again, checking the condition of the sails, the sheets, squinting up at the mast. By now, the muscles in my upper arms and shoulders had knotted into a single steady ache; Rex groaned whenever he sprawled on the settee, one bent knee in the air. He was fifty years old that summer. I'd just turned forty-eight. We were physically fit, or so we thought, but we hadn't expected how the constant motion would affect our backs, our knees. The damp salt air settled deep in our throats. We developed strange rashes under our arms, on the backs of our knees. Bucket baths, dipped directly from the sea, only left us feeling itchier, greasier.

Moth-like holes peppered our T-shirts, collars and hem lines unraveling.

I thought of our claw-footed tub back home, the master bath shower with its twin showerheads, the stack of soft towels in the closet. I imagined slipping into my good silk nightgown, walking barefoot through the house and out onto the lawn. The cool evening dew against my sun-toughened feet. Evan and Rex filling jars with fireflies. Perhaps that very evening, Toby would stop by – without Mallory, as he sometimes did – to sneak a forbidden hamburger, watch a little TV. All of it seemed unreal to me now, like something I had dreamed. Like traces of a life I'd lived as someone who was not me.

Hour after hour, I stared out at the swells, hoping to see something, anything at all. Whales, seagoing turtles, even the slice of a shark's dark fin. For a while, there'd been schools of dolphins, surfacing so close to *Chelone*'s hull that I heard their little wet gasps of amazement, saw their expressions, which were strangely human: expectant, curious, kind. Like saints, I'd thought, remembering my childhood collection of intricately painted figurines. St Francis had had those same kind eyes, brightly colored birds perched on his shoulders. But Rex and I had seen nothing living, aside from each other – and, inexplicably, a swarm of red-eyed biting flies – since leaving the Gulf of Maine and bearing southeast, into the open Atlantic.

Once, something hit the fishing line we'd trailed behind the stern, but by the time I worked the rod out of its mount, there was nothing on the other end — not even the ten-inch lure.

Once, as Rex fiddled with the single sideband radio, he tuned into a terse conversation in a language we did not recognize.

Once, I spotted something in the water that turned out to be a jerry can, the red plastic faded to a Valentine pink. I watched it through the binoculars, tracking it for as long as I could. When it finally slipped out of sight, I was ridiculously disappointed.

Still, every day, I learned something new. How to drink from a glass without spilling. How to walk without falling down. How to cook simple meals on a propane stove. How to eat those meals when *Chelone* heeled over and our table became a forty-five-degree incline. It was as if we'd stumbled upon a strange, magical kingdom, a place where down was up and up was down, where the ground flexed and trembled while the sky appeared solid, fixed. Even our vocabulary changed. At first, I fumbled with the correct names for things: *port* (left) and *starboard* (right); *bow* (front) and *stern* (back). Down the stairs (*companionway*), there was a kitchen (*galley*); a toilet (*head*); a main room (*salon*).

We didn't sleep in a bed, but rather, in a *berth*, which was located in a *stateroom*.

'It's like a foreign language,' I said.

'Don't sweat it,' Rex said. 'Another few weeks, and you're gonna be a regular Jack Tar.'

'A who?'

'A seasoned sailor, matey,' he said, giving me a fierce pirate scowl. 'Salt water running through your veins.'

But what ran through my veins was good, old-fashioned blood: I knew because I saw it constantly. My bare thighs were covered with bruises. I knocked my head on the hatch covers, stubbed the nail off my littlest toe. And then, one night, the barometer dropped. The healed-over break in my ankle seemed to glow, red-hot, beneath my skin.

The following morning, we encountered a line of squalls that hit very rapidly, one after the next. Rex was trying to put a second reef in the mainsail – lowering it partway, then tying it off – when the boom swung free and knocked him off the cabin top. He hit the safety lines hard before tumbling to the deck. I started forward, but he got up again, waving me back.

'Stay at the helm!'

I could barely hear him over the roar of the rain, the crack of the flapping sail. A white crest of wave detached itself, and suddenly I was standing in water. The lenses of my glasses were drenched; I couldn't see a thing.

'You okay?' I hollered, feeling another wave crack against

the back of my foul weather jacket. It was like being shoved by a human hand.

'Keep the bow into the wind!'

By the time I'd wiped my glasses clear, he'd already returned to the cabin top, where he finished tying down the sail. A few minutes later, he crawled back into the cockpit, right arm tucked against his side. Another wave broke over us, achingly cold, replenishing the water that had drained away.

'It could be worse,' he said. He was panting. I slicked my hair back from my forehead.

'Worse how?'

He forced a grin. 'We're making good time.'

Almost as he spoke, a watery light broke through the clouds. The squall line passed to the east, slipping across the surface of the water like the shadow of some great, dark bird. The wind gusted lazily now: twenty knots, fifteen, ten. Above us, the sun swelled like a blister. Steam rose from the cockpit benches as Rex, moving slowly, took the reefs out of the mainsail. A raggedy clatter came from below; I pushed back the heavy hatch cover. Books and plastic dishes covered the floor, canned goods rolling to and fro, apples and potatoes scattered everywhere. We'd gotten careless, leaving things out, neglecting to secure locker doors.

'That'll teach us,' Rex said. One front tooth was chipped.

'Your mouth,' I began, but he shook his head, peeled his wet T-shirt away from his shoulder to reveal a red and purple bruise the size of an open hand. I stared at it, appalled. It seemed to be getting larger, angrier, spreading from within, and I remembered, suddenly, horribly, seeing my face for the first time after the accident: two black eyes, a bridgeless nose, a protruding tongue. I hadn't been able to recognize it.

'It popped out of the socket,' Rex said, 'but then it went back in. We've got some of those instant ice packs, don't we?'

'In the first-aid kit.' I was already scrambling down the companionway. Rummaging through the mess, I couldn't stop seeing, again and again, the arc of Rex's body as it fell. Only this time, it missed the safety lines and landed in the water like a sack of grain. What could I have done to save him? Thrown him the life preserver we kept in the cockpit. Turned on the engine. Lowered the sail the rest of the way, secured the boom, brought the boat around. All the while keeping him in sight, because once you lose sight of something in the water, you're not going to find it again. Especially in the midst of a squall, when you can't see as far as the bow.

The large, orange duffel with our medical supplies had been flung from the locker above the forward berth all the way to the aft chart table. I thought of the force it must have taken to hurl such a heavy bag thirty-odd feet, and then I sat down, covered my mouth with my hands. I remembered thinking, after Evan's death, that I'd never be afraid of anything again. Suddenly, I understood how ridiculous that was, how childish, how petulant. We were still roughly four hundred nautical miles northwest of Bermuda. We might meet another tanker. We might be faced with more storms. We might strike a floating barrel or some other piece of rubbish, knock a hole in *Chelone*'s hull.

'Why are you doing this?' people had asked in the weeks before we left Wisconsin: Toby, my parents, Lindsey Steinke, the parents of Evan's school friends. Because there's no reason not to, I'd say. Because this is something we talked about doing, years ago, before Evan was born. Because we want to escape all the things that remind us of what we've lost. At the time, each of these explanations had seemed perfectly reasonable. Now, I was asking myself the same question, and none of the answers I'd given made sense. At that moment, I wanted nothing more than to turn the boat around, head back home.

Instead, I cracked open two packs of instant ice, carried them back to the cockpit, held them against Rex's shoulder. As it turned out, we were lucky. The bruise didn't get any larger. He was able to move his arm. Soon it was clear that the bleeding had stopped.

Still, Rex spent the afternoon slumped in the cockpit, shifting painfully, while I reorganized our supplies, stowed everything back inside lockers and hatches. Gradually, the winds died down, dwindling away into random, lazy puffs. Without a breeze, the sails luffed; the bow swung to and fro. Water gurgled in and out of the through-hulls – the small, round openings at the waterline – and the sound was like a deep, plucked string, a hollow pop-pop-pop. With each rise and fall of *Chelone*'s hull, our canned goods settled and rolled.

Thump, scrape, *thump*.

Bang, luff, *bang*.

At last, I lay down across from Rex, but it was too hot, too noisy, to rest. The ocean a molten circle around us. The very air shining, as if each molecule had caught fire. We had always been here, would always be here, in this small teak cockpit, the slow swells lifting us, dropping us, lifting us again.

Thump, scrape, *thump*.

Bang, luff, *bang*.

A discordant waltz that went on and on. Like a heartbeat. Like the slow, steady pulse of grief.

'Are you sure this is the hill you want to die on?' Toby said. He paused before a tank of angelfish, selected a net from the wall, and began to push it slowly, deliberately, through the water.

'Nobody's going to die,' I said. 'Besides, lightning doesn't strike twice.'

Toby cornered the angel he wanted, trapped it against the glass.

'Actually, it does.'

It was early June, the first time I'd been to the fish store since Mallory's letter had appeared in the *Pilot*. Toby didn't let on that he was surprised to see me, but I knew, as I perched on an overturned bucket, that he, too, was considering just how long it had been. He was, and is, a bear of a man: broad-shouldered, heavy-boned, his face partially, deliberately, concealed beneath a lion's tawny beard. When Evan was alive, we'd visited several times a week — Evan had loved the African fish, the piranhas and Jack Dempseys — and it was difficult, now, to look across the tank room and not see his determined little baseball cap gliding between the long rows. To keep myself from dwelling on this, I told Toby what Rex and I hadn't told anyone else, not yet: that we'd found a tenant to rent our house. That we'd just signed a contract on a sailboat in Maine. That, if everything went according to schedule, we'd be living aboard by the end of the month. I also told him that Rex and I were withdrawing the civil suits we'd filed, including the one against Cindy Ann.

'Rex said it was okay to let you know,' I said. 'If Cindy Ann hasn't been contacted yet, she'll be getting a letter soon.'

To my surprise, Toby shook his head. 'Rex will never withdraw that suit,' he said.

'I told you he just did. We did.' I was annoyed. I'd expected — what? Not thanks, exactly, but some kind of acknowledgment. The decision, after all, couldn't help but affect his relationship with Mallory, ease what I could only imagine was an awkward situation for them both. 'Look, we're leaving Fox Harbor,' I said. 'We just bought a sailboat. Didn't you hear what I said?'

41

Of all people, I'd assured Rex, Toby will understand. After all, whenever he wasn't in the fish store, he practically lived aboard the *Michigan Jack*: trawling for coho and sturgeon, netting smelt in season. He traveled to national breeders' conventions, fish shows, tournaments. He'd been on snorkeling and scuba diving trips all over the world. He also knew what it was like to stand out, to hear people whispering in your wake. He'd been born with a birthmark that covered his cheek, pinned his ear to the side of his head. His eye didn't open fully. His left nostril didn't match the right. It was, I'd often thought to myself, the reason my brother lived the way he did, drawn to things that lived silently, simply, under water.

'Tell me you're kidding,' Toby said, now.

'Do I look like I'm kidding?'

'Jesus.' He carried the angel, dripping, to the counter, where he held it beneath a UV light. Rough white patches appeared along its sides. 'You've got no offshore experience, and Rex is hardly any better off.'

'Rex has experience——' I began.

'Working on a cruise ship? Sailing with his dad? Come on.' Toby flicked the angel into the sick tank, where a stunned-looking molly already swam in circles. 'This is the big, bad ocean, Cowboy. People die out there.'

I glared at him, the age gap between us swelling – a deep, dividing stream – from a trickle to a roar. He wasn't taking me seriously. He wasn't being fair. As a child, I'd idolized him, longed for his approval, blushed helplessly at his rare, lasting compliments. *Cowboy*, he'd called me then, called me now whenever he wanted my attention, and the sound of his voice gliding over the word made me long to curl up again, young and small, swinging in the strong, snug V of his arm. Always, I'd been secretly, shamefully happy that Toby never dated, never seemed to have friends, beyond the distant correspondence of his breeding clubs and dive teams. Even after Rex and I were married, I'd often walked over to the fish store after work, joined him for a snack of summer sausage and cheese from a refrigerator crowded with fish heads, bone meal, bait. It was actually cleaner – and more wholesomely supplied – than the ancient, leaking fridge in his apartment over the mill. There he'd lived, alone, since he'd left my parents' house at twenty-five, accumulating miles of plastic tubing, broken aerators, aquarium pieces, artificial grasses, stacks of fishing bulletins, brochures, magazines. A table saw stood in the dining alcove. The bedroom held buckets in which he bred mice, mealworms, brine shrimp; the kitchen housed his dive gear and assorted boat parts. Somewhere beneath all the rubble was the broken-backed couch where he slept. The landlord, Mr Dickens, turned a blind eye to the lifestyles of his tenants, provided they turned a corresponding eye to the boarded-over windows, the broken appliances, the fact that the temperature seldom rose above sixty degrees in winter.

That hellhole, my mother called it. I myself hadn't seen the inside of it, now, for several years.

But I'd always loved spending time at the fish store, watching Toby putter about with his tanks, traffic passing by outside the window. 'How about a splash of something?' he'd say, pouring us each an inch of Maker's Mark. The two of us sipping that good amber fire. Feeling myself to be first and always chosen. The truth was that Toby knew me better, loved me better, than anyone, even Rex – Rex, who'd accepted this from the start, with remarkable, generous grace.

All of that had changed after Evan was born. And then, the year before Evan started kindergarten, Toby had begun seeing Mallory. She'd rented, it turned out, the efficiency across the landing from his place, four hundred square feet that had stood, unoccupied, for as long as I could remember. Through the open door, I'd seen the cracked walls, the ancient gas stove, the bathtub sitting in the middle of the kitchen, and I worried about her – or anyone, for that matter – trying to make the place habitable. Though Mallory, it turned out, was remarkably resourceful. She borrowed Toby's hot plate while she, herself, refurbished the stove, stored goat's milk in his fridge while she scoured the dumps for an antique ice chest. Soon there were reports that he was dropping her off for work at the Cup and Cruller. Shortly after that, Anna Schultz – my parents' former neighbor – phoned my mother, in Florida, to let her know she'd seen them at the Dairy Castle.

Together, you know, Anna had said.

I figured it was time to ask.

'I've been helping her out, that's all,' Toby said. 'I suppose the grapevine has us married.'

'No,' I told him. 'Just sleeping together.'

To my amazement, he'd blushed, blood rushing into his birthmark, leaving the other side of his face as pale as naked bone. I phoned my mother immediately.

'Well, you've got to admit, she's brave.' My mother spoke in her usual matter-of-fact way. 'Tackling a seasoned bachelor at her age. What is she – thirty, thirty-one?'

'Thirty-six,' I said. 'It isn't quite that bad.'

'Which makes her twenty years younger than your brother.'

'Nineteen.'

'Somebody's doing her math.'

'I'm an accountant. Math is my job.'

'Of course, it is,' my mother said.

Now, I turned to face Toby slowly, deliberately, keeping my voice steady. 'People die anywhere and everywhere,' I said. 'Driving to school at eight in the morning, for instance.'

'It wasn't your fault, Meg.'

I bristled. 'You're damn right, it wasn't my fault!'

'So why *do* this? It's as if you're trying to punish yourself. I'm just trying to understand why.'

It was like being fed a precise, round pill. Tears filled my eyes, but I swallowed it down, swallowed and swallowed until the ache in my throat was gone.

'If I really wanted to punish myself,' I said, 'I'd be trying to figure out what you see in Mallory Donaldson.'

'Okay.' His voice, unlike mine, had stayed even. 'I guess it's none of my business what you do.'

'It's none of my business what you do, either,' I said, staring at the chunky silver ring on his third finger. It was one of Mallory's peculiar designs, something she'd hammered and soldered into being. It surprised me, surprised my parents, too, that Toby would actually wear it. Then again, nothing about the relationship made sense, unless you considered – as Rex pointed out – that, before Mallory, Toby had always been alone. He'd seemed self-sufficient to me, perfectly complete, but perhaps this had never been true. After all, I'd seen the stares people gave him, women gave him, not to mention kids my own age when he'd pick me up at school. Arriving home from Madison on fall break, freshman year, I myself had been startled by the sight of his face. Try as you might to pretend otherwise, it would always be the first thing strangers noticed.

Suddenly, I was tired. I'd spent the whole day working on the house, steam cleaning rugs, recaulking the bathtub, getting the place ready to receive a tenant. Evan had been dead six months. Driving into town, I'd seen Cindy Ann's three daughters bicycling along the J road in tank tops and bright, summery shorts. *Amy, Laurel, Monica*. Each of those names a poisonous flower.

'Can't you understand,' I said, 'how hard it is to be here without Evan?'

Toby's hair had fallen in a tangle over his eyes. 'Won't it be just as hard somewhere else?'

'I don't think so.'

'Why not?'

'Well, for one thing,' I said, 'we won't have to deal with Cindy Ann anymore.' I waited for him to nod, agree. 'I mean, seeing her. Seeing her kids. Watching her going about her life as if nothing even happened.' Again, I waited. 'For Pete's sake, Toby, she's driving the same damn car. She killed someone, a human being, and it hasn't made the least bit of difference. She's still a reckless drunk.'

'Mallory says she's not drinking anymore.'

'Mallory would say that.'

'She says there are days Cindy Ann doesn't get out of bed.'

'I've had some of those days myself.'

The bubbling sound of the aerators filled the silence between us.

'But you *knew* her, Meg,' Toby finally said. 'You knew all those girls. You, of all people, know how hard it was for them, growing up in that house.'

Now I was angry. Of course I knew, as everyone else in town knew, that Cindy Ann's stepfather had shot himself in the shed behind the veal pens. It was the excuse people always gave: for Cindy Ann's failed marriages, for Mallory's shrill politics, for the middle sister, Becca, going door to door for the Jehovah's Witnesses. Cindy Ann's mother was barely in her sixties, and yet she was living in a nursing home, disabled by early Alzheimer's: hunched, forgetful, smiling. The only child she'd had with Dan Kolb — born when Cindy Ann was twelve — had been what was then called *mentally retarded*. He'd eventually died in his early teens. This, too, was blamed, implausibly, on Dan Kolb's suicide.

'So the family had problems,' I said. 'So what. That doesn't give Cindy Ann the right to drink however many bottles of wine she drank and then get into her car, the hell with everybody else.' I wanted to shake my brother, slap him; my neck and shoulders actually hurt with the effort of restraining myself from doing it. '*She* had a choice in all this, remember? Rex and I had no choice. Evan had no choice.'

'I know, I know all that,' Toby said, and at last, he was angry, too. 'Evan was my nephew, remember? You think it doesn't matter to me, too? You think I don't wake up every single day and think about how awful it is? I'm just saying I feel sorry for her, that's all.'

'*Sorry?*' I spat the word from my mouth, and then I told him what I'd told no one else: how I'd sat in the Piggly Wiggly parking lot, hands gripping the wheel, waiting for Cindy Ann and her ice cream.

'Maybe,' I said, 'you'd feel sorry for *me* if I'd actually run her over.'

'I would feel sorry, Cowboy,' he said. 'Sorry for you both.'

I turned, walked out the door. Hurrying past the front window, I caught a glimpse of him standing between the tanks: one side of his face, stricken as my own, the other half lost in darkness. The neon dartings of the fish all around him seemed like sparks flying out of his body. I understood I was losing something else, someone else. Someone precious.

I didn't go back.

And then.

Crossing the parking lot toward my car, the sky growing dark over the lake, I saw – not Cindy Ann Kreisler, but Cindy Ann Donaldson, sixteen years old. Hurrying straight out of our childhoods, out of the single, charmed summer we'd been friends. There was her Dairy Castle uniform. There were her regulation shoes, the white bib, the hair net and curved paper hat. I'd often met her at closing time, and together, we'd walked to the beach, where we sat on a slab of pale sandstone, sharing still-warm burgers she'd crushed into her purse. Looking up at the stars, the moon. Wisps of her hair flickering, soft, against my cheeks. Abruptly, I remembered the smell of her uniform: tomato ketchup and grease. I remembered, too, the odor of the shampoo she used to lighten her hair. She was struggling to pin her hat into place. One earring dangling, the other hung up in her hair.

Want to come to my house sometime?

Ducking our heads to step up into the attic. A double mattress in the center of the floor, a twist of pink sheets, a floral comforter.

I get the whole attic. It's because I'm the oldest.

I'd forgotten about the attic. They were dirt-poor, the Donaldsons. At the time, I thought it was cool. Shirts and dresses on a clothesline strung between the eaves. A cardboard box for underwear, socks. The thrum of Dan Kolb's voice from below, affectionate and warm, roughhousing with Cindy Ann's younger sisters. The slow, strained sound of Ricky Kolb's speech, incomprehensible to anyone outside the family. The smell of the veal pens behind the shed where, eventually, Mr Kolb would fire two shots: the first opening a hole in his chest, the second passing through his head.

I blinked. It wasn't Cindy Ann Donaldson, of course. It was Cindy Ann Kreisler's oldest daughter, Amy, late for work at the same Dairy Castle where her mother had worked thirty-five hours a week during the school year, fifty-hour weeks in the summertime. Same swing shift. Same wheat-colored hair. Why was a girl like Amy Kreisler working at DC? Amy was the daughter of Cindy Ann's first husband, the older man, the one with all that money. It was said that she'd never have to work a day in her life, if she didn't want to.

I knew the moment Amy recognized me because she lost

her grip on the paper hat. It kited away in the cool lake breeze. She turned, hesitated, let it go.

We passed each other in silence.

When I was pregnant, I took a course on hypnosis, in which we learned to say *surge* instead of contraction, *breathe* instead of push, *pressure* instead of pain. Once a week, we met at the hospital, in what was clearly an unused supply room: four pregnant women plus the instructor, an older woman who positively glowed with her good wishes for us all. Her low, beautiful voice led us through scene after imagined scene. *You are in your mother's kitchen, there's a warm, baking smell in the air. You are at the beach, the sun in your hair, the sound of the water like a song. You are breathing your baby down out of your body, and each surge fills you with excitement and strength.*

My favorite exercise involved imagining everything we'd ever heard about childbirth, all the images, positive and negative, as if they were painted on a tall, wide mural filling the walls. In our hands, we held a paintbrush and a bucket of black paint. Our job was to blot out the negative images, one by one, then fill the black spaces with whatever we pleased: an easy delivery, a healthy baby, our hopes and dreams for the future. I painted a baby with dark brown eyes, a thicket of curls like my own. I painted a bowlegged toddler, riding on Rex's shoulders, shrieking with delight. I painted family sailing trips, picnics on Lake Michigan aboard the *Michigan*

Jack, birthday parties, Christmas dinners, high school graduation. College and career — what would it be? Maybe some travel before settling down. A wife and children. Grandchildren. Rex and I blustering through the door, arms filled with overpriced gifts, just as our own grandparents had done.

Again and again, during the course of my labor, I returned to this exercise, forcing myself to open my eyes, to concentrate on my mural. Even when faced with the physical fact of my pain — which was, indeed, pain, and nothing like pressure at all — I was able to step over it, again and again, the way, walking along a city sidewalk, you step over patches of broken glass.

I boarded *Chelone* believing it was possible to step over Cindy Ann the same way, given enough distance between us. To blot her from my thoughts with imaginary paint. I did not yet understand that we'd been forever bound to each other like sisters, like lovers, like people who have known each other in the glimmer of some otherworldly life. That Cindy Ann had been woven into my heart like a violent act, or a secret child. That she, in her turn, carried me: a bumping beneath her ribs, a fluttering deep in her abdomen, an acid burn that bubbled up after meals. This, despite the old sleeping pills, the new high-tech antidepressants. Despite the drone of the court-appointed therapist's bored voice. Despite the guilty bottles of wine she still downed in the evenings, defiantly, helplessly. Or so she would admit to me later, much later, when I was able to hear. Her beautiful face twisted, transformed. Stricken with utter self-loathing.

The face from which, at sixteen years of age, I'd turned away.

One morning at dawn, a warbler fluttered into *Chelone*'s cockpit, perched on the rail, then slid, exhausted, onto the bench. It was my watch; I called out to Rex, who poked his rumpled head out of the companionway.

'What?'

Then he saw it, too.

For a moment, we just stared at it, stunned, disbelieving. We were hundreds of nautical miles from the nearest piece of land. I don't think we could have been more surprised if an angel had appeared.

Rex tipped freshwater into a bottle cap, nudged it as close as he dared. To my surprise, the bird drank immediately, lustily, tilting back its head to reveal its yellow throat. Within a few hours, it had revived completely, and by the following day, it flitted comfortably between us, pecking crumbs off the cockpit floor. We assumed it would stay with us, our mascot, our darling – after all, where else would it go? But all of a sudden, without any warning, it simply took off.

It was gone.

A small loss and, yet, how easily it swelled to fit the exact dimensions of each familiar, empty place. I sat in the cockpit, hugging my knees. Rex paced the deck, oblivious to the sun.

'What was the point?' he finally said.

'There's always a point,' I said.

He passed a hand across his eyes. 'I wish we'd never seen the goddamn thing,' he said.

Chapter Three

For the first days after the squall line passed, Rex and I were grateful to find ourselves becalmed. The ocean barely breathed beneath us, a dreaming animal, rumbling with content. We huddled beneath the shade of the bimini, slathered ourselves in sunscreen and zinc. We played cards. We read books. I polished all the ship's brass – pump handles, grab rails, the post supporting the mast – while Rex oiled the teak hatch covers, rubbed down the engine with grease. He was still moving slowly, babying his shoulder, taking prescription painkillers from the medical kit. The dark bruise had transformed itself into a bright tropical flower: a whorl of lavenders and purples, burnt umber, pale green.

After a week of stillness, we began to grow uneasy. We ran our refrigerator thirty minutes a day, just enough to keep things cool. Ice, of course, was impossible. We were out of fresh fruit and vegetables. We were down to six eggs, a stick of butter, a half-block of hard cheese. Plenty of rice yet, thank goodness. Plenty of chickpeas, black beans, kidney beans. I knew, exactly, what we had left, balances ticking inside my head. The last of our bread had sprouted an extraordinary halo of bright, blue mold, and though I'd brought along flour and yeast, it was too hot to think about baking fresh loaves. Besides, operating the stove – like running the refrigerator – drained power from *Chelone*'s batteries. Charging the batteries required running the engine. Running the engine required fuel. Already, we'd used roughly half of the one hundred gallons we'd brought on board, we agreed it was best to conserve what remained. We started using hand pumps to empty the bilge, the toilet. We switched from DC lights to kerosene.

Still, every afternoon, we turned on the single sideband radio. I'd discovered, by accident, a call-in show for offshore vessels, run by a slightly impatient-sounding man who called himself Southbound Two. One by one, captains across the Atlantic radioed in their *lats* and *longs*, then stood by, waiting for Southbound Two to advise them about potential storm systems, wind patterns, fluctuating currents. Despite repeated hailings, we were never able to make contact ourselves, but we overheard other vessels in our vicinity, all of them becalmed, all of them asking pretty much the same question: when can we expect wind? Southbound Two's response was not encouraging. We'd been caught within a sprawling high pressure system. Calm, clear skies reigned for over two hundred nautical miles. Rex marked our locations on the master chart with a lightly penciled *X* and, as the days passed, we kept track of everybody's progress – or, lack thereof. In a strange way, the people aboard these boats became our friends, though we knew them simply as disembodied voices, identified them only by the names of their vessels: *Reflections, We Did It, Clear Sailing, Easy Street*. We talked about them obsessively. We gave them nicknames, invented personal histories. We listened hard for background noises that suggested the slightest details about their lives.

One afternoon, a new vessel, *Rubicon*, hailed Southbound Two with *lats* and *longs* that were nearly identical to our own. The man's voice was distinctive, rough as a cartoon sailor's. 'Popeye the Sailor!' Rex said, looking up from the chart. That morning, he'd been back in the medical kit, rummaging about for more codeine. Now, his pupils were huge.

Popeye hailed again, crisp and clear, as if he were sitting between us. A series of high-pitched squeals rose and fell behind his words.

'They've got a dog aboard,' I said, emptying a can of chickpeas into the three bean salad I was making.

'Either that, or it's Olive Oyl,' Rex said, and he laughed at his joke a little too hard.

'I wish we could contact them, let them know they've got neighbors.'

'I'll try hailing after the broadcast. You never know, maybe we'll get through.' Rex scratched another faint *X*, representing *Rubicon,* onto the master chart. 'Seriously, that guy sounds like Popeye. Remember that show? And the one with the moose. Bullwinkle. Did you ever see Bullwinkle?'

Codeine made Rex chatty, nostalgic, the same way he got whenever he drank Scotch whisky. Which he'd been drinking a lot of, lately, after his evening watch was done. It helped the codeine, he said. It soothed his shoulder so he could sleep.

I covered the three bean salad, wiped down the counter with salt water. 'Do you think,' I asked, 'we could see them if we climbed the mast?'

'I'm in no condition to go up the stick.'

'Well, I am.' I grabbed the binoculars from their hook, slung them around my neck.

'You?' Rex said. 'You get dizzy going up a stepladder.'

His offhand laughter annoyed me all the more.

'Good thing this isn't a stepladder, then.'

'Meg,' he began, but I hurried up into the cockpit, worked my feet into my salt-stiffened shoes. I could hear Rex clambering after me, but I'd already scrambled forward, mounting the first of the narrow mast steps, trying not to consider what would happen if I slipped. Three-quarters of the way up, I stopped, raised the binoculars. There was no one else out there, nothing else, aside from our shadow like a dark slick of oil, floating lightly on the water.

'Anything?' Rex called. Looking down, I saw he was cupping his right elbow, relieving his shoulder from the weight of his arm. For the past few nights, despite his extra nightcap, he'd moved uncomfortably from the cockpit to the V-berth, from the V-berth to the settee, from the settee to the double berth. Suddenly dizzy, I pressed my cheek to the mast, hugged the firm bulk of it against my chest. I was worried about Rex's shoulder, what was clearly a constant, grueling pain. I was worried about the weather. I was worried that, along with *Rubicon* and all the other vessels, we were doomed to remain exactly where we were, drifting for the next hundred years in a kind of Twilight Zone. We were, after all, on the edge of the horse latitudes, the Atlantic's notorious dead zone. Named in the days before steam, when becalmed sailing ships ran low on supplies and jettisoned their cargoes of horses, cattle, whipping them up out of the holds, driving them into the sea. Farther south, the slave ships languished, generations of Africans dying of hunger, thirst, disease. Suddenly, I imagined all those skeletons below, an entire lost civilization: women rocking babies, men building shelters, livestock moving in slow, deliberate herds, picking their way across the ocean floor.

'Meg?'

I forced myself to scan the horizon one more time, careful not to squint, keeping both eyes open. The edge of the sea blended seamlessly into the edge of the sky, leaving no sense of where one ended, the other began.

'Nothing,' I said, and I started climbing down.

'You sure?'

I stopped. 'I *know* how to look.'

'*Sorry*,' Rex said, in a tone of voice that told me he wasn't.

I wished we had a crow's nest. I wished I could climb into it, curl up in a ball, out of sight. I wished I didn't have to continue my descent, which, of course, I did, one reluctant step after another.

This was the hardest part of each day: the hours of light remaining after we'd shut down the single sideband, after Rex had attempted, in vain, to hail any one of the half-dozen vessels all around us. The sudden silence — augmented by heat, confinement, monotony — left us irritable, snappish. We picked at each other, sulked, avoided each other's gaze. Below, in the cabin, the temperature rose past one hundred degrees; topside, the teak decks licked our heels like flames through the thin, rubber soles of our deck shoes. There was nothing to do but wait for dusk beneath the thin shade of the cockpit bimini, sipping tepid bottles of powdered Gatorade, sopping ourselves with seawater. Later, in the relative coolness of evening, we'd emerge, hunched and stiff, like bears from a cave. We'd apologize wearily, sheepishly. We'd put on our nightshirts, nibble trail mix and dried fruit. We'd nose through the galley lockers, the salon bookshelves, looking for an unopened package of crackers, a fresh magazine, the least thing we might have missed.

'Are you happy?' Rex asked, surprising me one night. 'Happier, I mean?'

The truth was this: I was thirsty. My tongue lay thick in my mouth. Hours often passed during which I didn't think of Evan even once.

'I'm all right,' I said.

Rex bit his lip. 'I don't miss him as much, out here.'

Had I wanted to weep, it wouldn't have mattered. My dry, burning eyes were incapable of tears.

In college, I took a public speaking seminar in which we studied mnemonic devices used by the Greeks. How had the great orators been able to remember long histories and speeches, seemingly endless panegyrics, without writing anything down? The professor explained that, instead of composing pages of words, the speaker created an architectural structure within his mind, then walked through the rooms and corridors, placing key points he wished to remember in windows and doorways, on ledges and hearths. Later, while giving his speech, he'd simply retrace his steps, collecting each item from its place, until he'd reclaimed them all.

Even at the time, this made sense to me. If I wanted to remember my tenth birthday party, I simply returned, within my mind's glassy eye, to Ooster's Restaurant and Ribs, inhaling its odor of popcorn and barbecue, peering into the display case with its assortment of sweet, frosted cakes. If I wanted to remember my grandmother, I imagined myself at St Clare's, settled into the pew beneath the statue of St

Augustine, the place where she'd always sat. I'd kept Evan alive in the overstuffed chair where we'd read bedtime stories; in a spatter of stains on the living-room carpet, where he'd managed to open a pen; in the garden, where he'd knelt to pat damp earth around the roots of trembling seedlings. Melons sprouted in eggshells. Pepper and tomato plants purchased from Wassink's Nursery. Marigolds to ward off rabbits and gophers and deer.

Now here I was, adrift in a place where he'd never lived, lost within a landscape that, during his lifetime, neither one of us could have imagined. A seascape, in fact, free of ledges and doors. Without angles, definition.

Without history.

That night, while Rex was on watch, I wriggled my way into the V-berth with a flashlight, opened the locker where I'd stowed the small, waterproof box that contained our passports and traveler's checks, cash, prescriptions, emergency numbers. At the bottom of the box was a plastic sleeve of photos: I slid them out, studied them deliberately, guiltily. My parents, arm in arm, on a Florida golf course. Toby at the fish store, grinning. Our house with its fieldstone walls, its watercolor views. And, finally, a single picture of Evan, taken a few weeks after Halloween, dressed up as SpongeBob SquarePants. He'd caught me out in the garage, slipping the costume into the Goodwill bag.

'I want to wear it next year!' he howled.

'But you'll be too big for it by then,' I said. 'And you might not even like SpongeBob SquarePants anymore.'

In the end, we'd agreed that he could put it on one last time. I would take his picture. If, by next Halloween, he still wanted to be SpongeBob SquarePants, I would travel to the ends of the earth, if necessary, to find him a costume just like it. Now, studying his face, enclosed by a corona of bright yellow cloth, I could see everything that had always amazed me most about his character: his determination, his methodical persistence, his insistence on the justness, the validity, of his ideas. If I told him 'We'll do it tomorrow,' he'd remember. If I said 'Let's save that for next week,' he'd never forget. He would have reminded me, come October, about this photograph. He would have considered earnestly, leisurely, all sides of the question of whether or not he still wanted to be SpongeBob SquarePants.

No photos, Rex and I had agreed before setting sail from Portland. No sentimental charms or mementos. Why subject ourselves to the inevitable questions? Why re-create, wherever we went, the same painful circumstances we'd hoped to leave behind? If anyone asked if we had children, we'd tell them the truth.

We'd tell them no.

On our twenty-first day becalmed, something white flashed on the horizon. Gradually, a ragged-looking motor sailer, single sail luffing, chugged into view. She was nearly twice the length of *Chelone*, though not much beamier, giving her the scrawny, raw-boned lines of an alley cat. Jerry cans of fuel formed a gypsy necklace around the edges of her deck. Two solar panels gleamed above the cockpit like dark, expressionless eyes.

Rubicon.

Rex eyed the vessel doubtfully. 'Looks a little like a plague ship,' he said.

Still, he hailed, first on the VHF and a few minutes later, when we got no response, on the single sideband radio. Nothing. Hurrying below, I found what had once been a white T-shirt. This I carried out onto the bowsprit, waving it like a flag.

'Are you trying to surrender?' Rex asked.

I ignored him.

'Even if they're looking our way, they won't be able to see you. They're too far off.'

'So let's motor after them.'

When Rex shook his head, I wanted to throttle him. Here, less than a mile away, were real, live human beings, people other than ourselves. Maybe he didn't care, but I certainly did. I was sick to death of talking about Bullwinkle.

'C'mon, how much fuel can it take?'

'It isn't only that, Meg. What if they don't want company?'

'Who wouldn't want company in the middle of the Atlantic?'

'We're not in the middle,' Rex said, and there was a weary edge to his voice. 'Nowhere near the middle, believe me.'

With that, our VHF began to crackle, and *Chelone*'s cockpit reverberated with the rough, cartoon voice of Popeye the Sailor:

'Chelone, Chelone, *that's one helluva name, hope I'm sayin' it right. This is sailing vessel* Rubicon, Rubicon. *Come back,* Chelone.'

To my surprise, Rex lunged for the microphone, sore shoulder and all, and I realized he'd been just as eager as I was for contact.

'Gotcha, *Rubicon*. You're a sight for sore eyes.'

'Ain't that the truth. How you doin' on freshwater?'

'Fine. You in trouble?'

'Just a minute.' There came that high-pitched barking sound, followed by a series of squeals, then the shush of a woman's voice. 'Sorry, our little guy gets excited. The membrane on our water maker's fouled.'

'Can't you clean it?' Rex asked.

Rough laughter filled the frequency. 'Problem is, you need the cleaning solution to do it. Wife tidied up a few weeks ago, and now we can't find a goddamn thing.'

There was a mild scuffling, followed by a woman's good-natured voice. 'Not that we could find anything before. I don't suppose you have a water maker?'

'Plenty of cleaner, too, I believe.' Rex glanced at me to confirm this; I nodded. 'Love to help you out.'

'I'll tell you what, *Chelone*.' Popeye was back on the air. 'We've got two pounds of ground chuck we've been saving for a special occasion. Come aboard with that solution, and we'll cook you up the best damn burgers you've ever tasted.'

Meat that did not come out of a can! Even now, I can't recall another invitation I've accepted with such eagerness, such gratitude. While Rex and Popeye (whose name, it turned out, was Eli Hale) worked out the logistics of rafting our boats together, I dug *Chelone*'s fenders out of stowage, and by the time I'd dragged them onto deck, *Rubicon* was already closing in. There'd be no time, I realized, to clean myself up, to change out of the filthy shirt I was wearing and into the less-filthy shirt I'd been saving. Dark crescents of dirt frowned beneath my nails. I glanced back at Rex, who was at the helm. He was bare-chested. The waistband of his shorts had rotted through, revealing a gray strip of elastic.

We're the ones, I thought, who look like a plague ship.

But my first glimpse of the Hales put me at ease. Like Rex, Eli was standing at the helm, bare-chested. Like Rex, the shorts he wore had seen happier days. Unlike Rex, however, he was short, heavyset, with dirty blond hair twisted into a thicket of tattered dreads. His belly was spangled with tattoos. Moments later, his wife burst onto the deck in cutoffs and with what looked like an old brazier. She was full-chested, freckled, with long red hair pulled back into braids. I liked her instantly. A tangle of fenders fanned out behind her; she flashed me a grin before working them free, expertly tying them along *Rubicon*'s hull.

'That should do, don't you think?' she said, eyeing my own row of fenders. Without waiting for an answer, she perched on the combing, legs extended, to fend off the impact of *Chelone*'s hull. 'I'm Bernadette.'

'Meg. My husband, Rex.'

'Christ almighty,' Eli called, jutting his chin at Rex's shoulder. 'What the hell did you do to yourself?'

Rex laughed. 'Bet it didn't hurt as much as those tattoos.'

'Can't tell you if they hurt or not,' Eli said. 'Drunk as a skunk when I got 'em.'

Our hulls kissed. Bernadette and I traded lines. Five minutes later, I followed Rex aboard, clutching the bottle of cleaning solution like a house-warming bouquet.

'You're a couple of funny-looking angels,' Eli said, 'but we're awful glad to see you anyway.'

The Hales, we learned, had been living aboard *Rubicon* for nine years. At the end of each summer, they headed south to the Caribbean; in spring, they made their way north again, eventually arriving in New Bern, North Carolina, where they owned some property. This year, their departure had been delayed by a medical appointment, but Bernadette was still hoping they'd make Houndfish Cay – another four hundred miles to the south – before hurricane season started in earnest. Nearly a hundred cruisers wintered there –

Americans, Canadians, a smattering of South Americans and French — anchored in a series of small, sheltered bays. Together, they homeschooled their kids, organized book clubs, participated in talent shows, fishing trips, dine-arounds. There was a pageant at Christmastime, an Easter egg hunt in April. The Hales had been lots of places, but Houndfish Cay was their favorite.

And of course, their little guy loved it there.

Rex and I exchanged the tolerant glances of people who don't keep pets.

'Where are you folks headed?' Eli asked.

I looked at Rex; he shrugged. 'Bermuda, for now. After that, we'll see.'

'Now that's the cruising spirit,' Eli said. 'Go where the wind decides to take you.'

Bernadette laughed. '*What* wind?'

Like farmers, the four of us stopped talking for a moment, stared reverently, beseechingly, at the sky.

'Well,' Eli finally said, 'I better take a look at that water maker.'

'Need a hand?' Rex asked.

'Won't say no.' He was already in the cockpit, tossing aside cushions and hatch covers, lifting the bench seat to reveal a wide access hole. With amazing agility for a man his size, he slithered down into it. Rex followed, moving deliberately, holding his right arm close to his side.

'Looks like he messed up that shoulder pretty good,' Bernadette said.

Up close, I saw she was younger than me, her pretty face weathered by wind and sun. Eli, on the other hand, seemed ageless. He could have been thirty-five, or sixty. The dreads, the tattoos, the excess weight: each was its own disguise. He reminded me, a little bit, of Toby. It made me like both of them all the more.

'Might have been worse, I guess.'

'Yes.' She responded seriously, as if I'd said something insightful, unique. 'No matter what it is, it can always be worse.' She glanced at the sky. 'I'm baking. Let's get into the air-conditioning.'

I must have looked surprised. '*Rubicon* has air?'

'You bet,' Bernadette said, unlatching the doors to the companionway. 'I told Eli from the start, I'm not going anywhere without AC.' A puff of cool air hit my face, along with the faint, familiar odor of bilge, and something else, something I couldn't quite place: pungent, fruity, unpleasant. Immediately I thought of the dog. But there was no sign or sound of any animal as Bernadette led the way down the stairs.

Despite *Rubicon*'s rough-looking exterior, her salon was comfortable, homey, fitted up with custom cupboards and shelves. There was a teak dining table, a desk with a computer, satellite TV. The couch was crowded with homemade pillows and stuffed animals. Framed watercolor island-scapes, signed by Bernadette, were affixed to the bulkheads. Somewhere aft of the galley, a generator hummed, powering the blessed air conditioner. If it weren't for the sounds of Rex and Eli at work — the growl of the water maker, dropped tools, muffled curses — I could have imagined I was back in Fox Harbor, sitting in the living room of somebody's ranch house. That, and the slight gliding feeling of the hull.

And the peculiar smell.

'Have a seat,' Bernadette said, heading for the galley. 'What would you like to drink? Apple juice okay?' Again, that flash of grin. 'We seem to be low on water.'

'Apple juice would be great.'

I sank onto the couch. The smell seemed stronger here. I could almost place it; I fought the urge to squint, as if that might help me see. And then, there it was: Cindy Ann Kreisler's house. Not the grand place where she lived now, but the farmhouse she'd grown up in, four square rooms off a shotgun hall, divided by stairs that led to the second-story bedrooms, the attic. At the back of the kitchen was a pantry Dan Kolb had converted to a room for four-year-old Ricky, who couldn't climb stairs, who couldn't walk, in fact, without holding on to a walker. Shelves lined the walls above a chipped countertop; below, there were cupboards, overstuffed with clothing, toys, stickered with Tiggers and Winnie-the-Poohs. A wall-mounted can opener still jutted from the space to the right of the doorway.

'How about crackers and cheese?' Bernadette called.

It was then that I noticed the wheelchair, secured behind the table with floor locks.

'Juice is fine,' I said.

It was smaller than any wheelchair I'd ever seen, with a strangely torqued back, a single footrest. A complicated web of embroidered straps formed a makeshift harness attached to the seat. Beside it sat a teak chest, high as a bench, roughly the size of a coffin. It, too, was affixed to the floor, its cover sealed with latches, a blue and white cushion resting on top. I was leaning forward to study it more closely when Bernadette came with our drinks.

'It's a bathtub, actually,' she said, and she tapped the box with her toe. 'Though it doubles as a bench. Eli built it that way. He built all these shelves and our table, too. He even built Leon's wheelchair.'

'Leon?' I was beginning to understand.

'Our little guy,' Bernadette said. 'Our son.' She gestured toward a closed door. 'He should be up from his nap pretty soon. You folks have kids?'

Perhaps for the first time since Evan's death, the question caught me off guard. I felt my face flush. 'Not really,' I managed; then: 'Not now. No kids.'

If Bernadette thought this was odd, her expression revealed nothing.

'Leon's eleven,' she said. 'He nearly died at birth. He can't hear, but he feels vibrations. If the engine isn't running right, he's always the first to know. Actually, I'm surprised he hasn't noticed you're on board.'

With that came the sounds Rex and I had heard over the VHF, followed by a series of scuffling thumps against the bulkhead. Bernadette laughed. 'What did I tell you?' She got to her feet, then paused, considering. 'It takes awhile, getting him up. You want to come and meet him?'

I was surprised to discover that I did. Back in Fox Harbor, I'd gone out of my way to avoid other people's children. Now, after so many weeks of isolation, the thought of seeing a child, even the child of a stranger, filled me with tenderness. Already, I was regretting the lie I'd told. Already, it seemed too late to take it back.

'It won't upset him?' I asked. 'Seeing someone he doesn't know?'

Bernadette shook her head. 'He loves people. Especially kids.' More thumps against the bulkhead; she crossed the salon, motioned for me to follow. 'That's why we want to make Houndfish Cay. He's got friends there, real friends, boys his age. They come over on their parents' skiffs, hang out with their Game Boys, listen to music. Boat kids, you know, don't judge like kids onshore. I guess they've seen enough of the world to accept when someone's different.'

Her steady blue eyes found mine.

'Everyone's accepting out here,' she said. 'Everybody has their story.'

Before I could feel the need to reply, she opened the portal to Leon's stateroom.

I remembered Ricky Kolb, the smell of his room off the kitchen, close-walled, dark. Leon was naked, except for a diaper, lying on his side. Not much bigger, at eleven, than Evan had been at six. His skeletal limbs wrapped around themselves as if he were made of a single muscle, everything clenched into a fist. Thick blond dreadlocks, like his father's, covered his head, but the wide-set eyes were Bernadette's. When he saw me, tremors of excitement nearly jolted him free of the thick foam wedges that propped him up, supporting his chest, cushioning his knees. It occurred to me that I was looking at the child Evan might have been, had he survived the accident. *Your son would not have been himself.* Doctors had stressed this, family and friends had alluded to it, Rex and I had repeated it to each other like a prayer. Better for him to be at peace than endure a lifetime of disability and pain. You grasp at such comforts the way a drowning person might reach for a piece of barbed wire. Because it is there. Because it is all you have.

'Sweetheart,' Bernadette said, leaning forward so the child could see her mouth. 'I've got a surprise for you. This is Meg.'

'Hi, Leon,' I said, leaning forward, too, and then, to Bernadette, 'What incredible hair.'

She nodded, sweeping it off his forehead with the flat palm of her hand. 'It was like that from the moment he was born. Just as thick.'

I wanted to tell Bernadette about Evan's hair — dusty-blond fuzz that had all fallen out, then grown back in, months later, darker than my own. I swallowed the words, tried again.

'He must have been a baby, still,' I said, 'when you and Eli went to sea.'

Bernadette had already changed Leon's diaper, flipped the wet one into the diaper pail. Here, then, was the smell I'd remembered: hand-laundered diapers, hand-laundered sheets. A flushed, wasting body like an overblown rose.

And, in this case, a broken water maker.

No rain for weeks.

What would have happened, I wondered, if Rex and I hadn't drifted into view? But I was learning you simply couldn't think that way. Not out here, where everything, it seemed, was a matter of chance, random luck.

'He wasn't quite two,' she said, tugging a T-shirt over his head. 'Everybody thought we were crazy.'

I couldn't imagine it myself. 'Weren't you scared?'

'I'm always scared,' she said. 'But he's outlived every prediction. And he's happy. That's what's important. Right, guy?' She bent to face him again. 'You're a survivor, isn't that so?'

Leon jerked his head. Once again, tremors ran, like

ripples, through his body. I glanced at Bernadette, concerned, but she was smiling broadly.

'Didn't I tell you?' she said, jutting her chin at the portal overhead. 'He always knows.'

She pulled the thick curtain, revealing Eli's sweating face. He gave us a thumbs up through the salt-spattered glass, mouthed a single, jubilant word.

Water.

Chapter Four

We ate dinner at the round teak table: hamburgers, canned green beans dressed up with slivered almonds, applesauce that Bernadette had made from her stock of dried apples. Leon sat in his wheelchair, watching our faces as we talked. He seemed restless, I thought, uncomfortable, and I wondered if this was because of Rex and me. From time to time, he jerked his head, cried out.

'What's up, honey?' Eli asked, massaging the child's stiff shoulders. 'This calm really gets to a person, doesn't it? Even an old salty dog like you.'

He and Rex were working their way through a six-pack, discussing the pros and cons of storm anchors, the nuances of single sideband transmission. Bernadette and I, on the other hand, had been talking about the homes we'd left, the people we missed. Again, it struck me how easily we might have been back in Fox Harbor. While there wasn't enough space for the men and women to physically separate themselves, the conversation itself had formed two discrete rooms, each with its own priorities, its own independent furnishings. A colleague of mine at Lakeview – old Fred Pringle, ears and eyebrows bristling with wiry, gray hairs – once told me that the difference between men and women was that a man, looking up at the night sky, wondered about the stars, whereas a woman looking up at those same stars thought, *I need to wash my hair*. Of course, I'd been offended. Of course, I did not – and do not – agree. But it occurred to me that Bernadette's sense of direction, much like my own, came out of a deep understanding of where she'd begun: a compass built of sinew, blood, bone, one that could never be damaged or lost. Eli, on the other hand, spoke of chart kits, headings. Like Rex, he looked up and saw only the stars, places he wanted to go.

As Bernadette slipped a bit of burger into Leon's mouth, I glanced at the men, who'd pushed their plates aside and wandered over to the nav station. There they stood, scrutinizing *Rubicon*'s GPS. Heads nearly touching. Exchanging coordinates, distances, frequencies like promises. Like kisses. Even their gestures held something like tenderness. But the words that they spoke didn't match.

'Are you ever lonely out here?' I asked.

'Yes,' Bernadette said, without hesitating. 'And no.' She shrugged, made a funny face at Leon. 'There are different kinds of loneliness.'

'What about the homesickness kind?'

She nodded, her red braids catching the light, and I

wondered how I could have thought of her as *pretty*. She was, in fact, quite beautiful. I couldn't keep my eyes from her face. 'I get that a lot, actually. My parents are gone now, but I miss my sister.'

'I miss my brother,' I said. It was the first time I'd admitted this out loud.

'I miss the house where I grew up. We had all kinds of animals, horses and cows, dogs. A dozen cats, at least.'

'I miss——' I began, then stopped. *Evan*. I imagined him curled up in the V-berth, coloring – *illustrating*, he would have said. I imagined him standing at *Chelone*'s helm, scanning the horizon for pirates. I imagined the friends he would have made, year after year, in a place like Houndfish Cay. But, no. If Evan were alive, we wouldn't have purchased *Chelone* in the first place. Never would I have taken so deliberate a risk, not with my own life, certainly not with his.

'What is it?' Bernadette said.

I blushed, shrugged, but she wasn't speaking to me. She was looking intently at Leon. Abruptly, his legs kicked out as one, striking the underside of the table.

'*Aah!*' he insisted. '*Eee!*'

And Bernadette said to everyone, to no one: 'Something's wrong.'

The lolling motion of the boat had changed. We turned to Leon in unison, listening now, with the whole of our bodies, the way he was listening, too. I could sense something build-ing around us, beneath us.

'Better take a look topside,' Eli said.

A grinding sound brought us all to our feet as *Chelone*'s hull rubbed up against *Rubicon*'s, long and hard, a lazy cat arching against a table leg. Glasses spilled; a fork clattered to the floor. Even before the second wave lifted us, everything seemed to be in motion. Rex was already at the top of the companion-way, struggling with the unfamiliar hatch; Eli hurried after him while Bernadette tightened Leon's harness, bent to check the floor locks that gripped the wheels of his chair. I cleared everything off the table, securing plates, bottles, and silver-ware inside the deep sink wells. Waves were coming regularly now, and after so many days of stillness, they felt larger than they actually were, unsettling. Exhilarating, too. Waves meant wind. At last, we'd be on our way. With a little luck, we'd be motoring into Saint George's harbor in just a few days. As I sealed the second sink well with its heavy teak cover, I heard Rex calling me from above.

'Meg! Squall line!'

'I don't believe this,' I said to Bernadette, bending to grip Leon's hands for a moment – his face was bright, triumphant – before straightening up, looking around. Somehow it seemed important to remember everything: the clever shelves, the teak bathtub, the paintings and books and curtains. This intimate glimpse into the lives of three people I believed I would never see again. Bernadette kissed my cheek, pressed a Tupperware container into my hands. 'Dessert. No, take it. It's the least we can do.'

'Gotta get these boats apart!' It was Eli calling now, and I scrambled topside just in time to see Rex leap aboard *Chelone*, his good arm extended for balance. As he ducked below to start the engine, I glanced at my watch. Eight-fifteen. The western sky burned red with sunset, but a black mass of clouds, webbed with lightning, choked the east. Crouching on *Rubicon*'s rub rail, I waited for the next wave to pass before I launched myself after him, Bernadette's Tupperware tucked beneath my arm. Gusts of wind pulsed over me; I dashed from cleat to cleat, collecting *Rubicon*'s lines. Rex engaged the throttle just as Bernadette appeared. We traded lines, and Eli gave a shout.

Chelone was free.

'Remember – Houndfish Cay!' Bernadette called as *Rubicon* wheeled away from us with amazing agility and speed. Lightning split the sky like glass, glittery pieces scattering across the dark water. I ran through the cockpit and down the companionway, the sound of the wind rising, thickening, reminding me of the tornado I'd seen once, as a child, touching down in my grandmother's fields. Safety lines hung at the foot of the stairs; I tossed a set up to Rex.

'Portals and hatches!' he shouted.

'Got 'em!'

The ocean was pitching now, a confusion of waves that splashed through the open portals. One by one, I screwed them shut, clinging like a monkey to the grab rails. I'd just reached the forward hatch when *Chelone* pitched forward into what seemed like an endless trough. A torrent of water knocked me down and I rolled beneath the table, sputtering, banging my head against the brass pedestal. More water poured through the companionway, flooding the bilge; *Chelone*'s engine sputtered, died. One by one, the floorboards covering the lockers began popping up, sloshing around like small, wooden rafts. Pulling myself onto the sodden settee, I wedged my torso between the table and the bulkhead just as the rain began: staccato, fierce, a battery of bullets. Abruptly, the forward hatch snapped shut, cotter pins stripped by the weight of the incoming water. Momentary darkness. *Chelone* pitched again, an interior wave rolling into the forward berth, soaking the mattresses, the bookshelves. And then, rearing back, we were swept into a chorus of lightning bolts, bright, singing spears hurled into the sea.

At the very moment I thought of the mast, there came a sound I couldn't have imagined, a sound I would hear only once again in my life. A boom that seemed to reverberate within my very cells, recalibrating flesh and muscle and bone. Blue wires of electricity crackled through the air. My forearms tingled; in an instant, the fine sun-bleached hairs were singed away. I thought about Rex, my parents.

I remembered, oddly, intensely, a small gray kitten I'd found, half-starved, when I was ten. Evan popped a red crayon into his mouth, spit out the bloody pieces, and I bit into an ice cream cone, half vanilla, half chocolate, a soft serve Dairy Castle twist. Something was about to happen, something important, I was certain of this, and then Toby's words came back to me, as if he were whispering in my ear.

Are you sure this is the hill you want to die on?

As quickly as it had come, the storm passed over us, continued on its way. I wriggled out from the table, calling, 'Rex! Are you up there?'

'More or less.'

Gray light filtered in through the portals, the companionway hatch. I waded across the flooded salon, stepping over holes left by the floorboards, avoiding the sharp edges of floating debris. Already, the seas were lying down, gusts of wind steadying into a smooth, stiff breeze. Climbing up into the cockpit, I glanced, again, at my watch. Only six minutes had passed since I'd stepped from the air-conditioned comfort of *Rubicon*'s salon and into the first, wet gusts of the storm.

Rex was still bent over the helm, eyes dull with pain, astonishment. The bimini had been completely torn away. Our propane tanks were gone. So were our jerry cans of fuel. At least the sails were intact, secured beneath the heavy sail covers.

'It hit the mast,' he said, his voice like a scratch.

I extended my bald, pink arms. 'I know.'

He'd woven the safety lines through the helm, tied them around his shoulders and waist. 'There wasn't time to put them on properly,' he said, straightening up a little, fumbling at the knots. Then he stopped, lowered his head again, rested it on the compass. 'It's my goddamn shoulder. That last wave felt like a ton of bricks.'

'Here,' I said, dropping to my knees, and I began to work on the knots. Darkness was falling, but you could still see the front in the distance, faint as a curl of smoke. Ironically, it was drawing all the wind after itself, unraveling the brief, lovely breeze. As my fingers picked and pulled, my mind overflowed like *Chelone*'s bilge, thoughts bumping into one another, piling up: Rex's shoulder, my stinging forearms, would they actually blister? Gallons of water sloshing around in the cabin. The lost jerry cans of fuel. The silent engine. My last glimpse of Leon, the floor locks, the harness which seemed, in retrospect, no stronger than a cat's cradle, a child's useless weave of colorful yarn.

The eastern sky was sprinkled with stars by the time I got the last knot loose. Rex stepped back with a groan. Something had been wedged between his body and the helm; it clattered to the cockpit floor.

'What was that?' I said.

'Don't know. It flew back into the cockpit, so I grabbed it.'

Miraculously, the emergency flashlight still hung on its

83

hook beneath the top stair. I clicked it on, swept it around the cockpit, and there, on the floor, between Rex's bare feet, was Bernadette's Tupperware. I picked it up, peeled it open. Together we looked inside. An exoskeleton of Ziploc bags. A bony lump of foil. And then—

Tollhouse cookies.

The smell of them rose, incongruous, into the damp, dark air: butter and egg, chocolate, vanilla. The odor of comfort. Contentment. Home.

'They're from Bernadette,' I said, and even to myself, I sounded pitiful, lost. 'I'm going to try hailing *Rubicon*. Make sure they came through all right.'

Rex gave me a weary look. 'That isn't going to work, you know.'

His voice sounded as thin, distant, as the last frail traces of wind.

'Why—' I began, then stopped. Clicked off the flashlight. 'Oh.'

Of course, the lightning strike would have fried our VHF, along with the rest of our electronics: radar, autohelm, inverter. Possibly our batteries were damaged as well. Not to mention the engine, half-submerged in salt water. And what about drinking water? We couldn't run the water maker without electricity – how much was left in the tanks?

I put my head in my hands.

'It's not so bad,' Rex said.

'You've reinjured your shoulder,' I said, without looking up. 'We're still becalmed. We spent an afternoon with people who' — I swallowed hard — 'are probably *dead* for all we know.'

'Dead?' Rex said, and I now heard him exhale: a sharp, exasperated sound. 'C'mon, Meg. They've been doing this for how long — ten years? You can bet they've weathered worse than a ten-minute squall.'

At that very moment, the cloud cover cracked, releasing the moon like a round-eyed yolk. One day short of fullness, it illuminated everything I didn't want to see: the open sky above us where the bimini should have been, the missing propane tanks, the standing water at the foot of the companionway, the motionless paddles of the wind generator.

'Forgive me,' I said, and now my voice rose, too, 'if I'm not feeling particularly optimistic.'

Rex got to his feet, picked up the flashlight, and hobbled past me down the companionway. Beams of light shot from *Chelone*'s portals, pooled along her hull. I listened as he sloshed across the salon, stopped, rummaged around in a locker. 'What is it with you?' he called up to me. 'Why do you always have to make things worse than they already are?' He reappeared with a leather-bound flask. 'My shoulder, for example. For Christ's sake, Meg, if something were seriously wrong, do you think I'd be able to move it like this?' Deliberately, fiercely, he raised his arm a couple of inches; I had to look away. '*Chelone*'s fine! She's built to take this and more. As long as we've got a sound hull and good sails, we can make it around the world.'

'Not without water,' I said. 'And we can't run the water maker without electricity.'

Rex lifted the flask, drank in slow, musical swallows. When he finished, he popped a whole cookie in his mouth, then gave me a forced, messy grin. 'I ran it yesterday during my first watch, okay? We've got a hundred gallons. We could stay out here another two months—'

'Two months!'

He swallowed. 'If we had to. *If*. Jesus, Meg. That's just what I'm talking about.' He took another swig from the flask, then shook it at me, a command. 'The point is, we've got plenty of water. C'mon. Bottoms up.'

I turned it over in my hand. 'Where did this come from?'

'Toby. He said I should save it for a time we really needed it. I'm thinking that might be now.'

Even before I tasted it, I knew it was Maker's Mark. The bourbon warmed my throat, opened a smooth, clean path through my chest, and I was back at the fish store, sitting on a crate as Toby glued thick panes of glass into a long, rectangular frame. It must have been well before Evan was born. It was certainly long before Mallory. For a moment, I felt better again, safe, as if I were a child, awakening from a bad dream to feel the comforting weight of his hand on my back – *shh-shh-shh* he'd say, drowsing me back into sleep – but then my eyes flew open, and I wasn't in bed, I wasn't a child, I was far from home, surrounded by thousands of gray miles of water, the black dome of the sky falling over me like an executioner's hood. I became acutely aware of my breathing. It seemed to me that, somehow, there wasn't enough air. By now, we'd been at sea for nearly five weeks – three of them becalmed. Soon Toby would have to notify the Coast Guard. Perhaps he'd already done so. Perhaps there were vessels looking out for us: tankers, cruise ships, customs patrols. And if one of those vessels should pass within range, I'd send up flare after flare. Let Rex go around the world, if he wanted, with his sound hull and good sails, his one hundred gallons of water. Let him survive without electronics and propane. I, for one, had had enough.

'Squalls like this one?' Rex was saying. 'They're wrinkles in the weather. I'll bet you the rest of this bourbon that we'll be under way in another few days.'

I wasn't certain I could make it through the next few minutes. The ocean like a flat black quilt all around us. The pure, cold gaze of the rising moon.

'Take it,' I said, and I put the flask down. When Rex touched my shoulder, I flinched, jerked away.

'Look,' he said, relenting a little. 'You're spooked, that's all. It's natural, under the circumstances, to feel a little anxious.'

'Anxious,' I repeated. My teeth were chattering. I'd broken out into a cold hard sweat.

'We're fine, Meg. Really. When we get to Bermuda, we'll have everything repaired. I'll even see a doctor, have an X-ray if you want.' He tipped his head back, looked up at the sky. 'In the meantime, what a moon! And that must be Venus – there, do you see? You could spend your whole life onshore and never see a sky like this one.'

Which sounded just fine to me. But Rex was rocking on the balls of his feet, the way he did whenever he'd been seized by an idea. 'I know,' he said. 'Let's go for a swim.'

I could have killed him. 'Right.'

'I'll knot a couple of lines, trail them over the side. When we're finished, we'll just climb back up again.'

Good god, he was serious. I peered over the side. 'What if something's down there?'

'You mean, like, *Jaws*? I think that happened closer to shore.'

'I am not going swimming in the middle of the goddamn Atlantic.'

'I told you, we're not in the middle. Nowhere near—'

'Stop saying that! Stop making everything a joke!'

'Then stop complaining! You think I don't wish we were under way? For Christ's sake, do you think I'm not sick to death of you, too?'

He was still holding the flashlight; now he took aim, as if it were a gun. Click. The world went blind with light. I lunged at him, twisting the beam back into his face. The flashlight spun up into the air, splashed overboard into darkness. We froze at the sound, dogs startled into reason. Gradually, my vision returned. A long spill of moonlight parted the water, ebbing and swelling like an elegant vase.

Rex held his shoulder, panting. My forearms burned where they'd twisted in his grip.

'Come for a swim, Meg,' he said. 'You'll feel better, we'll both feel better.'

But the very thought of being separated from *Chelone*, floating like a dust mote in the eye of all that space, made me feel, again, as if I couldn't breathe.

'I can't,' I told him. 'No.'

I climbed out of the cockpit and walked to the bow, the teak decks wet, cool, beneath my bare feet. Something I'd read once popped into my mind: *The distance to the ocean floor is farther than Mount Everest is high.* Don't think about it, I told myself firmly, taking deep gulps of air. Instead, I concentrated on the moon overhead – after all, wasn't that solid land? And I found my way back along a wandering path I hadn't taken in years, following the edge of the water treatment plant, skittering down to the beach below. The lights of Fox Harbor like a quiet glow. The sand littered with pop cans, plastic rings, crumpled bags. The Dairy Castle smell of Cindy Ann's uniform as we sat, side by side, on our slab of sandstone. Gorging on burgers, soft ice cream. Salt and sweetness, grease.

The taste of that adolescent hunger in our throats, powerful as sex, as secret.

The game that we played, looking up at the moon.

Keep your eyes open. Don't blink, no matter what.

The sandstone still warm beneath our shoulders. The only time, I realized now, the two of us ever touched.

Chastely, holding hands. Willing ourselves up out of our bodies, rising high and higher still, until — *don't blink* — we'd made it, we were there, we were walking on the moon's bright surface. Stepping over blue craters, floating on the vast Sea of Tranquility. Breathing together with our new moon lungs. Whispering in our soft moon voices. Looking down at the whole wide world with our blank moon eyes. There was nothing that world could have hidden from us. No way it could have shocked us, disappointed us. We knew everything, saw everything, Cindy Ann Donaldson and I, and we were not afraid.

It was then that I heard the splash.

'Rex!'

By the time I'd run back to the cockpit, he'd surfaced, whooping, sweeping the hair out of his eyes. 'This is great!' he hollered, and then he dove, flashing his bare, white bottom. I sat down on top of his discarded clothes, knowing he was lost to me forever. Already, his lungs were filling with water. Already, the great white jaws were opening beneath his feet. Already, his body was being carried away, piece by microscopic piece, the walls of the coffin split with moisture, roots working their long, cold figures through the seams. Beetles and sow bugs, mealworms and microbes, circling around and over again like the words to the childish rhyme I'd taught Evan myself, innocently, horribly, tickling his stomach, his armpits and chin: *the worms crawl in the worms crawl out . . .*

A wall of blackness seized me. My pulse thrummed in my temples and ears. As if from a great distance, I heard the sound of feet scrabbling against the hull, and then Rex pulled himself up over the cap-rail, one-handed, landing on deck with a messy wet flop.

'Look,' he said, eagerly.

'Damn you,' I said.

'No, Meg. *Look* at me.'

And I did. Saw the strange, sparkling outline of a body, Rex's body, otherworldly as any ghost. Every inch of his skin was glowing emerald green.

Phosphorescence.

The beauty of it stunned me. I'd seen it before, in *Chelone*'s wake: millions of tiny organisms, salt water's answer to fireflies. But I'd never imagined it could be so bright. Almost before I understood what I was seeing, the colors had started to fade. Still, when I rose to touch Rex's shoulders, my palms sparkled briefly, and the drops of water falling from him sparkled, too.

'I thought,' I began, but Rex pressed his fingers to my lips, salty and cool.

'Just this once,' he said.

I waited.

'I'd like you to do something for me.'

At that moment, I would have promised him anything.

'I want you to stop imagining the worst thing that can happen.'

A soft sound escaped me; I was startled into the truth. 'I can't.'

'Why not? What would be so terrible?'

The question hung between us, giving off its own peculiar light.

'If you imagine the worst thing,' I said, 'then it can't happen. Because you've already thought of it.'

Rex stared at me. 'Oh, honey,' he said.

And with that, I understood.

From the moment of Evan's birth – no, from the moment he'd first trembled inside me – I'd been on my guard, alert, anticipating every possible danger. I ate carefully, avoiding preservatives, additives, artificial flavors and colors. I stopped using the microwave. I ordered a special monitor so I could listen to the terrifying gallop of his heart. After he was born, I purchased another monitor – this one had a small wireless receiver that blinked every time he took a breath – and I placed air purifiers around the house, washed his clothes, and ours, in hypoallergenic detergent, took a three-year leave from Lakeview because I couldn't find anyone I trusted enough to care for him in my absence. Of course, I locked up all our cleaning supplies, moved matches and knives to high cupboards, glued padded bumpers to the sharp edges of the hearth, the coffee table. Of course, Evan always rode in his car seat. Of course, I buckled the straps in his stroller, his high chair, his baby swing. As he grew older, I taught him about stranger danger. I made him memorize his name, address, phone number. When we went to the mall in Milwaukee, he wore a little harness with a tether I kept wrapped around my waist, to hell with the dirty looks people gave me, the comments about overprotective mothers, about people treating their children as if they were dogs.

My child was not going to be lured away by a pedophile. *My* child was not going to dash out into the parking lot, onto the street, to be crippled by a passing car. Evan wore a helmet and training wheels whenever he rode his bicycle, and at the beach, I stayed beside him when he went into the water, never mind that he didn't go past his knees. I taught him to lie down during electrical storms, should he find himself out in the open; I taught him to crawl out of his bedroom, on his belly, in case of fire. I roused him from his bed during thunderstorms, in case there was a tornado, and led him to a nest of blankets in the basement, where we slept for the rest of the night. When walking along the lakefront park, if a strange dog happened to approach, I put my body between us, and I warned him, possibly frightened him, yes, about rabid raccoons and foxes and skunks.

And, of course, I expected there'd be broken bones, a tumble down the stairs, a fall from a backyard tree. I'd expected a stay in the hospital with a bad case of tonsillitis, a nasty dehydrating flu. I'd expected – and indeed, this had actually occurred – that one night, at supper, he'd stop breathing, a wild, shocked look on his face, and I'd have to turn him over and whack his back, hard, to dislodge a partially chewed piece of meat. And car accidents, okay, they could happen, did happen, and that was why we avoided I-43 during rush hour, on holidays, during bouts of sleet and ice. That was why we didn't drive on New Year's Eve, or Superbowl Sunday, times when, as my mother liked to say, the *crazy drunks* were out. Middle-aged men, I imagined, with beer bellies, noses swollen red as stop signs. Teenagers crammed into a beat-up car, goofing around, the radio too loud.

I'd never imagined the face of someone who'd sat, in fourth grade, in the desk behind my own. Someone who'd driven me home from a party on the night I turned sixteen. Who'd become, after that, for the summer which followed, the closest friend I'd ever had. Who'd confided something that had struck me then as so unthinkable, so terrible and strange, that I'd pushed it out of my thoughts, sweeping our friendship right along with it, but wasn't that just part of being young, falling in and out of friendship in the easy, fluid way that kids all around us fell in and out of love, day to day, week to week? Someone I hadn't really thought about in years — in truth, tried not to think about — because thinking about Cindy Ann Donaldson still triggered the same feelings of uneasiness, shame. And perhaps Cindy Ann herself felt the same way, for never once, in all the court documents, the police reports, the careful transcriptions, did she mention, even obliquely, that we'd ever been more than acquaintances. Neither, for that matter, did I.

Certainly, I'd never imagined a crisp December morning, Christmas presents already wrapped and hidden, the first pink blush of sunrise in the air. I'd never imagined, nudging Evan into his booster seat, that the kiss I left on his forehead — more a hasty temp check than a true mark of affection — would be the last one I'd ever give him. As I'd approached the intersection, I'd never imagined that the vehicle to my right was slowing out of inebriation, inattention. That it would accelerate to ninety-five miles an hour as soon as I looked away. That the face of the driver belonged to a woman. That this face could have been my own.

This was the thing for which I could not be forgiven, for which I could not forgive myself. I'd never seen any of this coming. Even in the split second before the crash, I hadn't so much as suspected that it was, already, too late.

I wiped my eyes, stared into Rex's face, saw my own pain

mirrored there. Magnified. He looked away, stared out across the water, and for the first time, I thought about what it would be like: to literally jump ship. To leave everything behind.

Let go.

I stripped my T-shirt over my head. 'Okay,' I told him. 'Let's swim.'

We balanced on the cap-rail, holding hands.

'On the count of three,' Rex said. 'One.'

I jumped, pulling him along with me.

As soon as my feet touched water, I lost my grip on his hand. Sound filled my ears as I plunged down and down, opening my eyes upon blackness. For a moment, I panicked, but then, looking up, I saw a faint, silvery glow, like the light at the end of a long, dark tunnel, and I began moving toward it, arms and legs thrashing in a vortex of bubbles that carried me, faster and faster, toward the surface, until I broke through, tossing back my hair. Gasping with the shock of it, the unexpected joy. Cool water soothing my forearms, my salt-scabbed skin, cupping my whole body like a palm. Rex splashed toward me, dove beneath me, surfaced with a playful roll, and we floated on our backs above the abyss, above unnamed fish and terrible jaws, above civilizations lost for good. And I thought about how easy it would be, to float through the rest of my life this way, not looking down, not looking back. Sailing across the surface.

At that moment, I believed that it was going to be enough.

Suddenly, the air swelled with motion. The paddles of the wind generator started to turn: once, twice, accelerating into a humming spin. Rex grabbed at a trailing line as I clung to the other. We were laughing, shouting, shrieking up at the sky, tasting that sweet, beautiful wind, which would freshen, hour by hour, until — by the following morning — we'd be under way once again.

Thousands of miles away, my parents were just sitting down to dinner in their town house, which was exactly like all the others in their development, each lot overlooking a wide retaining pool that Realtors — and now my parents, too — referred to as a *lake*. Thousands of miles away, Toby was closing up the fish store, turning out lights, checking thermostats, setting frozen bait out to thaw. Pressing his good eye against the cichlid tank. Imagining, briefly, he'd been born another creature: smooth-scaled, graceful, anonymous.

In her efficiency apartment over the mill, Mallory was listening for the sound of his truck as she prepared the evening meal: vegetarian lasagna, salad, her own rich whole grain bread. Just north of town, in our fieldstone house, our tenant was riffling through the videos in the den, bored, lonely, wondering what in God's name had ever possessed him to leave Chicago.

And in the house she'd inherited from her first husband, Cindy Ann Kreisler was sitting at the kitchen counter, rereading the letter from her attorney, Carla Gary, a letter which, by now, she'd read so many times that the creases had begun to soften and tear, like the folds in a love note, or a favorite recipe. Enclosed along with the letter were photographs, six of them, taken by a private detective. And these, according to Carla, were merely the tip of the iceberg. Her proverbial hands were tied. All she could do, at this point, was try to negotiate an out-of-court settlement.

Move into a modest rental, Carla advised, and sell the second car. Get rid of the housekeeper, the expensive club membership. Document any monies you give in support of your mother. Be prepared to present yourself as you truly are: a single mother, fallen on hard times, struggling to live within a limited trust allowance.

'I can find no evidence,' the letter concluded, 'that Rex and Megan Van Dorn intend, or ever did intend, not to pursue this case to its full closure. In the future, do not listen to rumor or hearsay which may, in fact, be constructed as a means of deliberately misleading you to the advantage of the plaintiff. I am your attorney. I am here to represent you. All information regarding your case should come from my office alone.'

Part Two | Houndfish Cay

Chapter Five

Imagine a woman rising on a dark December morning, cursing beneath her breath, the sound of the bedside alarm going off for the third time. The pain at the back of her head like the most insistent cliché: a pounding, a drumming, a hammering with ice picks. Imagine her teetering on the edge of her bed, feeling herself on the brink of something worse than the usual despair, the sense that everything is getting away from her, the bills, the instructions for the housekeeper, the weekly shopping lists. The roof is leaking. The cats' teeth need cleaning. It's time for her annual pap smear. On and on, a hundred small things: irritating, necessary, meaningless. In fact, she considers going back to bed, letting the girls spend the morning at home, eating Fig Newtons, watching DVDs.

But, no. Cindy Ann Kreisler gets up.

A mile and a half away, I am getting up as well.

Imagine her pleading with the girls to hurry-scurry as she pours out three bowls of Cheerios, divides the last splash of milk. Hurry-scurry as she herds them out to the Suburban, part of her last divorce settlement, a behemoth of a thing, solid as a tank. She'd been lucky about the car, even her divorce attorney said so, and afterward, he'd hugged her – his fat belly hard and tight against her – and told her she was brave, getting out of that marriage when she did, the heck with appearances or what people would say, the heck with trying to make it work when it was clear that the guy was having problems, seriously, he was a menace to himself and others, no ifs, ands, or buts.

Get hit once, you're a victim, she'd quipped. *Get hit twice, you're a fool.*

But then she remembered she'd used this line with the divorce attorney before, and that he hadn't smiled. He didn't smile now. He gave her a card with a number written on it – the meetings, he said, were at the Lutheran church – and she'd meant to call the number, she truly had, thinking that, perhaps, the attorney himself might be there. After all, how else would he have had that number? How else would he have known about the Lutheran church, about the people who'd been sober for five years and more, the medallions they got to prove it? Perhaps he might ask her out for coffee sometime, after. Perhaps he might put his arms around her again, and this time, she wouldn't be taken by surprise, she'd have the sense to hold on tight, a man like that, settled in his work, even-tempered, and the weight, well, she'd just have to get used to that. What mattered, she told herself sternly, was kindness. What mattered was finding someone who loved you for what you were under your skin. Bees and butterflies were fine for kids, but she wasn't a kid, she was a grown woman, widowed once, divorced twice, with three growing daughters to think of.

But she hadn't called the number, although – and she was proud of this – she'd been making herself wait until after the girls had gone to bed, limiting herself to two bottles of wine, no hard stuff, no cheating. Certainly, there could be nothing wrong with that. Certainly she deserved it, a little quiet time to herself. Only, last night, Amy had gone to bed late – she'd been studying for a test, she said – which meant Cindy Ann couldn't open the first of her bottles until after midnight. Somehow she'd opened three bottles, maybe four, though she couldn't believe she'd drunk that much, couldn't believe she wouldn't have remembered going down into the basement, to the cedar-lined closet, and lifting the lid of the low, wicker chest where she kept an extra bottle or two, just in case, tucked beneath the girls' outgrown coats.

But the next thing she knew, the alarm was ringing. And ringing.

And ringing again.

Christ, she was late. Her head ached. It had started to snow. Backing out of the driveway, her rear fender kissed the Haldigers' mailbox, and she pulled away dragging a tangled string of Christmas lights. Later Evie Haldiger would say that she'd seen everything from her breakfast nook, that she and Roy had shaken their heads as they'd watched the Suburban zig and zag its way down the street. Not that they'd thought much about it at the time. That was Cindy Ann Kreisler for you, what could a person do? Poor girl, married to that older fellow who'd up and died on her, though what did she expect? And then those other two good-for-nothings, each one worse than the last. The first one, at least, had left her well settled. Still it had to be tough, a young woman like that, attractive, all alone in that house, and with those three girls to care for.

In the backseat, the girls had started to quarrel in the high singing voices they used only with one another. Cindy Ann's headache gripped the back of her skull like an external force, something cold-blooded, evil. The sound of the quarrel, its familiar refrains and endless, silly verses, made her long to swerve off the road, plough through the snow fence beyond the shoulder, hurtle down into the frozen belly of the ravine. Certainly that would be easier than dropping Monica and Laurel off at the grade school, Amy at the high school, each of her daughters disappearing without so much as a wave or a backward glance. Easier than returning home to the disapproving stare of Mrs Railsbeck, who'd raised seven children of her own without so much as a cleaning lady, thank you very much. Easier than getting properly dressed, running errands, checking in on her mother at the assisted living center, all the while thinking of those bottles in the fridge, their twin, elegant necks, their crisp, clean glow. Easier than gathering the girls after school, running them to dance class, piano lessons, soccer. Easier than sitting down to the lasagna or tuna casserole Mrs Railsbeck had left in the oven while the girls complained, or fought, or giggled, or related endless details about their day. The grandfather clock sounding out the quarter hours. The evening wearing down like melting wax. Dribbling closer, closer still, to the moment when, at last, she could open that first chardonnay, pour herself a crisp, cool glass, the initial sip like goodness, like a mouthful of clarity itself.

But, of course, Cindy Ann stayed on the road. She loved her girls. She wouldn't have done anything to harm them or, for that matter, anybody, including herself. It was only that she was particularly tired this morning. It was only that the days had grown so dark — you forgot, each summer, what the winters were like, year after year, in Wisconsin. It was only that she'd just turned forty-five, fifteen years older than she'd been when David passed, and still there wasn't a day she didn't wonder how her life would have been different, if. She'd been numb with grief when she'd married Laurel's father, Scott — he'd been after the trust money David left, she could admit that now — and as for Andy, well, all she could say was that he'd been different, before. Before he'd proposed. Before he started drinking so much — *much* more than she did, that was a fact. Before he began to look at Amy in a way that Cindy Ann recognized. At least, she reminded herself now, she hadn't not-seen that look, insisted on not-understanding it, the way that Mum had done. At the time, Monica had still been in diapers. Still, Cindy Ann had thrown him out.

Her attorney had been right. She was brave. She was that.

At least, in her darkest moments, there was always that.

Only now, here she was, single again. Middle-aged. The mother of three daughters, ages seven to sixteen, each of them bearing a different last name. How on earth could she meet someone new, begin all over again? Who, after all, would want someone who'd already been married three times? Who wouldn't assume what Cindy Ann herself had been suspecting ever since the summer she, herself, was her oldest daughter's age: that there was something fundamentally wrong with her, repellant, scarred, stained?

'Skank!' That was Amy.

'Slut.' That was Laurel.

Monica kicked her heels against the back of Cindy Ann's seat.

Enough.

Turning onto the Point Road, Cindy Ann snapped on the overhead light so she could see their faces in the rearview. 'Keep it up,' she promised, pumping the brakes so hard that their heads snapped forward and back. 'I'll pull over, make you walk, I swear it.'

Three pairs of eyes observed her patiently, scornfully. She wasn't going to make them walk. They knew it, and they knew their mother *knew* they knew it. The moment she sped up again, they'd resume their bickering, which was, in fact, delightful to them, an invigorating exercise of wit, a warm-up for all that awaited them in the close, crowded hallways, the overheated classrooms, the echoing gymnasiums of Fox County's public school system.

Imagine the Suburban tunneling between the plough drifts in the early morning haze. Imagine it approaching the yield sign, the flashing yellow light that foreshadows County C. Headlights striking dark patches of ice. Pale twists of dead cornstalks, lumps of hardened snow. Imagine the hushed, expectant faces of the girls, who love one another, need one another, in desperately equal proportions. Imagine the pleasurable tension they feel, returning their mother's stare.

Someone stifles a giggle. Somebody sneaks a pinch. At last, Cindy Ann slows down for real, turns in her seat to face them, the Suburban traveling forward as if by intuition alone, a headless warrior, a blinded horse.

Yes, I understand.

Because at this moment, it's incomprehensible to Cindy Ann that the world could be larger than what she sees. Everything and anything that matters is here: her children, her daughters, this external, tri-chambered heart. All her best wishes, her tenderness and longing. Her past and her future.

Her reverence and hope. So that when she faces forward again, accelerating as she does so, it's easy to dismiss the glimmer to her left — astonishing, quick as a falling star — as a tremulous illusion, a trick of the eye. Her feet, after all, are snug in their boots. There's a prickle of static in her hair. A commercial on the radio, something about peanut butter, the crunchy kind, even as one of the girls draws a high, sharp breath.

No, this cannot be happening.

That long-buried thought, rising to the surface like a fish, like an eel, shooting out of its deep cave.

And then, the first ting of metal against metal, unyielding as an unwanted kiss.

Cindy Ann Kreisler touched, with her index finger, the line of Carla Gary's letter containing my name, a name that, even after twenty-odd years, sounded wrong to her, unfamiliar, strange. *Megan Van Dorn*. In her thoughts, I was still Meggie Hauskindler: narrow-hipped, solemn-eyed, the sort of girl who favored bulky sweatshirts, jeans tattooed with a ballpoint pen. Cindy Ann wore patchwork skirts she made herself, Indian-style blouses, beads. Sweet perfume that belonged to her mother. Mum never minded, the way some mothers did. She let Cindy Ann wear her jewelry, too, as often as she liked: turquoise earrings, funky toe-rings, bracelets set with bright, tumbled bits of glass.

'You're a lovely girl,' Mum used to say. 'It's only right you should wear lovely things.'

Lovely. Cindy Ann closed her eyes, bent her head until it rested on the cool, smooth surface of the letter, the photos spread out on the counter like a dark halo, circling her head. Her stomach muscles ached from the gym; her neck was stiff, too, from where she'd pulled it, hauling trash. Three days a week, she reported to the Highway Department with a half-dozen other violators. There she strapped on a dirty orange vest and walked beside whatever stretch of road they'd been assigned, picking up litter with a grab-stick. Nine A.M. to three P.M., Mondays, Wednesdays, and Fridays. It was July. She'd been doing this for five months.

Five hundred hours, the criminal judge had said. *That should keep you out of trouble.*

Sometimes, passing cars would slow, heads turning to gawk. Occasionally, someone threw something, a can or a bottle, a wad of fast-food wrappers. Today, it had a been a shoe. A single high-topped sneaker, whizzing past Cindy Ann's ear. Carlton Schmidt, their supervisor, picked it up. He was soft-spoken, a widower, a Sunday morning usher at St Clare's. All of them sweated like pigs as they worked, especially now that the cooler, June weather had turned, but the thing about Carlton – they talked about it sometimes, among themselves – was that he never, ever broke a sweat. He seemed genuinely happy to see them in the morning. He addressed them as mister and misses. He never acted as if he were speaking to a bunch of petty criminals, which is what, for the most part, all of them were. Shoplifters and vandals. People who'd been too stupid not to get caught.

'Kids,' he said, with a mild sigh, stuffing the sneaker into Cindy Ann's bag. He didn't bother to write down the license. Nobody ever bothered with that.

But now, it was Friday evening. The air conditioner hummed. The girls were all in bed, thank God, even Amy, who had only worked until nine – her throat hurt, she'd said, there was something going around. The blinds in the wide, bay window were closed, the new, thick curtains pulled tight. Cindy Ann could hear the quiet hiss of the ginger ale she'd poured just in case Amy came back to the kitchen, pretending she needed something: cough drops, hot tea. Pretending she wasn't checking up on Cindy Ann. Which, of course, was exactly what she was doing. Because Amy had found the letter, the photos, which had shown Cindy Ann sitting down in exactly this spot. Taken from the street, which meant – according to Carla Gary – that they were perfectly legal, admissible. What an idiot she'd been, letting down her guard. Believing what Toby Hauskindler had told Mallory: that the Van Dorns were dropping the civil suit. *Ha*. The Van Dorns had set her up, that much was clear. And what made it even worse was that they'd used her own sister to do it.

Not that Cindy Ann owed the Van Dorns or anyone an

explanation for those photographs. Not that she didn't have the right, in the privacy of her home, to enjoy a glass of wine if she wanted to, the hell with some goddamn court order. The hell with her therapist, with Carla, with Mal. The hell with Amy, always watching her, always worrying, as if she were the mother and Cindy Ann the troublemaker, the child who couldn't be trusted. Amy, who insisted on working this job, putting all her money into six-month CDs, buying stock, investing in government bonds. For the future, she said. If we need it, she said. We have to be practical, Ma, in case the Van Dorns take everything.

Cindy Ann got up, rolling her neck from side to side. She listened at the foot of the stairs. Then she slipped out into the garage, popped the trunk of the Lexus, and lifted her gym bag, carefully, onto the concrete floor. Inside it, underneath her sweats, was a soft cooler stocked with a cheap corkscrew, two bottles of chardonnay. Cindy Ann had bought the cooler from a specialty place at the mall, chatting loudly, deliberately, with the young cashier about an engagement gift for her sister. As if she believed that Mallory's engagement to Toby Hauskindler was something to be celebrated. Especially now, after what he'd done, tricking them that way. Besides, for Christ's sake, he was almost *sixty*. Probably a pervert, too. Cindy Ann had seen enough of the world to know what was what. Once, he'd even asked *her* out — it had been thirty years ago, but still. Perhaps he'd forgotten, but Cindy Ann sure hadn't.

'They could take this on a picnic,' she'd said to the bored cashier. 'Wouldn't it be romantic?'

The cashier nodded glumly, but Cindy Ann kept on talking. Everything she did these days was done with an eye toward what it might look like to someone outside herself, watching. Apparently, the Van Dorns' investigator had followed her every day for a week, snapping pictures, asking questions, sifting through her trash. Cindy Ann felt the way she had after a date had taken her to a Milwaukee bar where (she'd learned afterward) the women's room mirror was, in fact, a long panel of one-way glass. What had she done as she'd stood before that mirror? Reapplied her makeup? Checked her teeth? Adjusted her boobs? It wasn't the thought of what she had done so much as the idea of someone watching her do it as she stood there: clueless, ridiculous, shamed. The way Dan Kolb had watched her, years before. Not that it mattered anymore. Once, before Mum went into assisted living, Cindy Ann had gone up to the attic – vacant now, the mattress infested with mice, swallows looping in and out through the broken windows – and there was the gap leading into the crawl space, plugged with her algebra homework. She tugged the yellowing pages free, unfolded them like a map. Theorums, proofs, a few lines of correction in Mr Hector's back-slanting hand. She'd loved algebra and, especially, geometry. She'd signed up for trig, which was college track, too, but then switched to vocational after she accepted the

DQ promotion. Sixteen years old and already night manager, complete with a grown person's salary, benefits, talk of her own franchise down the line. Dan Kolb bragged about it to everyone, how smart she was, how responsible, and there was nothing fake or forced or sly in the way he spoke of her then.

That was what made it so hard, even now. The sense that he'd admired her, loved her, as a real father should. The nagging feeling, wrong as it was, that, perhaps, she was the one who'd misunderstood.

Cindy Ann lifted the gym bag back into the trunk. At the kitchen door, she paused, listened again – but no. It was fine. The girls were sleeping, all of them. She was safe. She was free. Somehow she'd made it through yet another day: an hour at the gym with her personal trainer, another hour of Pilates, followed by her daily visit to Mum, doing Mum's nails, washing her hair, taking her to lunch in the cafeteria. 'Life goes on,' Mum said with a sigh when Cindy Ann showed her the menu. Every day, the same seating arrangements, the same salad bar, the same choice of soups. No wonder people got confused. 'Have you been here long?' Mum asked as Cindy Ann got up to go. 'Would you have time to wash my hair?' And then, community service, the flying shoe, the hot sun. Off-loading bags of trash at the dump, raccoon-size rats rustling through the scraps, a flurry of seagulls rising and falling like a single, sentient creature. Cindy Ann pushed herself hard, harder still, the same way she pushed herself at the gym, flinging the bags as far as she could. It was important to be fit, to be strong, to be ready — for what, she couldn't exactly say.

It was the readiness that was important.

But all of that was done for the week. The younger girls had been picked up from school. There had been the stop at the video store, the carry-out pizza, paper plates in the den. The slow migration upstairs, the brushing of teeth, the one-more-book bedtime routines. And, finally, Amy's key in the door.

Now Cindy Ann wanted to whoop, to laugh, to lie down on the floor and sob. Instead, she opened the first chardonnay and sipped directly, neatly, from its small, cold mouth. The other she placed in the cupboard beneath the sink, leaving the door ajar. It would only take a second to tuck the open bottle beside it, close the door, reach for the ginger ale. Not that this would be necessary. Lately, Amy came home so tired that she slept in her clothes, on top of the covers. The way Cindy Ann herself had once slept. She knew firsthand what it meant to stand in front of that Frialator, hour after hour, the swift spats of grease that transformed themselves, over the course of your shift, into a single, excruciating itch. The gradual, rising ache in your calves. The hot coins of pain in your heels. Not that she couldn't do it again, if she had to. And she probably would. The truth was that David's trust was exhausted, most of the principal gone. Once a month, she wrote a check to cover Mum's resident fee, her medical care, her prescriptions.

And then there were the girls' various lessons, her own club membership, her personal trainer. There was Mrs Railsbeck and her tidy habits, her thick casseroles, her thin-lipped smile. There were credit card payments, car payments, insurance payments, the rising cost of living. There were payments on the equity loan she'd taken on the house five years earlier. And, of course, there was that goddamn court-appointed therapist, a girl who looked no older than Amy and, frankly, had no more sense. Dr Cantreau, for this was her name, thought Cindy Ann should go back to school, and because Cindy Ann wanted a good evaluation, she pretended she believed this was actually practical, possible.

Have you thought, Dr Cantreau had asked, *about what you might like to study?*

Landscape architecture, Cindy Ann had replied.

Remembering this now, she laughed. She wasn't even sure, exactly, what the hell a *landscape architect* did. The phrase had simply popped into her head. But perhaps, she thought, raising the bottle again, she could work for a landscaping company, trimming hedges, mowing lawns, planting flowers. Eventually she might even go into business for herself – why not? She liked being outdoors. And she definitely needed the exercise. It wasn't as easy as it used to be, toning her abs, taming her thighs, despite running fifteen miles a week, lifting weights, going to Pilates, Spin, Jazzercise. She'd been lucky, she thought, to get assigned to the highway crew instead of, say, a hospital, or a prison, or a place like the one where Mum lived. Or a morgue. There was this group of mothers that wanted anyone convicted of DUI to work so many hours in a morgue.

But Cindy Ann hadn't been convicted of DUI. She hadn't been convicted of murder, or manslaughter, or even reckless endangerment. She was guilty of involuntary manslaughter. *Involuntary*. Because that's what it had been. How could the Van Dorns or anybody think that she'd meant to kill an innocent child? She'd been hung over, yes, but there was nothing illegal about driving with a headache, driving when you were tired. For Christ's sake, half the damn state of Wisconsin would be in jail if this were the case! She'd had coffee to drink for breakfast, black coffee, nothing else, nothing in it, and she'd taken a lie detector to prove it. And as long as fingers were pointing, who was to say the whole thing hadn't been Meggie's fault? She'd been running late, too, after all. She hadn't seen Cindy Ann either. And now, this whole business with leaving Fox Harbor, moving onto a boat, sailing around the tropics. Hardly the actions of grief-stricken parents, and plenty of people around town agreed, although Carla Gary assured Cindy Ann that a judge wouldn't see it that way. Especially when he or she was shown the photos of Cindy Ann, drinking wine – three bottles, glass after glass – alone at her kitchen table. Cindy Ann standing in the checkout line at Lifetime Liquors. Cindy Ann, in her robe and slippers, lugging the recycling bin to the curb, dark green necks poking up from beneath the girls' cola cans like periscopes.

No. The Van Dorns' attorney would argue the Van Dorns had been driven to extremes by the force of their grief, unable to live in the house, in the town, in the community where they had lost their only child. And Cindy Ann, in fact, understood what they'd done. She herself would have moved to a cave in Siberia if it meant that she'd never have to think about any of this ever again.

The first bottle of wine was gone, but that was okay, the first always went that way. It was the second that Cindy Ann savored, sipped, until her mind slowed into reason, each thought glowing singly, like a firefly, beckoning, easily caught. She would not be going back to school to study landscape architecture, computers, education. Forget about the money it would cost. Forget about the time. How could she go back to school, read all those books, take all those tests, when she couldn't even write a simple letter like the one she'd been trying to write for more than a year? She'd started it, for the first time, just after the accident. She'd started it again after the sentencing. She'd tried, yet again, after she'd run into Meggie in the freezer section of the grocery store.

The last time she'd tried had been the night Mallory phoned to break the news of her engagement to Toby. That night, writing in fat, angry scrawls, Cindy Ann had filled six pages, top to bottom, telling Meggie how she hoped that she was somewhere at the bottom of the ocean by now, that her house and its tenant would burn to the ground, that her brother would go off on one of his dive trips and never come back, leave Mallory alone.

I wish I had never met you, she wrote. *I wish that you didn't exist.*

But, of course, you couldn't send a letter like that, even if you did know where to send it, particularly since the purpose of your letter was to say something utterly different. I'm sorry, was what Cindy Ann wanted to write. Good god, I am so sorry, I am so goddamned sorry I just don't know what to do. The very letter, she knew, that Carla Gary was afraid she might write, even now, even after what the Van Dorns had done. Afraid that it would end up in the hands of the Van Dorns' attorney. Afraid that it would appear in court alongside those terrible photographs, which would leave no doubt that Cindy Ann wasn't honoring the terms set down by the criminal court. She was, in fact, in violation. She could end up actually going to jail.

Cindy Ann wiped her eyes. The second bottle of wine was gone, but it hadn't taken her far enough in the direction she wanted to go, leaving her stranded by the side of the highway, cars passing by in a long angry blur, her nose and forehead starting to itch with sunburn, sweat, dust. The orange vest like a carapace, holding in the heat. The smell of exhaust and the moist, stagnant ditch. The heft of the grab-stick. The bump of the trash bag against her hip and thigh. Wads of newspaper, magazine subscription cards, waxy cups with leaking plastic lids. Crushed cigarette cartons, torn panty hose. Random socks, scrunchies.

A child's faceless doll.

Condoms. Blood-soaked maxi-pads.

A flea collar. A gutted purse.

But mostly, fast-food wrappers: fat bags filled with rotted McNuggets and the gooey remnants of Blizzards, slimy salads, exploded pies, desiccated fries like bits of human bone. These days, there were at least half a dozen chain restaurants, sprouting in clusters, mushroomlike, at the edges of Fox Harbor. Not like when Cindy Ann was in high school. Then, everybody just ate at DC. Not only high school kids or tourists heading north on their way from Chicago, but families, old people, bachelors. No matter what shift you worked, it was always busy, people standing in line. Not like nowadays. More than once, she'd taken the younger girls for dinner, timing their arrival with Amy's break, and they'd been the only people in the restaurant. Looking around, you could see that the place was getting run-down. The doors and window frames needed painting. Some of the floor tiles had cracked. Still it was hard to believe that so much time had passed. There was the booth, over by the window, where Mum and Dan Kolb liked to sit, sipping like sweethearts from the same cup. *The love of my life*, Mum liked to say. The narrow table, by the stack of high chairs, where Meggie waited with a book for the end of Cindy Ann's shift. The pay phone Cindy Ann had used to call Meggie, the only time she'd called anyone, ever, while she was supposed to be working.

'I caught him this time.'

'Caught who?'

'My stepdad. In the crawl space.'

Listening to Meggie breathe, Cindy Ann could picture the look on her face, the one that meant she was trying to erase the lines connecting the dots. She was like that, Meggie. If you told her something bad about someone, a teacher, for example, she'd defend them, make excuses. It was something Cindy Ann liked about Meggie, usually. It was what made her think of Meggie as a good person, somebody to be trusted.

'What was he doing?' Meggie said, and Cindy Ann had wanted to reach through the phone lines to slap her.

'What do you think?' she said, hating the way her voice shook. 'Spying on me, that's what. Watching me. With his dick out. He made me touch it.'

Meggie said, 'Oh. God.'

'Meet me after my shift, okay? I need to figure out what to do.'

A bag filled with hamburger buns. The broken neck of a beer bottle. Plastic wrap. Fish sticks. Endless cigarette butts. A cup of soft serve ice cream, still capped; Cindy Ann lifted it, gingerly, with the grab-stick and discovered that it was frozen, fresh. She wondered why someone had thrown it away. It crossed her mind to save it, but no. Of course not. Still, what a shame.

How she'd loved that soft serve ice cream, especially the Dairy Castle specialty, *Twist*: half vanilla and half chocolate, the two flavors swirled into one. The night she'd phoned Meggie, she filled two extra large beverage cups with *Twist* – one for each of them – layering them both with cherries, nuts, crumbles of brownie, chocolate sprinkles. They'd walked to the beach, the way they always did, only tonight, neither of them spoke. Instead they ate doggedly, deliberately, tongues cupping the cold, smooth surface of their spoons.

'I suppose I should tell somebody,' Cindy Ann said, and Meggie said, without looking at her, 'Nobody's going to believe you.'

Even before she'd finished the sentence, the clarity between them, the good understanding, had started to soften, fade. The summer of their friendship like a photograph dropped in water, its decomposition accelerating as each minute passed. So that by the time school started one week later, it wasn't surprising to either of them that Meggie had opted out of study hall, though they'd signed up together only last May. Meggie elected to take a class, instead, to help with her college applications, she'd explained. Cindy Ann started carrying her bag lunch to the home ec. lab, rather than joining

Meggie in the cafeteria. And then, the DC night manager quit, and Cindy Ann was offered the position. She left college track for vocational. After that, she rarely saw Meggie at all. When she did, in the halls, they both smiled and waved, as if nothing whatsoever had happened.

At least, Meggie never told anyone at school, though she'd told her brother, of course. Cindy Ann had seen it in Toby's face, that time he'd asked her out. Probably Meggie had told her parents, too, because Meggie was the sort of girl who told her family everything; who turned in all her homework on time; who believed in things like hard work and good manners. More than once, over the years, it had occurred to Cindy Ann that she herself had wanted to believe in these things, and Dr Cantreau had even suggested her relationship with Meggie had had far more to do with this longing than it did with Meggie herself. But what did it matter? The friendship had been over now for – what? Thirty years? It had ended as quickly, as cleanly, as it had begun. There'd been no reason to think about it.

Until Mallory got involved with Toby Hauskindler.

Until the accident.

And, now, this fucking engagement.

'Why wouldn't they believe me?' Cindy Ann had said, her voice sounding thin, young, unreliable, even to her own ears. '*You* believe me, don't you?'

'Maybe he didn't mean it,' Meggie said, and she was

speaking rapidly, breathlessly. 'Maybe he thought you wanted him to.'

And Cindy Ann had gulped the *Twist* from her spoon, bit at it, swallowed it down so fast that a fist of pain blossomed in her forehead, as if Meggie had struck her there. There were times, like tonight, when it seemed as if her head still throbbed from the force of that blow. All those times she'd come home late from work, undressed, lain down naked in the heat. Reading with the light on — five minutes, ten. Sounds behind the walls. The click of a door at the top of the stairs. Was it just her imagination? A couple of squirrels in the eaves? And then, the night she'd caught him, how he'd pleaded with her, begged her, tears streaming down his face. But even as he'd wept, his hand was closing over her own, pulling her back into the ringing of hangers, the crumpling of shoe boxes as they wrestled and fought. Suddenly, he was angry. *Come on, you can do this for me.* Small, tear-shaped Christmas ornaments skittered around their shoulders; a ribbon of tinsel glittered in his hair, catching the distant light from the hall. For a split second, everything seemed normal again. He was, after all, just Dan. She laughed, and he rolled on top of her, trapping her hand between his penis and belly, her body between himself and the floor.

I didn't really do anything, he said afterward. *And I could have. Remember that.*

She was cursing aloud now, furious, filled with immense

self-loathing. Of course, Toby would have told Mallory. Mallory, too, would be wondering what Cindy Ann had done to encourage a guy like Dan, a man so devoted to their mother. There simply would be no putting this behind her: not now, not ever. Easiest simply to avoid them both. The way she'd avoided Meggie – no, it was Megan, Meg – year after year, chattering too brightly when they happened to meet at the Cup and Cruller, on the jogging path. And then, one day at the playground, who should appear but Meg herself, looking flushed and fat and pleased, a two-week-old baby strapped to her chest.

'Our miracle boy,' she said.

That day Cindy Ann happened to have all the kids: her own three girls, plus her sister's boy, Harvey, everybody playing on the swings. At the sight of the baby, they came running over, crowding close to see. Carefully, Meg lowered herself and the baby onto a bench. Still sore, Cindy Ann could see that. Still raw and shocked and tender. Something within her softened, made room, and she lifted her own baby, toddling Monica, into her arms, kissing her buttery cheeks.

'Congratulations,' she'd said, and she'd meant it.

And Meg had said, 'It doesn't feel real. None of it seems real.'

'That's just the way it is for a while.'

'I've wanted this for so long, and now it's like I'm not really here.'

'You won't feel that way, later on,' Cindy Ann said. 'It's just that you're tired, that's what does it.'

'I am tired,' Meg said, and she shook her head. 'God. How long does it last?'

Cindy Ann said, 'I'll let you know.'

And both of them had laughed.

Now Cindy Ann wasn't angry anymore. She was crying, sobbing, choking on the same, swollen lump of grief. She'd plugged the gap with her old math assignments, but this only meant that he came into her room. Each time, he'd be weeping. *Take off your shirt. You don't have to touch me. Just pretend I'm not here.* But after the next time he'd grabbed for her hand – the anger in him visibly rising, a sudden flush, like fever – she moved downstairs to Ricky's room, slept in Ricky's bed. Mornings, she woke to the feeling of his red, wet lips on her forehead. How delighted he was to find her there! Ricky. The only pure thing, she thought. The only good person on this earth.

'Nightmares,' she told her mother, who accepted the explanation.

Then it was fall. School had just started. One night, Dan began teasing her, lightly, good-naturedly. How would she ever find a boyfriend, sleeping with her own stepbrother? She'd replied – looking him straight in the face – that if he wanted to talk about why she couldn't sleep in her own room anymore, she'd be happy to call the school guidance counselor, no, the principal, first thing tomorrow. They could all sit down together, have an honest chat. Maybe the police would like to sit in on the conversation, too. Maybe the police would like to hear what Dan had to say.

They were sitting at the table in the kitchen, eating supper. Everybody stared at her: Mum and Mallory, Becca and Dan.

And Mum had said, 'Cindy Ann, my heavens!'

And Dan had said, 'Lena, it's okay.'

'I'll kill myself, first,' Cindy Ann had said. 'I'm telling you right now.'

'Relax,' Dan said. He'd recovered himself. He even managed to smile. 'Everyone just relax. Cindy Ann, what I said was in poor taste, and I'm sorry, Okay? Everything's okay.'

But it wasn't okay, and after supper, after the dishes – Dan Kolb always helped with the dishes – he'd done the chores, checked the livestock, then shot himself, twice. Through the chest. Through the head. It was a cold, clear night in September. People three miles away had heard the shots.

The love of my life, Cindy Ann's mother had called him.

If at first you don't succeed, kids at school had said.

'No,' Cindy Ann told Amy, who was kneeling behind her. 'Don't. Just leave me be.'

Arms locked underneath her breasts.

'No, I'm all right.'

But Amy was pulling her up to her feet.

'You're on the floor, Ma. I'll help you get up the stairs.'

'Don't make me go up there. I won't go up there.'

She couldn't stop crying. She sobbed into her hands. She'd killed Dan Kolb. She'd killed Meggie's child. And now, Mallory was going to marry Toby, binding herself to everything he knew, everything Cindy Ann had done.

'You can't let the little girls see you this way,' Amy said, her hand on Cindy Ann's back, rubbing small steady circles. 'Ma,' she said, and now they were in the living room. Now they were on the couch. They were crouching together on the cold tile floor of the downstairs bath.

'No,' Cindy Ann said again, and she was leaning against the sliding door that led to the patio outside, to the hot tub, to the in-ground swimming pool, her forehead pressed to the cool, clear glass.

'How about some coffee?' Amy was saying, 'If I make you some coffee, will you drink it?'

'You must hate me,' Cindy Ann said.

'I hate everybody,' Amy said.

Chapter Six

Three weeks in Bermuda while Chelone sat on the hard, scorched electronics strewn across her deck. Rex at the pay phone, hour after hour, arguing with the insurance company. Our small, rented cottage with its wide front porch, flowerboxes bursting with jacaranda, honeysuckle. The luxury of clean sheets. The daily paper. Ice. White painted rooftops, pink hotels, towering cruise ships like fat, layered cakes. At the center of the harbor, an ancient shipwreck, its metal hull eaten into lace.

Calling my parents, our first night ashore. *Yes, we're okay. Yes, we miss you, too.*

My father's voice so old, frail, positively shaking with relief. *Make sure you give Mother your address. Toby has something to send you.*

Logging on at the Internet café, sending brief, timed messages to Toby, Lindsey Steinke, Evan's former classmates at Harbor Elementary, giving them the coordinates so they could follow our progress on a classroom chart. Afternoons talking with the other cruisers, people from Sydney, Barcelona, Quebec. From Fernandina Beach, from Fort Lauderdale. From Cedar Falls, Iowa. The inevitable questions: *You guys have kids? How old are your children? Any grandchildren yet?* Evenings at Freddie's, a waterside restaurant, listening to the whispers as we passed through the bar: *That's them. Struck by lightning.*

Cold beer. Fish and chips.

Nothing in those whispers about a dead son.

We walked the cobblestone streets holding hands, deliciously anonymous.

And then, the Bahamas, a trouble-free passage – *We've earned this!* Rex said, jubilant – from Saint George to the Abacos. We followed sand paths the color of cream to a shallow beach studded with starfish and conch. A series of leisurely day sails south: to Green Turtle Cay, Great Guana, Marsh Harbor. Million-dollar sport fishing boats, rocking lightly in their manicured slips; Bahamian fishermen out on their skiffs, hand-casting nets, poised as herons. Weathered conch shells, the color of paste, piled into low-lying fences, like stones. Single-room houses, built on stilts. A flock of young girls in their Sunday best: white dresses, white frilly socks, white shoes.

Cracked, careful singing. Old English hymns.

A week hunkered down in Man O'War Cay, waiting out a category two hurricane. Roiling skies, bursts of wind.

Everybody drinking, playing cards. The harbor so crowded we hopped between the boats like gulls, blown from deck to deck.

Man O'War birds floating high overhead. Dark crosses. Red throats like fat, broken hearts.

But don't you regret not having children?

'Meg and I are each other's children,' Rex said.

A swift, clean passage southeast to Eleuthera, where local guides led us through the Devil's Back Bone. Taunted by pods of pilot whales, schools of gray dolphin, pale, speckled young. Pink sand beaches. Bonefishing tours. Raw conch salad, pickled in lime. Another passage, this time to Cat Cay. To San Salvador. To Rum Cay, where we plucked spiny lobster from the ocean floor. Nights anchored comfortably in ten feet of water, no other cruiser in sight. Mornings awakening to water so clear it seemed as if *Chelone*'s hull were resting on the bottom.

A sea turtle, wide as a tabletop, surfacing off the bow.

Flying fish, sand sharks, leopard rays.

Less than a mile off Houndfish Cay, we saw our first houndfish, thick as my thigh; it tail-walked twenty feet across the surface of the water. An omen, I decided, as we closed on the narrow channel — marked by a single, half-rotted buoy — into Ladyslip Cove. And there she sat, anchored just off the marina, in the midst of a cluster of twenty-odd boats. No mistaking those alley cat lines. No mistaking the belly, the tattoos, the dreadlocks of the man in the cockpit who stopped, stared, raised his broad hand, as if they'd been expecting us all along: Eli and Bernadette Hale.

August passed into September. September passed into October. We were invited to cocktail parties, a pig roast. We were shown the best snorkeling spots, the deep holes to jig for grouper. Rex joined the men for their weekly poker game; I dingied to shore for morning yoga on the beach. Halloween night, we walked down to the tip of the island, where the boat kids took turns reciting *The Legend of Sleepy Hollow*.

No children, we explained. *Just each other. Just us.*

We thought we might stay for the Thanksgiving pageant.

We talked about sticking around until after the New Year's Eve bash.

I still have the charcoal sketch that Bernadette made of us during that time, sitting in a tidal pool, babying cups filled with Junkanoo soda and rum. Beneath the clear green water, our legs are intertwined into a single, stout mermaid's tail. We are smiling. We are deeply tanned, fit, even fierce. We look exactly like the people I'd hoped we might become, back when I first imagined the warm Gulf Stream, open skies, a citrus sun. The sort of people who have never experienced any real disappointment.

The sort of people who always have gotten exactly what they've wanted.

* * *

By the time we learned of Toby's engagement, it was the middle of December. Rex carried the wedding invitation back from Echo Island, twenty-five miles from Houndfish Cay, along with fresh provisions, liquor, and a refill on the prescriptions he'd been taking for his shoulder. I'd spent the morning doing laundry: washing it in one bucket, rinsing it in the next. It had rained the night before, and all across the cove, women were pinning wet armloads of T-shirts and shorts to safety lines. Radios were playing. You could hear laughter, an occasional sneeze, the intermittent buzz of a dingy heading to shore. The odor of detergent drifted through the air, shimmering in a thick, sweet cloud, as if the smell came from the island itself, from the jacaranda trees that surrounded the marina.

In the afternoon, when the tide had turned, I put on my swimming suit and dove overboard, swam the five hundred yards to *Rubicon,* where Bernadette and Leon were fishing from the cockpit. Kicking around the bow to avoid their line, I nearly ploughed into the resident dolphin, Alvie; he gave me a hard-nosed bump, plunged, vanished in a rising rush of bubbles.

'Look what the tide washed in,' Bernadette said as I pulled myself up the swim ladder. She and Leon were nestled together in the oversize hammock. Leon's face was listless, drawn; still, when he saw me, he raised his fist.

Hello.

'Leo-the-lion,' I said, wringing out my hair. 'Catch anything?'

'Not yet.' Bernadette got up to check the pole, which sat in a mount on the combing. Even before she'd reeled the line in, I could tell that the bait was gone. 'That's the third time in ten minutes,' she said, with an unhappy glance at the bait bucket.

'I'll fish with Leon for a while,' I said, 'if you've got other stuff to do.'

Bernadette's face brightened. As always, the cockpit was cluttered with tubes of watercolor paints, brushes, sketch pads sealed in plastic. A half-finished painting, something new, was taped to the portable easel.

'I'd work a little more while there's light,' she said, turning her face toward Leon. 'If you don't mind, Bud. And you know how I feel about using live bait.' She gave a little shudder; the gold in her red braids caught the light. 'It's that little crunch when the hook goes through the shell—'

'So work, then. We'll crunch.' I bent over Leon, tickling his bare arms and chest with my still-dripping hair. A smile passed over his mouth, though it never quite reached his eyes, and I felt something harden at the back of my throat, an ache that I couldn't quite swallow. A few weeks earlier, in the middle of the night, he'd spiked a fever high enough to send him into convulsions. Since then, he'd been sleeping more and more. He didn't want to swim, or play video games, or push around the marina in his chair. When his friends came by, he closed his eyes, signed *No* and *Go away*. Day after day, he dozed in the hammock or stared idly at the dimpled water, watching Alvie romp among the boats like a friendly dog.

'What do you think keeps grabbing the bait?' I asked him. 'Crab? Barracuda?'

I watched his lips closely, the way he'd been watching mine, until I caught the shape of a *B*. Leaning over the safety lines, I spat into the water. A four-foot barracuda shot from beneath *Rubicon*'s hull, tilted its round, black eye toward the surface. Half a dozen needlefish appeared as well, clustering around the floating coin of saliva. Each time I swam in the cove – or for that matter, anywhere along the cay – I knew that there were barracudas, nurse sharks, jellyfish. But true to my promise to Rex, I'd stopped imagining the worst thing that could happen. I'd taken off my jewelry, my wedding ring, anything that might beckon to an underwater eye. Beyond that, I simply didn't allow myself to think about it, the way I didn't think about Toby, or my parents, or even – most days – Evan. *This is your life now*, I told myself fiercely, chanting the words like a prayer. *These people are your family. This beautiful place is your home.*

'Guess we won't catch much with him hanging around.'

Leon blinked once, deliberately. *No*.

'We could take the dingy over to the pier. Try there for a while.'

No.

'Tired of fishing?'

Two blinks. *Yes.*

'Tired in general?'

Yes.

'You're not feeling great today, are you?' I said, and I slipped into the hammock beside him. Bernadette had made it out of thin, silky line; she knew how to weave and macramé, sew clothing and canvas, twist rags into rugs. She braided fat ropes out of split palm fronds, which she worked into baskets and bowls. There wasn't an inch of *Rubicon's* interior that didn't shine with her touch, from the earthenware cups and plates she'd thrown, to the paintings that covered the bulkheads. Eli, on the other hand, could make absolutely anything run: pumps, compressors, electronics. He was also a crack fisherman. Mornings, he took off early on the dingy, returning with flounder, snapper, grouper. Afternoons, Leon at his side, he puttered with *Rubicon's* systems, planned alterations and improvements.

'You romanticize things,' Rex said, whenever I talked about the Hales.

'Between them, they can do just about anything.'

'Most people who've been cruising as long as they have can, too.'

'And look at how they are with Leon,' I said. 'The way they accept him for who he is. No bitterness. No disappointment.'

'You don't know that, Meg.'

'Of course I do. I see them every day.'

'They see us every day, too,' Rex said, and he paused to let his words sink in. 'Would you say they really know either one of us?'

I bit my lip. 'I feel bad about that.'

'Don't. It's a kindness. You don't come all the way out here because you want to wade through other people's baggage.'

'But Bernadette and Eli don't *have* baggage,' I said. 'That's what I'm trying to say.'

'Everybody has baggage.'

Still, there was something between them, an open contentment, a satisfied warmth, that spilled over onto the rest of us who knew them, during that time. It was in the way Eli touched Bernadette whenever he passed her on deck. It was in the way she took her time rubbing sunblock into his shoulders. It was in the way they called each other *honey*, as if the endearment were still new to them, sweet. Nights, as Rex and I sat in *Chelone*'s salon, reading by the light of our kerosene lamp, we could hear Bernadette's lazy chuckle, Eli's Popeye laugh. And I'd look over at Rex, sipping a Scotch, lost in another game of solitaire, and I'd feel as if we were ghosts, shadows, people who'd lived so long in the world we had nothing left to say. I tried to remember what it was that we'd talked about once, Rex and I. Work, of course. Family and friends. Things we'd read in the paper. Things we'd seen on TV.

Evenings after supper, we'd go for long walks along the bluff, and though I couldn't remember having said much during those times, I couldn't remember feeling lonely.

'They have a child between them,' Rex said, getting up to pour himself another drink. 'They have more to talk about than we do, that's all.'

'The way we used to,' I said.

'Right. When we had Evan.'

'I'm talking about before we had Evan.'

'You romanticize things, Meg.'

The conversation had come full circle. Rex sat back down, took another sip of Scotch.

Now the hammock swung to and fro, settled into the gentle motion of the hull. *Hmm*, Leon said. *Hmm*, I said. The vibrations traveling between us like a whisper, like a song, and I remembered Evan crawling into our bed on Saturday mornings, smelling of pilfered corn chips, snuggling his body against me. The sharpness of his toenails, the boniness of his feet. The fragile bird-cage feeling of his ribs as they expanded against my own. The one-year anniversary of his death had come and gone. A year had passed since we'd cuddled up this way. A year since he'd lifted his face to mine, demanding a *kiss-kiss* — never just a kiss.

'It's because he gets so many,' Rex had liked to say. 'He doesn't know it's possible to get only one at a time.'

Bernadette glanced over at us, smiled slightly, returned to

her work. She was painting, I realized, the laundry; bright smears of color seemed to ripple off the page. Something about the way she leaned forward, the slope of her strong, young shoulders, reminded me, abruptly, of a dream I'd had: Cindy Ann Kreisler and I, walking together along some nameless road. Other women were walking, too, and there was a feeling of . . . heat, was it? Shame? But the air was cold, the distant clusters of trees gone gold to brown to skeleton-bare. Hoarfrost covered the ground. From time to time, Cindy Ann would pause, stoop, poke with a stick. There was something, in the dream, that I wanted to do for Evan. There was an overwhelming desire to put things right.

'He was running a little temp again last night,' Bernadette said, and I realized I must have slept. Leon, beside me, was sleeping, too. 'Eli wants to take him back to the States, have him seen by some specialist there.'

The dream-fragment was like a name on the tip of my tongue, something that should have been easy to remember: obvious, effortless. But the moment I spoke, it vanished. 'Where?'

'Miami Children's. You know the couple aboard *Camelot*? They're retired pediatricians and they know this woman, a pediatric neurologist—'

Her voice broke off as the aft hatch opened, revealing Eli's tousled head. 'Hey,' he said. 'I thought I heard voices. Rex back from Echo yet?'

'Should be on the five o'clock ferry.'

'If he's got the balls.' Eli grinned. 'Lost everything but, the last time.'

Tonight was poker night. By seven o'clock, half the men in the cove would be crowded around *Rubicon*'s long galley table, shouts of laughter ringing from the open portals, the odor of grilled fish, coconut, and rum drifting in waves across the cove.

'We're dealing you in, too, right, Sport?' he called to Leon, rapping his knuckles on the cabin top. 'Buddy?'

'Honey,' Bernadette said. 'Let him sleep.'

'He's been sleeping all day.' Eli climbed from the hatch like a bear emerging from a hollowed-out tree. 'Bud? Leo-the-Lion?' He squeezed Leon's shoulder; the child's eyes fluttered beneath his closed lids. I sat up, and it struck me how pale Leon was, despite his dark-tanned skin. For a moment, I thought he'd stopped breathing – but, no. There was the faint, frail motion of his ribs.

'Christ, he's really out,' Eli said.

'It's the heat,' Bernadette said, briskly. 'I should have taken him inside, but then Meggie came by––'

Meggie. No one in the world ever called me that, now. Only Bernadette.

'It isn't the heat,' Eli said.

'He's been sick, that's all. He just needs a little more time.'

Eli said nothing. He stroked Leon's hair.

'We're keeping him hydrated. We're giving him antibiotics. We're doing everything that a hospital would do. Even Dr Matt says so.'

Dr Matt was Leon's pediatrician and, also, I gathered, an old family friend. Prior to *Rubicon*'s first offshore passage, he'd taught Bernadette how to start an IV, perform an emergency tracheotomy, administer injections. Between her medical library and her eye-popping assortment of pharmaceuticals, she was certainly better equipped than, say, the walk-in clinic at Echo, where Rex went to get the new pain medications he was taking for his shoulder. The difficulty was contacting Dr Matt – or, for that matter, anybody else – during emergencies. The pay phone at the marina had been broken for as long as anyone could remember. There was a so-called Internet café at the back of the island liquor store where, for a ten-dollar purchase, you could log on to the owner's aging desktop for ten minutes at a time. But the dial-up connection was unreliable, slow; more often than not, it took the full ten minutes just to connect. If you wanted to send mail, research something on the Internet, you had to pony up for another bottle of rum.

Eli knelt down beside the hammock, pressed his mouth to the palm of Leon's hand. 'Rest then, Sport. It's okay. You can stay up for the game later, how about that?'

'Which reminds me,' Bernadette said, turning to me. 'There's a bunch of poker widows meeting over at Island Girls later.' She wiped her hands on her paint-spattered shorts. 'Audrey Mueller and Pam Thomas for sure. Maybe Carole Daniels, if she can get the twins to bed.'

'As long as she doesn't bring them this time.'

'She won't. Pam made her promise.'

I laughed. Pam, a retired mortgage broker, was nothing if not direct.

'That new girl might come, too,' Bernadette said. 'The really young one, you know, who's been coming to yoga? Sailed in alone on that Cape Dory?'

'Jeanie Mc-something,' I said.

'Jeanie McFadden,' Eli said. He was standing now, squinting at something out in the bay. 'Quite the sailor, from what I hear.'

'She plans to go around the world,' Bernadette said.

'Alone?' I said.

'Worse,' Eli said. 'With two goddamn Jack Russell terriers.' He shaded his eyes. 'Isn't that T-Rex? There. Nine o'clock.'

A small, dark shape seemed to hover in place. No, it was moving after all. Moments later I could see it was approaching the channel, and there were the points of the bandana Rex tied, pirate-style, over his head. He was sitting to the right of the outboard, guiding the tiller with his left hand, and I couldn't help but notice, as he came into the cove, that it was his left hand he raised in response to Eli's hail. Some days, the troublesome right shoulder was better; other days, it was worse. In Bermuda, we'd had it x-rayed, but the plates had come back negative. The clinic doctor had prescribed anti-inflamatories, more painkillers, a single shot of cortisone, as well as a series of exercises, which Rex was supposed to do twice a day.

'Shoulders can be tricky,' this doctor had said. Beneath his white coat, he'd worn bright Bermudan shorts, black socks pulled up to the knee, leather wingtip shoes. 'Especially at your age.'

Afterward, Rex and I had laughed about it. *Especially at your age* became a running joke between us. But Rex's shoulder had never fully healed. And he'd stopped the exercises, the anti-inflammatories, everything except the pain medications, which were nearly as easy to get, in Echo Harbor, as rum. Now I watched as he cut the outboard, drifted in, kissed the edge of the dingy against *Rubicon*'s hull. He looked exhausted, his cheeks red with sunburn, and I felt sorry for him, yes, but I also felt annoyed. Once again, I'd volunteered to make the trip to Echo, but Rex had insisted, as he always did, that it wasn't safe for me to go alone. Whenever supplies ran low — or if we needed to check e-mail, use the telephone — he was the one who dingied north to hop the King's Point ferry, while I stayed behind, kept an eye on the boat. It was true that the harbor was a rough-and-tumble place, choked with waterfront bars, liquor stores, foul-smelling conch stands. Set back from the water, up a steep road strewn with dog waste, was the grocery store: a windowless warehouse, constructed from a series of hinged, aluminum sheets. Beside it stood a strip mall, shops selling marine supplies, chart kits, cheap clothing. There were rough, paved roads, a few taxicabs, scooters you could rent by the hour. A single-strip airfield, where – so we'd been told – you could look down on the wreckage of half-submerged planes, even as your own struggled to rise above the water. The harbor was shallow, littered with trash, wandering moorings, rusted-out hulls. The only time we'd tried to sail *Chelone* through the narrow inlet, we'd wound up running aground.

'Good trip?' Eli called.

'Ferry ran on time, for a change,' Rex said. 'Got something here for Buddy. How's he feeling?'

'Better,' Bernadette said, just as Eli said, 'Not great.'

They looked at each other, looked away.

'He's sleeping right now,' I said.

Rex handed Bernadette a package. 'Can he eat Junior Mints? They're nice and squishy.'

'He loves Junior Mints,' Eli said.

'I'll say he does,' Bernadette said, laughing. 'Look.'

We all turned toward the hammock, and there was Leon, clear-eyed, smiling. *What*? he signed eagerly, eyes fixed on the package, as if he already knew what was inside. And for a moment, I thought that Bernadette was right. Leon was going to get better. All he needed was rest and time. Just like Rex's shoulder.

'Anything special for me?' I asked, climbing down into the dingy. Fresh fruits and vegetables were hard to come by, but occasionally Rex would find a bunch of carrots, a few battered apples, a single orange, priced like gold. Last time, it had been three dark plums, sweet, though hard as stones.

'Maybe.'

'What?'

'Wait and see.'

He raised his eyebrows mysteriously, and wrinkles I'd never noticed before erupted across his forehead. Lately, he'd been putting on weight; his beard was grizzled with curly gray hairs the texture of wire. An old man's beard. I'd told him so. I'd pleaded with him to shave it.

'He's toying with you,' Bernadette said, laughing, and she hiked her upper body out over the rub rail, leaning down to kiss me good-bye. 'See you at 'Girls, okay?'

'What should I bring to the game?' Rex asked.

Eli laughed wickedly. 'Just your cash.'

As we motored away, I waved to Leon, but he didn't look up. He was just like any other eleven-year-old boy, intent on the promise of candy. The sky was blue. Out in the bay, the Gulf Stream shimmered green. There was nothing in that moment to suggest I would never see him again.

By now, it was low tide. The shorebirds were out, herons

and snowy egrets, sandpipers and gulls, multiple species flocked together on the newly emerging sand bars. Idly I watched them from *Chelone*'s stern until Rex started handing up the groceries. One by one, I swung the bags over the safety lines, deposited them on the cockpit floor. There were tinned meats and packaged cookies, powdered milk and peanuts, onions, potatoes, plantains. Too many bottles of Scotch, rum. Diet cola, Gatorade.

'Spaghettios!' I said, lifting a super-size can from one of the bags. 'I haven't had these since I was, like, ten.'

Rex climbed the swim ladder without looking at me, and for the first time, it occurred to me that something might be wrong.

'What is it?' I said.

He sat down beside me on the cockpit bench, worked his hand into the pocket of his shorts. 'I thought about not giving this to you,' he said, and he pulled out a quartered envelope, smoothed it on his knee. It was constructed from homemade paper, oversize and square, and even before I saw Toby's and Mallory's names in the corner, I understood that it was an invitation, guessed what it probably meant. It had been sent care of our cottage in Bermuda. It was postmarked the thirtieth of July. Who could say how long it had been in transit before it had actually arrived? Someone had added the name of the boatyard where *Chelone* had been repaired. But how had it wound up at Echo Island? Perhaps another cruiser, someone we'd met at Freddie's, had carried it south, looking out for us, hoping our paths would cross. Rex told me he'd spotted it at the Echo ferry dock, pinned to a bulletin board along with dozens of other lost letters, want ads, notes. *That couple struck by lightning – Houndfish?* had been written in bold capital letters across the bottom.

I remembered, then, my father saying that Toby had something to send us. I'd imagined – what? Something for the boat? Some small, useful gadget? A good luck charm? But nothing had come, and as soon as *Chelone*'s repairs were complete, I'd forgotten to think about it.

Until now.

'I got through to your mother,' Rex said. 'She assumed we already knew. Everyone thinks we know about this, Meg.'

'So why didn't she say something in her e-mails?' I began, then stopped. Even at the Internet café in Echo Harbor, you had limited time to download your mail, respond, surf the net for a bit of news. There were only three computers. There were restless lines of people, waiting, and you paid, of course, for each minute. *Are you going to congratulate Toby?* my mother had written, shortly after we'd first arrived in Houndfish. When Rex relayed the message, I'd assumed – we'd both assumed – that it had something to do with his fish, his cichlids, perhaps another breeder's prize. Obligingly, on his next trip to Echo, Rex had sent Toby a line that read, *Why should we congratulate you?* Something to that effect. When we hadn't heard anything back, we'd blamed the distance. My mother, being my mother, hadn't mentioned it again.

I opened the invitation.

Toby and Mallory's wedding would take place on the day after Christmas. The actual exchange of vows – led by a justice of the peace – would be held aboard the *Michigan Jack*: sleet, snow, or freeze. Afterward, there'd be hot tea and a vegetarian lunch at the Indian restaurant downtown. At the bottom of the card, Toby had written a single, sloping line: *Hope you can be there.* Below it, in a back slant that must have been Mallory's, two simple words.

Please come.

Rex was reading over my shoulder; now, he made a sharp, sarcastic sound. 'Right. You, me, Cindy Ann and her kids, all sitting down for a nice dish of curry.'

'Are Mom and Dad going?' I asked.

'They're driving up next week. That's all I know because we got disconnected. When I tried to call back, the seven wouldn't dial.'

'There's more than one phone at the ferry dock, Rex!'

'Actually, Meg, there are four. One had no dial tone. One dialed spontaneously when I picked up the receiver. One *had* no receiver.'

'She probably thinks you hung up on her,' I said, imagining my mother replacing the receiver, waiting for Rex to call back. Imagining Toby, reading Rex's e-mail, his face flushing dark with hurt. 'I suppose it would all be even worse if we were there,' I said, speaking more to myself than Rex, and Rex said, 'Do you ever wish we hadn't dropped the civil suit?'

The question took me by surprise.

'Why?' I finally said.

'I want to know your answer.'

'If we hadn't dropped the suit,' I said, avoiding the question, 'we'd be meeting with Arnie every other week. We'd be in and out of court.'

'Not necessarily.'

A dingy approached *Chelone*'s stern; it belonged to a neighboring ketch. Two men sat on the forward seat while a third, Paulie Mandler, clutched the tiller.

'T-Rex!' he called. 'Losin' again tonight?'

'You'll find out soon enough.'

'Okay, then. See you at the game.'

We waited, smiles fixed to our faces, until Paulie pulled away.

'The thing is,' Rex said. 'I've been in touch with Arnie. I talked to him today, in fact.' He shrugged. 'No sevens in his number.'

I couldn't have been more shocked if he'd confessed to having an affair. Stunned, I picked up two bags of groceries, carried them down the companionway. Rex followed with an armload of clean clothes, which he tossed into our stateroom. Then he poured himself a drink – the last of the Scotch from a bottle he'd promised, three days earlier, would last him at least a week. He took a sip. Another. He said, 'Anyway. Remember, before we left, I told you that he'd hired this private detective?'

I said, 'Could you bring down the rest of the grocery bags?'

'Don't you want to know what the detective found?'

'It doesn't matter what he found.' I was sorting and stacking cans of food, slapping things onto the countertop: green beans, fruit cocktail, soup. 'We withdrew the suit.'

Rex went topside, returned with the last of the groceries. Then he squeezed past me into our stateroom and shut the door. I could hear him opening drawers, putting away our clothes as I unpacked the perishables from their melted ice packs. When I looked up again, he was dressed in fresh shorts and a short-sleeved polo, his uncut hair slicked back into a nub of ponytail. The ponytail appealed to me about as much as the beard. It emphasized his high forehead, with its receding hairline, its chronic peeling sunburn. 'Cindy Ann's attorney wants to settle, Meg.'

'I'm not getting dragged back into this.'

'So give Arnie permission to handle things for you.' He paused. 'That's what I did. Before we took off, in fact.'

I couldn't stop shaking my head. 'We dropped the suit. That was six months ago. You told me I could tell my brother, and I did. Don't tell me what I told him wasn't true.'

It was not a question.

'Six months ago,' Rex said, 'I told Arnie that you'd – we'd

– developed certain reservations. And Arnie advised me, as I would have advised any client of my own, that people often make these decisions in haste. Then, later on, when they've had some time to think, they change their minds. They get a second wind.'

I stared at him. 'You're telling me we didn't drop the suit?'

'But wait until you hear—'

'You've been talking to him all along!'

'—buying liquor at the discount store! Shit-faced drunk in her kitchen, lit up like a goddamn diva in a spotlight! The detective got photos, Meg, dozens of them.'

And that was all it took. Instantly, all the old anger kicked and bit and punched its way out of my heart. I was coming down County C toward the Point Road. I was watching the Suburban slow for the yield, and I did see it slow, I made certain of it, before I glanced away. I was staring at the cemetery plot that would hold the body of my child as soon as the ground thawed enough for the backhoe. I was rocking, naked, in the same bed where Evan had been conceived, screaming into my pillow, unable to let Rex touch me.

'I know,' Rex said. 'I know.'

Again, we heard the sound of a dingy drawing near. There was a knock on the side of the hull.

'Ahoy, *Chelone*!' This time, we recognized the voice of Marvin Thomas, Pam's husband, a retired ophthalmologist. 'Rex-man, need a lift?'

'Be right up,' Rex called. To me, he said, 'You can have the dingy. I'll catch a ride with someone after the game.'

'How much is it?' I asked, softly. 'The settlement?'

'Two hundred thousand.'

'Peanuts.' I spat the word. 'To someone like her, that's pocket change.'

But Rex shook his head. 'She's uninsured. Her trust is nearly spent. She took out a loan on the house before the accident.'

'She must have equity there.'

'The first forty thousand is protected by Wisconsin statute. She walks away with that much, at least, no matter what we do.'

Outside, Marvin's dingy motor flooded, choked, died. You could smell the belch of gas fumes as it started up again. Rex downed the rest of his drink in a gulp.

'I want to see those photographs,' I said. 'I want—'

But then my throat closed up. I couldn't say anything more.

'You know what?' Rex said. 'The hell with the game. Let me run up and tell Marv I've decided not to go.'

'No,' I said. 'If you don't go now, half the cove will be stopping by to ask if something's wrong.'

'You shouldn't be alone with this.'

'I've got the dingy,' I said. 'I'll head over to the 'Girls. I'm okay, I'll be okay,' I said, turning my head to avoid the sour taste of Scotch.

'Sorry,' Rex said, and then I was sorry, too, but it was too late. He was already up the steps.

Gone.

I tuned the single sideband to the BBC, tried to focus on world news as I dumped the perishables into the sour-smelling well of the refrigerator. The post-election scandal was heating up in Florida. The Middle East peace talks were falling apart again. Blood-colored liquid sloshed around at the bottom; the trap was blocked with a butter wrapper, eggshell, bits of cheese. It was time to clean it properly, thaw the layer of ice that was clinging to the cold plate. It was time to take everything out of the lockers, wipe the shelves down with diluted bleach. The trash bags were full. The floors needed washing. The brass grab rail in front of the stove begged for polish, as did the compression post. Outside, in the cockpit, the teak was overdue for staining and sealing. The hull's gel coat had lost its shine.

And this was only the beginning of all the things that needed to be done, tasks we'd fallen behind on since landing in Ladyslip Cove, since deciding we might as well stay until the end of the hurricane season, until Rex's shoulder had enjoyed all the benefits of a good long rest. Engine maintenance, through-hull checks. The head had developed a leak. There was a short in the bilge pump motor. *Chelone*'s batteries weren't charging as efficiently as they should. Perhaps, I would stay in tonight, put some time into the boat.

Clean the galley properly. Reinventory supplies. But suddenly, it all seemed overwhelming, and I threw myself, facedown, on the settee. Of course, I still thought about the civil suit. Of course, I still wondered if we'd been right – if I'd been right – to insist we let it go. Of course, I'd been hoping all along that Toby's stubborn attachment to Mallory would fade, that we'd return to Fox Harbor in a year to discover Cindy Ann had moved away. Somehow, we'd step back into our lives as if we'd never left them. Our tenant would vanish. Our jobs would reappear. One night, we'd come home from work to find Evan sitting at his place at the table.

Bullshit.

I was crying so hard I bit my tongue, tasted my own salty blood. Evan was dead, he'd been gone a whole year; still, I couldn't believe it. Toby and Mallory were engaged to be married. Cindy Ann still lived up the road, where she'd probably live forever and ever.

Unless she were forced to sell.

I thought, again, of the dream that I'd had, the two of us, walking by the side of the road: silent, stooping, rising. I imagined the photos the detective had taken, Cindy Ann with her head thrown back, raising her glass in a toast. Cindy Ann laughing, like a woman in an ad, lips parted, wet with shine. She looked nothing like Rex looked when he drank too much, and he *had* been drinking too much, night after night, there was simply no way not to see it. A couple of drinks before supper. A glass of wine with dinner, maybe two. The glass by the sink as he washed the supper dishes — I've got it, he'd say, why don't you go for a swim?

Come with me, I'd say.

I'm fine right here.

Want to play cards?

Not really.

A walk on the beach, then?

Ask Bernadette.

Drunk, his features unhinged themselves. His eyes grew puffy; his jaw lengthened, slack. Want anything? he'd say, pouring himself another drink, another Scotch, always another Scotch. Sitting in the amber-green glow of the kerosene lamp. Playing solitaire. The soft slap of cards against the table. Maybe, it wasn't just the alcohol. Maybe it was the combination of alcohol and the painkillers he'd been getting from the clinic. Or maybe it was just that he was aging so fast. Chronic pain could do that to a person. Make him seem older than he actually was. Make him drink more than was good for him. Make him seem like a stranger, someone vaguely unappealing, the friend or family member of a loved one you must, as part of the package, put up with at birthdays, holiday gatherings.

'We could fly back to the States,' I'd said. This had been several weeks earlier. 'Get your shoulder looked at by a specialist.'

'What would we do with the boat?'

'Put it in a slip. Eli would watch it.'

'That's too much to ask during hurricane season.'

'It's just that I'm worried about your—' I began, thinking I knew where the sentence was going, 'your drinking.' Quickly, I amended myself. 'Self-medicating, I mean. That's what it's called, when you drink out of pain. It's not that I don't understand why you do it.'

To my surprise, Rex laughed. 'If it's true that I'm *self-medicating*,' he said, 'then there's no need to travel three thousand miles to see a doctor, is there?'

'Rex.'

'Meg.' He poked my arm teasingly. 'Aw, c'mon. Look around. If you're worried about how much I drink, take a look at Eli.'

'He's not on medication.'

'Those warnings have more to do with legal protection than anything,' Rex said. Then he shrugged. 'But okay. After we're under way again, I'll clean up my act. I promise.'

'In January,' I said.

'January, February, whenever we get *Chelone* back in shape.' He gave me a quizzical look. 'What's the rush? We're happy here, right? And it's not like we're expected anywhere else.'

But I wouldn't have called it happiness that kept us in Lady-slip Cove. It was something closer to inertia, a deepening sense of ennui. Weeks had passed since we'd taken *Chelone* out for so much as a day sail, and when I thought of Jeanie McFadden, traveling alone with her dogs, her plans, I was envious. Restless. Longing to be back on the water, in motion, skimming across the surface. Falling into sleep at the end of each watch with such fullness, such force, that there was no room for thought, no choice beyond necessary oblivion, the closest thing I'd found, since Evan's death, to peace.

Now, breathing in the musty odor of the settee, everything seemed pointless. Worthless. I couldn't think of a single thing I truly wanted to do. It was exactly the way I'd felt before Rex and I had purchased *Chelone*, sailed off into what, I'd hoped, would be a new life, far from shore. Only now, here I was again. Here we were. Right back where we'd started.

No.

I got up, pumped water at the galley sink, splashed at my tear-swollen face. Then I went into our stateroom, searched through my locker for clothes. A miniskirt with a tropical print. A bright tank top. My old swimming suit to wear underneath. I threw off my torn shorts and faded T-shirt, dressed, put on earrings, pinned back my hair. Lipstick, eyeliner, mascara. Bronzer, which I dusted over my shoulders and cheeks.

I would go to Island Girls, damnit. I'd meet up with Bernadette and Pam, Audrey and Carole, whoever else was there. I'd drink and I'd dance and I'd have a good time, the hell with Arnie and his photographs, the hell with Cindy Ann and Mallory, the hell with Toby, too.

Why should we congratulate you?

It had been, I decided, the perfect response. What else could we have said? *As long as you're happy, we'll overlook the fact that your fiancée's sister murdered our son.*

I could feel the flames of my anger building, burning my regret, drying my tears. When I looked in the mirror one last time, there was no trace of sorrow anywhere.

'Got to get my game face on,' Rex used to say, facing a full day of arguments in court. Unlike most other attorneys we knew, he seldom had a drink when he came home from work, though he'd certainly enjoyed a glass of good Scotch, a shared bottle of wine, on the weekends. Instead, in the years before Evan was born, he'd fix himself a stack of peanut butter crackers, then head upstairs to his study. *The crow's nest,* he called it. There, sitting at his father's antique drafting table, he'd page through his collection of nautical magazines, his chart kits, his scrapbooks of neatly sketched sail plans, hull designs. I'd come home from work to find him studying lists of boats for sale, items circled, underlined, margins thick with notes.

After Evan was born, I'd find both of them up there, Evan tucked into the baby sling. By the age of two, Evan could tell you the difference between a sailboat and a motorboat. By four, he could talk about the Gulf Stream, point out the Caribbean on a chart. At six, he and Rex were making plans to build a wooden skiff in the garage. I'd follow the trail of cracker crumbs, the smell of peanut butter, to find them in the crow's nest with their heads bent over a set of blueprints, each of them holding an identically chewed grease pen, Evan talking, talking, talking.

'Look at this one, Mom, look at her lines,' he'd say, spraying me lightly with crumbs, and Rex would say, smiling, pleased, 'Isn't she a beauty, Meg?'

'She's a beauty, all right.'

Both of them would beam as if they actually believed I could see the difference between one little rowboat and another. What I liked to look at were the couples on the sailboats in Rex's collection of magazines. And there always were couples, women and men, roughly the ages of Rex and me. There were clasped hands, glasses of wine. There were sunsets the color of oranges. A sense of connection that seemed to run as deep as the ocean itself.

How close, I often thought, two people like that could be. How well they might come to know each other. No distractions. All that time. What a wonderful thing for a relationship.

Chapter Seven

There were three places to meet friends for a drink on Houndfish Cay. The first was the Ladyslip marina, which operated its own bar and restaurant, complete with white tablecloths, candles, good wine. It catered to the owners of the long, sleek yachts that occupied most of the slips, and the only time Bernadette and I had eaten there, we'd felt out of place with our sunburned noses, our calloused hands, our salt-scrubbed clothes. The second restaurant, Glory, four miles to the south in Martin's Cove, was run by a Bahamian couple who specialized in what I'd always considered midwestern food: pork sandwiches, Jell-O salad, baked macaroni and cheese. Getting there required a long, sweaty hike, too rough for Leon in his portable chair, so we didn't go often, although when we did, we spent the entire afternoon: diving for lobster off the rocky beach, shopping at the island market, enjoying homemade ice cream sold, by word of mouth, out of an elderly woman's kitchen. As we licked our cones, she'd pack a pint of peppermint into a bag of ice. 'For that boy of yours,' she'd say, and she wouldn't let Bernadette pay for it, either.

And then there was the Island Girls Pub and Grill, which was actually a grounded yacht, flung thirty feet ashore during a hurricane. Two women had claimed it, along with the tractor that washed up beside it, and proceeded to fix it up. They installed a generator, added a porch to disguise the ruptured hull, decorated everything with red Christmas lights. Finally they painted the tractor in swirls of green and neon pink, hung a matching sign from its bent steering wheel, and declared themselves open for business. Patrons could sit inside at the bar, or else claim a rusting metal table outside. Open barrels served as grills, arranged in a glowing crescent, and when the 'Girls got crowded, Gaylee might ask you to pull your own hot dog or burger. Miriam, her partner, seldom spoke, not even when you spoke to her first. She handled the cash, kept an eye on the bar, while Gaylee circulated brightly among the tables, teasing the regulars, helping out the staff, which on weekends included three waitresses, in addition to a grill man and cook.

Every now and then, there was live music, too. Tonight was one of those nights. Even before I stepped off the dirt road that wound past the marina, following the path toward the beach, I could hear the thud of overamped bass, the wandering strains of 'Margaritaville'. A few shouts of laughter, like shouts of rage, came from somewhere – the Cove, perhaps, or the honeymoon villas for rent behind the marina — falling all around me like a meteor shower. Sound carried differently, unpredictably, out here, especially on the outskirts of twilight. You might call to friends thirty feet away, and receive, in response, shrugs and gestures. You might pass the swim-up bar by the pool and overhear, in excruciating clarity, the whispered argument of a newlywed couple hunched against the bright, tiled wall.

Of course, my parents would be going to the wedding. Driving all the way there and back because my mother refused to fly. Bundled head to toe like arctic explorers, both of them complaining, bitterly, about the cold. Neither of them had come north since Evan's death, and it had struck me more than once that, without a grandchild to entice them, it was likely they'd never set foot outside of Florida for the rest of their lives. Of course, all that would change if Toby and Mallory were to have—

Children.

Mallory wasn't young anymore; still, it was a possibility. The thought was like a violent cramp, and I walked faster, trying to escape it.

Sand burrs caught in my sandals. Lizards rattled through the dry leaves, darted across the wide, flat surfaces of the scrub palms. Wild pigs lived on this island. So did bright flocks of parrots, descendants of exotics that escaped from captivity, survived. So did approximately 150 Bahamians, most of whom fished with hand-cast nets, worked at the marina or the villas. One family was known for the boats it built; another made custom sails. Women sold baked goods, seashells, crafts. There was a one-room schoolhouse. There was a Pentecostal church. The closest full-service hospital was a ferry ride plus a single-engine flight away. Still, a land developer had purchased most of the western arc of the island; a few weeks earlier, a barge had arrived, depositing bulldozers, backhoes, sacks of concrete. Now there was talk of the Echo Island ferry coming directly to the Cove. I'd spoken about it with Glory's owner, a woman everybody called Hal. In fact, her name was Halleluiah, which she'd tell you, if you asked, each syllable rolling from her mouth like clear water conjured from stone.

Praise God, she said, that everything go forward. Praise God there should be work for us all.

But aren't you afraid that the island will change? All these foreigners moving in?

Her smile was that of the victor, inscrutable and sly. Every person that come here among us come that much closer to God. Every man, woman, and child that eat my good food get a little bit of Jesus inside them.

I dropped back to a walk. Breathing hard, I ducked to avoid a low branch, dark with sap. Poisonwood. The rash it triggered, so they said, made poison ivy seem no more significant than a mosquito bite. Bernadette had warned me, early on, about the poisonwood trees, the same way she'd warned me about nurse sharks, about jellyfish, about the half-wild dogs that prowled the island in rough-coated, glittery-eyed packs. Potcakes, the Bahamians called them. A little of this, a little of that, unlikely scraps cooked together in one pot. Harmless, people assured one another, but still. Out on the paths, alone, it was best to keep a stone in your pocket.

Considering this, I bent to scoop up a fist-size King's crown, heavy as a mug.

Sharp claws scrabbled against my hand.

I dropped it with a muffled yelp. Hermit crab. It motored away. At the same time, something crashed through the underbrush, trailing a rippling green wake. Spooked, I stopped. Listened. The thrum of the band, the thick bass beat, had been swallowed by the hush-hush-hush of the surf. A twig snapped. A banana chit startled, wings scissoring the air. Though I'd walked here dozens of times before, the waning light – tinged with shades of cobalt, steel – made everything appear sharp-edged, unfamiliar, shadows lolling like tongues. Something was watching me. Following me. I began to walk again. Rounding a bend in the path, I saw another stone, mottled like coral, the size and shape of a robin's egg. I bent down to grab it, and as I did, I was swept by the sense, no, the *certainty*, that I'd done this before, not once, but hundreds of times. Reaching for the bag slung over my shoulder, my arm rasped against the orange vest I wore, only it wasn't my arm, my vest, my body. I was looking down at someone I didn't recognize. Beyond the blinking yellow light, on the other side of the intersection, a small, white cross poked up through the weeds. It was tilting to the side, one arm propped against the ground, which was littered with paper cups, plastic bags, curling strips of blown tire. The sky was low, overcast. The cold wind failed to stir the dull, frost-tipped grass.

My God, I thought, understanding where I was, and for the second time in my life, lightning passed through my body. I could not see. I could not recall my name. I fell, facedown, on the sandy path as a great wailing rose all around me.

Rough hands pulled at my shoulders.

'What the hell,' a man said, his face close to mine. 'What was it?' he said. 'Where did it go?'

Blinking, I could just make out the baseball cap he wore, a boat logo stamped on its brim. TOP BILLING. Beside him was a woman; she clutched at his arm, crushing it against her full breasts.

'Are you hurt?' she said. 'Was it some kind of animal?'

'I'm not sure,' I said, struggling to my feet. I was still holding on to the egg-shaped stone; I dropped it as if it had scorched my palm. Overhead, the sky had passed from twilight into darkness.

'Probably a goddamn wild dog.'

'Or a panther,' the woman said, nervously. 'I think there are panthers. Are there panthers?'

'Where are you headed? We'll walk you, won't we, Iris?'

the man said. He was pink-cheeked with sunburn, his neck haloed by a thin, gold chain. I realized he was waiting for me to answer. Iris waited, too.

'Island Girls,' I managed to say.

'That's where we're going,' the man said, and he put a fatherly arm around each of us, propelling us along the path. 'Nowhere in the world like the 'Girls. I told Iris, you've never seen anything like this place.'

'I've never seen a panther either,' she said. Her pants were the kind issued in travel magazines, little zippers sewn around each thigh so the legs could be removed in hot weather. She wore a pink fanny pack and matching pink sneakers. Tooth-colored braces on her teeth. I clung to each precise detail, proof that I'd returned from wherever, whoever, I'd been. Still, I was afraid to look down at myself, afraid I'd see a body that wasn't my own. Taller, fuller through the chest and hips. Pale hands with long fingers.

A chunky silver ring.

'There's a lot Iris here hasn't seen,' the man said, conversationally.

'Teddy's right about that,' Iris agreed.

'We met at the ticket counter.'

'I'm supposed to be visiting my sister in Cleveland.'

'Iris is a teacher.'

'I'm going to lose my job over this,' Iris said, and her expression was equal parts desperation and cheer.

By now we were climbing the rise to the beach; I could see the red haze of the Christmas lights, smell the cooking meat. I was starting to feel better. I was finding explanations. Something had startled me and I'd fallen. Whatever it had been, these people had heard it, too.

'You going to be okay?' Teddy asked.

I nodded, pointing to a table by the cinder block stage where Bernadette sat with Audrey and Pam. Carole Daniels was there, too, and the new girl, Jeanie McFadden. No sign of the twins. At a nearby table, Gaylee took orders, swatting at her ankles with a notepad.

'My friends,' I said. 'Thanks.'

But Teddy had already turned to Iris, his hand on the small of her back. 'How about a nice Frozen Girlfriend?'

'A what?'

He steered her past the smoking grills, up the crooked porch steps, toward the bar. By now Bernadette had spotted me; she waved me over, the others twisting in their seats to say hello. Every table was full tonight, packed with groups of cruisers I recognized from Ladyslip, King's Point, Martin's Cove. At the edge of the beach, couples were dancing. More couples sat on blankets. Just beyond the surf, sailboats and trawlers were anchored in a twinkling constellation, some with lighted Christmas trees strapped to the tips of their bows.

'Are you okay?' Audrey said, raising her voice to be heard.

For the first time since I'd fallen, I allowed myself to look down. My skirt, familiar, but torn. My own legs, streaked with mud and sand. Gingerly, I touched my knee, beaded with crystals of blood. Pain. The sting came as a strange relief.

'I thought I heard something following me,' I began, but then I stopped, started to laugh. How stupid it all seemed now. 'I started running and tripped. I guess if there'd really been anything there, it would have dragged me off and eaten me.'

'You look as if that's what happened,' Pam said.

Bernadette squeezed my wrist; her hand was ice cold, as always. *Cold hands, warm heart*: it was something my mother said.

'Little bastards,' Carole said, kicking at the bugs under the table.

Pam said, 'You told us they were in bed.'

'Not funny.'

Gaylee came over with her notepad, aimed her pen at my knee. 'Good one,' she said, with a whistle of admiration. 'Can I get you something for the pain?'

'One Frozen Girlfriend,' I said.

Frozen Girlfriends were the Island Girls' signature drink, the key to the pub's success. They were made of rum and ginger, pulverized ice, peach liqueur, and a mystery ingredient that very possibly might not have been legal. They smelled of high school, of bubble gum and lip gloss; they were the color of fresh cotton candy twisted around a paper cone. They tasted like what, as a little girl, I'd imagined pink champagne would taste like, and this was what got people into trouble. The drink seemed harmless. Innocent. It wasn't. You ordered one, paced yourself, nursed it through the night. Only the greenest of cruisers ever ordered them in pitchers. Above the bar, a hand-lettered sign declared: MANAGEMENT NOT RESPONSIBLE FOR FINANCIAL INVESTMENTS OR ROMANTIC PROPOSALS MADE WHILE UNDER THE INFLUENCE OF A FROZEN GIRLFRIEND.

'Truth serum,' Gaylee replied, whenever somebody questioned her about the secret ingredient.

Miriam, who'd invented the drink, said nothing, of course, whether you asked or didn't. She took your cash, made your change, slipped the bills into a lockbox. Nobody could understand how she and Gaylee had gotten together, though every now and then an unhappy rumor lifted its diamond head. Something about Gaylee having been married. Something about a child, a girl, who'd gotten in some kind of trouble. Something about Miriam – Gaylee's longtime admirer – convincing Gaylee to chuck everything, leave it all behind.

By the time my drink arrived, the band had gone on break. 'You look different somehow,' Bernadette said.

I took my first sip. It tasted so good that I'd swallowed a third of it before I realized what I was doing.

'I feel different,' I said, wiping my mouth with the back of my hand.

'Different in what way?'

'I'm not exactly sure.'

'Easy there,' Audrey said as I took another drink. 'You don't want to end up like her.' She rolled her eyes toward the tractor, where a woman in pink sneakers and a pink fanny pack sat teetering on the seat. Iris. She was singing into an imaginary microphone, belting out the words to 'Red, Red Wine'. Below, Teddy swayed a little, calling up encouragements.

'Why not?' Jeanie said, and she lit a cigarette. 'As long as she's having fun.' She was tall as a basketball player. Skinny. One arm tattooed with a butterfly, the other with a fat bumblebee.

Carole turned toward Bernadette and me; she'd been talking about the twins, and now she roped us happily, eagerly, into her story. 'So we're just about ready for bed last night, when Jamie crawls out of his berth. Turns out he's sleepwalking – can you believe it? Before we can say boo, he pulls down his PJs, piddles right there on the floor.'

'I'm never having kids,' Jeanie said. One bare, coltish knee poked over her plate; she picked at a toenail, studied what she'd found.

'It isn't all like that,' Audrey said. She was a graceful, gentle woman in her early seventies, the leader of our morning yoga sessions. She and her husband, Earl, had raised four children, some of whom had children of their own, all of whom descended on the Cove each year at Christmastime, bringing an assortment of friends, spouses, sweethearts. 'If it were, then the human race would have died out a long time ago.'

'The planet would be better off,' Jeanie said.

Pam laughed. Carole kept on talking.

'We barely get that mess cleaned up when Joshie appears. Same funny look on his face. Before we can stop him, he's hosing down the galley shelves, top to bottom.'

Bernadette nudged me under the table; Audrey caught my eye. Even when Carole left the twins at home, you wound up feeling as if she'd brought them along.

'I hope you made *them* clean it up, at least,' Pam said. She and Marvin had no children. Instead, they'd adopted half a dozen dogs: potcakes, strays, hopeless cases of every kind. Every morning, you'd see Marv in the dingy, motoring them to shore to do their business, fighting for balance in the midst of all those mismatched ears and spotted tongues.

'But they were *sleepwalking*,' said Carole. 'It wasn't like it was their fault.'

'Maybe they were just pretending.' Jeanie blew a jet of cigarette smoke into a hovering cloud of gnats.

'You can't pretend to sleepwalk.'

'Sure you can.'

'Not like that.'

Audrey said, changing the subject, 'At least they didn't set the boat on fire.'

'Well, that's the thing,' Carole said. 'I can't stop wondering what they'll do *next*.' Her good-natured smile became rabbity, anxious. 'Why do you think they're doing it? Maybe they're mad about something. Maybe I toilet trained them wrong and that's why they're pissing in my pots and pans.'

'The subconscious mind will assert itself,' Audrey said.

Pam groaned. 'Spare us the Freud.'

'No, she's got a point,' Bernadette said, jumping in all at once, the way you make up your mind to enter cold water. 'If Carole had twin *girls*, would *they* be pissing all over her house?'

'It's biology!'

'Freud was a misogynistic shithead—'

'But the stuff about boys and their mothers—'

There was less than an inch of pink left in my glass, but I didn't remember drinking it. And I wasn't feeling the effects of it in the least. This wasn't like me. It *wasn't* me. There, on my index finger, I could still see the shadow of that chunky silver ring. Cindy Ann's ring. I'd noticed it in court and again, later, at the grocery story. Of course Mallory would have made it. It was like the one she'd made for Toby. All of Mallory's jewelry had that same, heavy look.

I stood up, bumping the table with my thighs. Everyone scrambled to catch their drinks.

'Down in front,' Pam said.

Again Bernadette's cold hand found mine; this time, I pulled it away. There was nothing on my finger but my own pink skin. There'd been nothing on the sandy path where I had fallen. I signaled Gaylee for another drink.

'You go, girl,' Jeanie said.

It was after the band came back from break that time began to dissolve.

I remember telling someone I'd seen a panther. Someone at a nearby table said they'd seen it, too. Someone else had encountered a herd of wild pigs, complete with yellow tusks and tufted tails, and Jeanie actually stubbed out her cigarette to describe something she'd encountered offshore: dragon-eyed, silver-scaled, rising from an oily pool.

'Your imagination,' Carole said.

'I think I know the difference,' Jeanie said, 'between water and my damn imagination.'

Then Carole was gone and we were on the beach, dancing, singing along with the band. The band's shaggy-headed drummer danced with us. Iris and a heavyset woman danced, too. For a while, I found myself dancing with Teddy; he whooped happily when I stumbled, barefooted, onto his toes. Hadn't I been wearing sandals? Hadn't I worn a tank top over my swimming suit? Then Teddy was gone, and Bernadette and I were swimming together like mermaids, like beautiful long-tailed fish, and I was sixteen years old, skinny-dipping

with Cindy Ann in the iced clarity of the lake. Afterward, the
air felt warm against our skins as we dressed, slapping at
mosquitoes, tugging our wet shorts over our hips. How safe
we felt in the darkness, screened by the thick stand of trees at
the base of the bluff. It never crossed my mind that anyone
could be watching. Lying on Cindy Ann's mattress in the attic,
reading, studying, quizzing each other for tests, I felt like a
princess in a high, walled tower, the wide fields below like a
flowering moat. What did we talk about? School, classmates,
what we wanted to do with our lives. I don't think we ever
once talked about Dan Kolb. A couple of times, we tried on
clothes, getting ready to go out. A small fan turned its head,
side to side. *No*, it said. *No, no.* A single wasp buzzed in the
eaves. The voices of Cindy Ann's sisters in the garden drifted
through the windows like faint, sweet scent.

Cindy Ann's mother off to work at the post office. Dan
Kolb below, minding Ricky, his son. Dan had been the hired
man, arriving the same year Mallory was born. When George
Donaldson walked out on his family, Dan had stepped in:
neatly, seamlessly.

There were two wooden doors at the top of the attic steps.
The one to the left opened into Cindy Ann's room. The one
straight ahead led to a narrow crawl space, stuffed with
household odds and ends: broken toys, mismatched furniture,
snowsuits and sleds and saucers. Mr Kolb had promised he'd
turn that crawl space into a closet for Cindy Ann, an actual

walk-in closet with an overhead light and built-in shelves. He'd even started working on this, hauling boxes of junk to the shed; he'd used red marker on Cindy Ann's wall where he planned to install louvered doors. All this had taken place in spring, before my sixteenth birthday, before Cindy Ann and I became friends. By the time we were up in her room, on that particular August day, the red outline on her wall had become invisible to us, the way that the wall itself was invisible, made of rough, knotted pine. The slats didn't fit flush against one another; the plaster between them had crumbled away. The paint, too, was peeling off in strips: papery, translucent, like sunburned skin.

'Did you hear that?' I said.

'Hear what?' Cindy Ann said.

But I knew that she'd heard it, too, because she reached over, turned off the fan. What we'd heard had been a cough or, rather, the sound of someone suppressing a cough. It had come from behind the wall, from behind the red outline sketched on the wall.

'Your dad,' I said, because that's what Cindy Ann called Dan Kolb, even though, of course, he was her stepdad.

'He's downstairs with Ricky,' Cindy Ann said.

'Maybe he's working on the closet,' I said.

She got up, knocked within the outline of the louvered doors as if she believed they were already there, as if she were a child playing house. 'Hello?'

Silence.

We felt it then, the presence of someone, waiting. Mr Kolb, it had to be. Only why didn't he say something? Why didn't he knock back?

Cindy Ann sprang toward her bedroom door, catlike. 'Wait,' I began, but she'd already flung it open, grasped the cracked glass knob on the crawl space door. This door, like Cindy Ann's, was badly warped, which meant it couldn't close completely. Instead it rested lightly against its swollen frame. Cindy Ann threw herself at it anyway, shoulder first, like a TV cop. I saw it give slightly, suspiciously, then spring back.

'You try.'

Cindy Ann shoved me forward, and I caught the warm, slick knob in both hands, infected by the same determination. We were foxes on the scent of a rabbit. We were dogs, baying at a treed 'coon. We would flush him out, dig him out, demand an explanation. For several minutes, we fought with that door until, suddenly, Cindy Ann stepped back.

A high, shrill cry rose from below.

'Ricky,' she said, and together we turned, thundered down the steps. There he was on the living-room floor, sobbing, banging his head against his fist. That was why you had to watch him all the time. When he fell, his walker slipped out of range, so he couldn't get back on his feet. It took Cindy Ann half an hour to calm him, rocking him, kissing him, peeling his hands from his face. I fixed three glasses of Kool-Aid, washing out the jelly jars I found in the sink. When Becca and Mallory appeared, I divided what was left in the pitcher, and we were all sitting around the kitchen table when Mr Kolb appeared.

He hadn't come in from outside. The kitchen door stood opposite the table, so we would have noticed, if he had. Nobody ever used the front door to the house. The living-room TV, in fact, stood against it.

'What, none for me?' Mr Kolb said, eyeing our glasses. Then, noticing Ricky's face: 'What happened? Rick, were you hitting yourself? Did something upset you?'

He looked at Cindy Ann anxiously, curiously.

'You left him alone,' she said.

'Jeez, Rick, I'm sorry,' Mr Kolb said, and he pressed his lips into Ricky's matted hair. 'Did you get in a tight spot? Did you take a little spill?'

He pulled up a chair, settled close to Ricky's side, stroked the red plane of Ricky's cheek with a gentleness that made me think of Toby. Then he scooped up Mallory, settled her onto his knee. I waited for Cindy Ann to ask where he'd been, but she said nothing, so I said nothing, too. We all were going to pretend that nothing weird had happened. Frankly, I was relieved. Probably it meant nothing. Probably he'd just been working back there, with headphones on, or something. Maybe all the crap inside the closet had blocked the door. I busied myself cleaning up the kitchen, washing the dishes, scrubbing the countertops. After a while, Cindy Ann joined me. She dried everything and put it away. She took out the trash and mopped the floors, and we were just starting in on the windows when Mrs Kolb walked in the door.

'My goodness, girls,' Mrs Kolb said. She looked like a police officer in her postal service uniform. 'What a lovely surprise.'

She kissed Mr Kolb, who kissed her back. They were like that, the Kolbs, and it fascinated me. My own parents never kissed back then – not each other, certainly not Toby and me. It was why I'd always made it a point to kiss Evan first thing in the morning. I kissed him again when I dropped him off at school. I kissed him in the afternoon, as soon as he got in the car. I kissed him when I put on his pajamas and I kissed him when I tucked him into bed.

Kiss-kiss? he'd ask. *Kiss-kiss!*

Not *kiss*. Never *kiss*.

'Don't take Leon to a hospital,' I told Bernadette. 'At least, if something happens, here you're going to be right there with him. He won't die calling for you, wondering where you are.'

I was trying to explain myself clearly. I was trying to say what I meant. It was difficult, though, because each sentence kept getting away from me. It was like lobbing a ball from the top of a cliff: I simply couldn't predict exactly where it would end up. So I began again. I began again. The way that it made me feel, seeing Mr and Mrs Kolb kiss. Whenever they kissed, they closed their eyes. *The love of my life,* Mrs Kolb liked to say.

At sixteen, I had never been kissed – at least, not by someone who counted, which meant someone who wasn't related to me. Neither had Cindy Ann. Cindy Ann and her sisters kissed on the lips. Rex always kissed me before he left for work and again, at night, when I went upstairs. There in his study. His sailing magazines. Peanut butter, crackers. Kindergarten breath.

Evan's breath. The last time I kissed Evan.

That was it. There it was.

I told Bernadette.

My voice was hoarse from shouting. I wanted to be heard over the band. Only the band wasn't playing anymore. The band, in fact, was gone. All of the tables were empty, too, except for the one where I sat with Bernadette. She was stroking my hair, and Audrey, hello, was holding my hands very tightly. Pam was there, too, and Jeanie. Gaylee. I was wearing my bathing suit, gritty with sand, and my skirt, which clung stickily to my hips.

I realized I'd been talking for a long, long time.

'So did he keep molesting her – your friend?' Pam asked. 'Your ex-friend, I mean.'

The truth was this: I hadn't wanted to know.

'That's hardly the point,' Audrey said, quickly.

'He's a bastard, regardless,' Pam agreed. 'I didn't mean that he wasn't.'

'Still,' Jeanie said, lighting another cigarette, 'that sort of thing happens all the time. It's no excuse for driving drunk with your kids in the car and everything.'

'Excuse, no,' Bernadette said. 'But maybe an explanation.'

'I don't accept that,' Gaylee said. Her voice was soft, strange.

'Excuse, explanation,' Jeanie said. 'Who fucking cares? My parents were killed by a drunk driver, okay? The guy had cancer. He died four months later. He never even had to go to jail.'

For a moment, no one said anything. Sea sounds swelled to fill the gap. Out of the corner of my eye, I saw Miriam move between the citronella torches, arm raised like a sickle, smothering each small flame.

'Hey, it's okay,' Jeanie said. 'Life sucks and then you die.'

'Not always,' Audrey said. 'No.'

'Right,' Jeanie said. 'Sometimes you just die.'

And Bernadette said, 'It's a shame that he died before you had a chance to forgive him.'

Once again, nobody spoke.

'Why should she have to forgive anybody?' I said, and now I couldn't keep the anger from my voice.

Bernadette met my gaze. 'I didn't say she had to.'

'Well, I'm glad he's dead,' Jeanie said. 'I'm glad his kids don't get to have him.'

'But it wasn't their fault,' Audrey said.

'Like it was mine?' Jeanie said. She nodded at me. 'That's

what's so shitty about your kid dying like he did. Because *her* kids didn't. That's just so wrong. There should be, like, a law or something.'

'An eye for an eye,' Pam said, nodding. 'It's there in the Bible for a reason.'

'That's right,' Gaylee said.

'And so the world goes blind,' Audrey said.

'Only the assholes,' Jeanie said.

'I used to feel that way,' Bernadette said. 'After Leon was born. After we realized the extent of his brain damage. If you'd told me then that Dr Matt would be a friend, I'd have said – well, I don't know what I would have said. I certainly couldn't have imagined it.'

I grew so dizzy I thought I might faint. 'Why?' I said. 'What did he have to do with it?'

She was looking at her hands. 'He was the doctor on call. The doctor who delivered Leon. I thought I told you this.'

'You didn't,' I said.

'You told me,' Audrey said.

'I don't even think about it much anymore,' Bernadette said. Then she sighed. 'Matt was addicted to narcotics. He'd been fired from hospitals in three different states. We didn't know that, of course. Our regular OB was on vacation, so when I went into labor, Matt got called.' She was still looking at her hands, the delicate map of each palm. 'Matt misread the ultrasound. He got belligerent when the nurses tried to correct him. He was dropping things, cursing. It was a nightmare.'

'He dropped Leon?' I said, horrified.

'No,' Bernadette said. 'But Leon was over ten pounds, and it took – well, he was injured, we both were injured.' Again she sighed. 'When I woke up, I was told my baby wouldn't live, that he wouldn't ever know us if he did.'

'But certainly,' I said, stiffly, 'you *did* something about what happened. You prosecuted – Matt.'

'Well, of course we did,' Bernadette said, her voice suddenly sharp. 'What do you think? We'd just let him go on hurting people?'

'So what happened to him?' Jeanie said.

Bernadette shrugged. 'Not much. He lost his license. There was an insurance settlement. He had to go through rehab. At the hearing, he just sat there with his attorney. He didn't even look at us.'

I said, cautiously, 'That's how it was with Cindy Ann.'

'Six months passed and then he wrote to us, this truly awful letter. He said he thought about Leon every day, and how depressed he was, and I wrote back and said, We think about him every day, too, we're depressed, too, because we're the ones taking care of him, trying to figure out a life for him. I mean, I was just livid. But he kept writing and I kept writing and, eventually, we took Leon to see him. This was a few months before we moved aboard *Rubicon*. He wrote out a list of all the equipment we'd need, all the medicines and their dosages. It's funny, but Leon really liked him from the first. We visit Matt every summer, now, whenever we go back to New Bern.'

Pam said, 'If I had a kid, and someone did something like this, I'd visit him, too. On the day he went to the electric chair. I'd be there to pull the switch.'

'He didn't kill Leon.'

'He might as well have.'

Bernadette's head snapped forward. 'That's not for you to say.'

'He killed the person Leon was supposed to be. I mean, what kind of life is he going to have? How will he feel when he's a grown man and you still have to wipe his butt?'

'Quality of life—' Audrey began, indignant, but Bernadette put a hand on her arm.

'No,' she said. 'Let's say Matt did kill Leon. Let's say Leon died when he was born. Let's say that we're in, I don't know, Florida, and there's a jury and judge who will actually sentence Dr Matt to death. Then what?' Bernadette said.

'Zzzt,' Jeanie said.

'You bet,' Gaylee said, in that same, soft voice.

Bernadette shook her head. 'I could pull that switch myself. It wouldn't make any difference.'

'But of course it would,' Gaylee said. 'It does. It did.' She lifted her chin. 'I had a child, too, you know. She was waiting for the bus at the end of the drive. Three men pulled up in a car. I was watching from the window, from the window of *our home*, but by the time I got outside they'd taken her.'

Even Jeanie sat motionless, cigarette burning like a hard, red eye.

'Two of them were juveniles,' Gaylee said, 'but the oldest, he was nineteen. We had to petition the court, but I got to be there when he died. I would have given the injection myself, if they'd let me do it.' She was standing now, bending over Bernadette as if she meant to kiss her on the mouth. 'Tell me I should forgive what they did to her. How they dumped what was left of her when they were done. How they joked about it. Bragged about it.'

'Honey,' said a voice no one recognized, melodious and calm. I looked up to see Miriam, her eyes fixed on Gaylee. Behind her stood the derelict yacht that was their home. 'That's enough, now. Let's go.'

'She was thirteen years old,' Gaylee said. 'She was thirteen.'

Strings of Christmas lights slashed the darkness.

'Honey,' Miriam said.

'Tell me you wouldn't fall down on your knees and pray for those bastards to die.'

'I can't tell you what I would do,' Bernadette said, 'any more than you can tell me.'

'I could tell you,' Jeanie said.

'Me, too,' I said.

You could not have distinguished our voices.

'Let's go,' Miriam said again, and she guided Gaylee away from us, past the last glowing barrel, toward the entrance to the yacht. As they stepped up onto the makeshift porch, the Christmas lights vanished, swiftly, soundlessly. In the unexpected dimness, Jeanie and Pam rose, too. Pam cocked her head at me as if to say, *You coming?*

'I'm going to tell you something,' Jeanie said to Bernadette. 'You're deluding yourself.'

'Perhaps,' Bernadette said.

'Either that, or you're full of shit.'

'Perhaps,' she said again.

I stayed behind with Bernadette. For a long time, neither of us spoke. My head ached. My eyes burned. My stomach was a sour ball of fire.

'I'm sorry,' Bernadette said, 'about your son.'

I touched her arm, the way she might have touched mine. 'I'm sorry about what Dr Matt did to Leon.'

'He almost killed me, too, you know. I can't have any more children.' She made an odd, rueful face, as if she'd broken something meaningless and small: a cup, a glass figurine. 'But I just couldn't hate him anymore.'

'But you do,' I said. 'Of course, you do. Anybody would.'

'I forgive him, Meggie,' she said. 'I forgave him years ago.'

'Well, what if he hadn't been sorry?' I said, and I thought

of Gaylee's daughter. I thought of Jeanie, alone in the world. I thought of Cindy Ann at her kitchen table, drinking wine, breathing air, while Evan's body rotted in the ground.

'He wasn't sorry,' Bernadette said. 'He never apologized, not once. To this day, he insists it was all an accident, a misunderstanding involving procedure. I forgive him for that, too. *I* forgive him. *Me*. This has nothing to do with him.'

My teeth were chattering wildly. 'Jeanie was right,' I said. 'You are deluding yourself. No one can forgive something like that.'

Bernadette's face in the moonlight: pale. Her hair, in its braids, a corona of fire. Behind her, a flurry of stars filled the sky. 'Hasn't anyone ever forgiven you,' she said, 'for something you shouldn't have done? Something you failed to do?'

She could have been painted on velvet. She could have been a vision, described in a papyrus scroll. She could have been looking into my heart and reading every last thing ever written there.

'Not like that,' I said.

'Are you certain?' she said.

I opened my mouth, then closed it. Got up. Walked away.

Chapter Eight

Imagine a woman stumbling along a solitary trail, the eastern horizon dark as glass, overgrown branches beating at her like sharp, balled fists. The pain at the back of her head like the most insistent cliché: a pounding, a drumming, a hammering with ice picks. She is positively aching with righteousness and rage, yet, already, the first few tendrils of regret have begun to emerge like quiet assassins, like slim, venomous snakes. She wonders what it was, exactly, that has made her so blindingly angry. Bernadette's capacity for forgiveness? The idea of forgiveness itself?

You're deluding yourself. Even if this were true — and it is, there is no doubt in her mind on that point — why should it matter? What difference can it make? Why does it feel like a personal attack?

Somehow, she's passed the turnoff to the marina; the path dead-ends at the back of one of the new condominium developments. There are shrink-wrapped blocks of cream-colored tile, bags of concrete, a stack of small, kidney-shaped swimming pools. Cursing her mistake, she cuts between the skeletal frames until she reaches the water. From there, she follows the shoreline back to the marina, picking her way along the rocky strip of beach until, at last, she emerges from behind the restaurant, startling a couple kissing passionately by the pool. They stare at her as if she is an apparition. Her feet are cut, bleeding. They stick to the wooden slats as she steps up onto the pier. It is only when she reaches the dingy dock that she understands she's been hoping, all along, that she might still catch up with Bernadette. Say something. Say anything.

But *Rubicon*'s dingy is gone.

By now, it is well after midnight, closing in on dawn. Still, the marina is wide awake. People stand in their cockpits, drinking, talking, listening to music. Halogen beams shoot like dealership spotlights from the tall tuna towers of the sport fishing boats, and the air is thick with the odor of grilled fish, barbecue, the musty odor of rum. The fish smell makes the woman's mouth water unpleasantly; she sits down at the edge of the pier, feet dangling, waiting for the feeling to pass. Out in the cove, mast lights wink like fireflies. She can just make out *Chelone*'s, taller than the others, brighter. By now, Rex's poker game is over, and she hopes he has gone to bed instead of sitting up, waiting, worrying. The last thing she wants to do is face him, explain what has just happened, admit that she's thrown a fat, knotted rope into their past. By tomorrow evening, the truth will have boarded every last boat in the Cove. They will no longer be anonymous.

For the first time since their arrival, they will find themselves alone.

Christ, her head is aching. The soles of her feet sting horribly, and there's an unexplained burning – like a ringing in her ears – at the back of her neck, across her shoulders, down one arm. The burning seems to be expanding. Perhaps, she thinks, it's the stories she's heard, all that rage taking root beneath her skin, traveling like a dark, fierce vine: Jeanie's story, Gaylee's story, Bernadette's, her own. For a moment, she tries to imagine Gaylee's daughter, forever thirteen, holding Evan by the hand; she places Jeanie's parents beside them, like dolls, watching over them both in a place of warmth and light. Here, too, she glimpses the man with his cancer, the shadows of the three young men in the car. The lion lain down with the lamb. How she longs to believe in something like this, but she does not. Cannot. There will never be closure, she sees that now. There will never be explanations. People hurt each other and are hurt in turn. Children pass through like seasons. Lightning bolts fall from the sky.

How can one live in a world like this, and then keep on living, after it happens? The violent act, the car crash. The murderous illness, the shrill disappointment. The terrorist act, the war, the plague, the tornado that snatches your house and leaves your neighbor's standing, down to the potted plants on the porch, the swing set, everything intact. Such random abominations! The woman's headache grips the back of her skull like an external force, something cold-blooded, evil, and for a moment, she thinks about how easy it would be to simply fall forward off the pier, slip into the shimmering silence of the water. Her body would be found, of course. An accident, people would say.

But, no. The woman stands up.

I, Megan Van Dorn, force myself to stand.

There's a wobbling ladder attached to the pier and I ease myself down, step by step. The dingy floats just a few feet away like a faithful horse: round-bellied, patient. Hours seem to pass before I'm able to coordinate my hands with my body, twist around to grasp the line, pull the bow in close. By now, the sky is turning pink. My skin is catching fire. Stepping into the dingy, I cry out, then simply cry, for the cut bottoms of my feet have landed in three inches of salt water, spilled oil, gasoline. I can't get the engine going. It takes dozens of pulls on the chain before I realize I've forgotten to pump the gas line; then, when the motor catches, I twist the throttle in the wrong direction, wind up choking it dead. It's this headache, I tell myself, longing for aspirin, a glass of cool water. It's this sunburn consuming my shoulders and chest. The dingy pulls away, then jerks into a curve; I've forgotten to untie the line, which I should have done from the pier. In the end, I pry it off the bow cleat, abandon it, dangling, in the water.

Back to the boat. It's all that I want: a drink of water, the dark salon. I'm halfway to the channel when I realize, with a start, that I can't see *Chelone*, can't find her anywhere. What the hell, I think, what the *fuck*. Circling the Cove, again and again, and though I recognize the boats I see — *Extravagance, Flyboy, Great Blue, Donovan's Dream* — I can't make sense of the way they are arranged, can't find my way to where I know *Chelone* must be. Cutting short around *Gator Bait*, I foul the propeller on her anchor chain, just as the first ray of morning sun spits its poison light across the cove. What the hell's the matter with me? Where is the goddamn boat? I'm drifting now, the engine dead, the propeller quite possibly broken, when, suddenly, I understand.

I'm not hungover. I'm intoxicated.

Still intoxicated.

I am driving drunk.

I'd driven drunk only once before, for roughly half a mile, on the night of my sixteenth birthday. It was the end of May. It was closing on the end of the school year. Somebody's grandparents had a summer cottage. Somebody decided we should all break in, throw a party there — who would ever know? Somehow the whole thing evolved into a birthday party, my birthday party. Sweet sixteen. Girls who'd never spoken to me before mouthed *Happy Birthday* as they passed in the halls; boys whispered, *What do you want for your birthday?* in low, delicious voices. Word of the party spread to kids as far away as Horton, and by the time Friday rolled around, you could feel the momentum building like a rogue wave, feeding on its own widening power. In the school parking lot, kids opened the trunks of their cars to reveal kegs, stacks of wine coolers. Somebody scaled the gymnasium wall and hung a shiny banner that proclaimed, HAPPY BIRTHDAY! Somebody wrote HAPPY BIRTHDAY in whipped cream across the windshield of the principal's car.

'I don't like the idea of you driving alone,' my mother said. 'I mean, honey, you only got your license today.'

She and my father had made it a point to be home for dinner that night. Toby had shown up as well. We'd ordered a pizza from the new Pizza Hut, which we ate at the dining-room table, good cloth napkins draped across our knees. A yellow cake from the bakery. Neatly wrapped gifts, which my mother had chosen: a cardigan, earrings, a gift certificate for books and cassettes. Of course, she had to photograph me opening each one, Toby smirking in the background, making rabbit ears over my head. Everything had been perfect until I'd asked to borrow the car. At lunchtime, I'd walked downtown and passed my driver's test. Now, as my mother gaped in surprise, I held out my newly minted license, a poker-faced player who reveals the winning hand.

'I won't be alone,' I said. 'I'm picking up Stacy.'

'At least,' Toby said, scooping frosting off my plate, 'if you loan Meggie the car, you know she'll be with a safe driver.'

'How can a fifteen, excuse me, *sixteen*-year-old be a safe driver?'

'Beats me,' Toby said. 'But she is.'

I looked at my plate, flushed, pleased. Toby, in fact, had taught me to drive, taking me out with my learner's permit, making me parallel park, again and again, beside a stack of hay bales at the mill.

My mother sighed. 'Where is it you and Stacy want to go?' she asked, resigned, and for a moment, I had a change of heart. Nowhere, I wanted to say. I was only kidding, Mom, relax. How easy it would be to skip the party altogether, stay home, watch the videos she'd rented for us all. But I said nothing. It was my sixteenth birthday. You couldn't stay home on your sixteenth birthday, no matter how much you liked being with your family, especially when there was a party going on, the sort of party where everyone who was anyone planned to be. And even if there'd been no party, I would have found another reason to slap my license down on the table, too casually, saying, *So, can I borrow the car?* I wanted my parents to believe that I was capable of having a life beyond them, that they didn't know me as completely as they'd thought.

'We're meeting some friends at Dairy Castle,' I said. This wasn't exactly a lie. We'd arranged to collect Stacy's boyfriend there, along with some of his friends, before heading on to the party.

'Take my car, then,' my father said. It was the first time he'd spoken. 'It's heavier. You'll be safer.'

Across the table, Toby grinned. 'Good idea.'

My mother's car was a Mustang, a two-door with some zip. My father drove a Pontiac nearly as old as I was. Sitting behind the wheel was like piloting a ship. 'Thank you,' I said. 'I'll be home by one.'

In the past, my curfew had always been midnight. My mother opened her mouth, then closed it. My father sighed but did not object.

When I stepped outside, Toby followed, walked me over to the remodeled barn where my parents kept their cars. The night was cold and clear, and we could see, in the distance, the lights of the Schultzes' clapboard house. Our split-level ranch house stood on ten acres, part of a subdivision still known around town as 'the old Brightsman farmstead'. In the ditches, in the ponds, in the puddles scattered like coins across the flooded lawn, millions of peepers were singing.

'I don't suppose you and Stacy know anything about a big party on the lake,' Toby said. He opened the door for me with the exaggerated gestures of a gentleman. 'Somebody's birthday, from what I hear.'

I got behind the wheel. 'Can't be much of a party,' I said, sweetly, 'if old folks like you know about it.'

He poked my shoulder. 'If you wind up drinking, don't try to drive. Call me and I'll get you. No questions asked.'

'Nobody's going to be drinking,' I said.

'Cowboy,' Toby said. 'I'm ugly, not stupid.'

'No, you're just stupid,' I said, but it didn't come out right. I hated it when Toby joked about his looks, because, of course, he wasn't really joking at all. He'd rested his hand on the edge of the window; suddenly, I reached up, placed my hand over his.

'I'll be fine,' I said.

Quickly Toby moved his hand away – embarrassed, I think, as I was. But the comforting flicker of warmth stayed between us. Earlier, as I'd risen from the table, my mother had risen, too. She'd nodded, helplessly, saying, *Well*. And my father had said, *Sixteen years*. And I'd understood how much they loved me, how difficult it was to let me go.

I'd never driven my father's car before; now I discovered I could barely see over the wheel. Backing down our long, curved driveway, I felt the way I'd felt at nine, trying on my mother's high-heeled shoes. Still, I was grateful for the Pontiac's wide seats and deep wheel wells when Stacy and I arrived at the DC. Eleven kids were waiting on the curb. Two couples volunteered for the trunk, while the rest sat, stacked, on one another's laps. The underside of the Pontiac scraped, sparking, as we pulled away. I drove too slowly, cautiously. I was terrified I'd get pulled over.

'Speed up a little,' said a voice in my ear. Literally. It was Cindy Ann Donaldson. I realized it was her thigh squashing mine, her foot I kicked whenever I braked. 'If you drive too slow, you draw attention to yourself. That's what my stepdad told me when I first got my license.'

I nodded. This sounded reasonable.

'Happy birthday, by the way,' she said. She was the first person to say it.

'Thanks,' I said, dully. The hell with appearances. I was wishing with all my heart that I'd stayed home.

By the time we found the party, it was after ten o'clock. Cars lined the dirt road leading to the cottage; more cars were scattered every which way on the lawn, underneath the trees. There was nowhere left to park that wasn't ankle deep in mud, so I turned around and dropped people off, remembering, at the last minute, to release the necking couples from the trunk.

'You could park down at the beach,' Cindy Ann said.

'I guess I'll have to,' I said.

'Want me to come with you? I don't mind. I'm not big on parties, to tell you the truth.'

I looked at Stacy's retreating back, her boyfriend's arm slung around her shoulder.

'Sure.'

Eventually, we wound up at the state park, nearly two miles away. Even before we got out of the car, we could hear the singing of the peepers; as we walked, the sound seemed to shimmer in the air. By now, I was feeling sorry for myself. It was my sixteenth birthday, after all, and here I was, abandoned by my friends. A cold, damp wind blew off the lake; I buttoned my jean jacket up to my chin, my mood plummeting along with the temperature. Unlike Stacy, I didn't have a boyfriend. I wasn't particularly talented. I didn't have a clue what I wanted to do with the rest of my life. Cindy Ann glanced at me, but I kept my gaze on the ground. The last thing I needed was to start crying, which was exactly what I was about to do. And it would be worse than crying in front of a total stranger, because, even though we hadn't exchanged twenty words since grade school, I knew Cindy Ann, and she knew me, the way people know each other in towns like Fox Harbor. I knew that she worked at Dairy Castle. I knew that her family farmed veal. I knew that she had a retarded brother, and that she was good with him, good to her sisters, who were younger than she was by several years.

She'd stopped walking. I stopped, too.

'Listen,' she said. The sound of the peepers was swelling steadily, shrilly, as if it were taking physical shape: a flying saucer, a mythical beast, the face of an angry god. The clouds blew back to reveal a sharp-jawed moon. Neither of us moved.

'Why are they doing that?' I whispered.

'They're mating,' Cindy Ann said.

If Stacy had said the word *mating*, I'd have giggled. When Cindy Ann said it, I did not. I was struck, instead, by the mystery unfolding all around us in the half-thawed fields. Life breeding life. For the first time that night, I understood that something was beginning for me, rather than ending, and I didn't feel like crying anymore.

Gradually, the sound subsided. The wind kicked up, spitting bits of frozen rain. Without speaking, we continued to walk, biting our lips against the chill. By the time we reached the cottage, we were both out of breath, stomping our feet, beating our numb fingers against our hips. Light poured from the windows, cut by the dark thrash of shadows. The stereo was set so loud I could feel the thump thump of bass inside my chest.

'Peepers,' Cindy Ann said, and then, as if some spell had been shattered, we climbed up the steps single file, each of us walking alone. By the time I understood what she'd meant, she'd already disappeared into the crush.

Immediately I understood that the original impulse of the party — all its good-natured naughtiness — had mutated into an ugly, angry destructiveness. Broken dishes crunched beneath my feet as I passed through the kitchen into the living room. Kids were writing on the walls, flooding the toilets, stomping on lampshades. I found myself shoved into the dining room, which held a child's wading pool, filled with blood-colored liquid.

'Wapatooli,' a girl said. She scooped up a cupful, handed it to me.

'What's in it?' I asked.

'Booze and Hi-C. Drink it now before the guys start swimming.' She nodded toward a group of seniors, who'd stripped down to their boxers.

I took a sip, expecting it would taste unpleasant, but all I could taste was fruit punch. I was thirsty from all the walking. I drank. I thought to myself, It's my sixteenth birthday. I thought to myself, What can one drink do? I stood in the alcove by the entryway, like someone in a dream, watching as boys I'd thought I knew vandalized the family photos, one by one. In the kitchen, girls were spreading pieces of bread with jelly, ketchup, mayonnaise, then sticking them to the walls in elaborate designs. More kids kept arriving. Somebody opened the windows. Somebody pulled the garden hose inside. A water fight broke out.

'This is crazy.' Cindy Ann had reappeared. 'Let's get out of here before somebody calls the cops.' She looked at the empty cup in my hand. 'I hope you didn't actually drink that.'

I had, in fact. Several times. The cup had seemed to refill itself, again and again, like magic.

This time, instead of walking beside the road, we slogged along the bluff, following the footpath as it gradually sloped, down and down, toward the state park. Behind us, we could hear wave after wave of sirens converging on the cottage, the high wail blending with the sound of the peepers, creating an otherworldly cry all its own. I was sorry for Stacy and the other kids I'd driven, but I had my own problems. I wasn't feeling well. The first time I got sick, it utterly surprised me. The second time, I understood. Each time, Cindy Ann waited in silence, holding back my hair, then urging me to keep on walking, helping me, catching me when I stumbled.

'We've got to move the car,' she said, but when we finally reached the parking lot, I locked myself in the outhouse next to the boarded-up Welcome Center. The ageless, frozen stink seemed to issue from somewhere inside my soul. I threw up some more. After a while, Cindy Ann knocked.

'C'mon,' she said. 'You can get sick at home.'

'My parents can't see me like this,' I said.

'We'll go to my house.' She spoke through the half-moon cut into the door. 'Everyone goes to bed early 'cuz my mom gets up at four.'

'What if she wakes up?'

'She won't. My stepdad might, but he'll just laugh.'

I opened the door, stepped outside. Even the moonlight hurt my eyes.

'Give me the keys,' Cindy Ann said, and I stared at her as if she had suggested I give her one of my lungs.

'It's my dad's car!'

'So what?'

'You can't,' I said, speaking slowly, trying to make myself clear, '*drive* my dad's *car.*'

'Neither can you.'

I made it out of the parking lot, narrowly missing a tree, bouncing over the frost heaves. Then, mercifully, I pulled over, slid out of the driver's seat.

In the end, Cindy Ann drove us to her house, where I telephoned Toby from the kitchen phone. He arrived, half an hour later, in his truck. Cindy Ann followed us home in the car her mother used to deliver the mail – the steering wheel was on the wrong side – and then she drove Toby back to her parents' house to pick up his Ford. In the morning, the Pontiac was safe in the garage, my mother and father none the wiser, and on Monday, Cindy Ann Donaldson plopped down beside me in the school cafeteria as comfortably, as naturally, as if she'd been sitting there, day after day, since the beginning of the year.

'Wapatooli Girl,' she said.

'Bite me,' I said.

We grinned at each other. I was so happy to see her. I remembered the singing of the peepers. I remembered the way she'd held back my hair. Someone was shaking my shoulder. It annoyed me, because I wasn't doing anything, I wasn't bothering anybody, all I wanted to do was sleep. Everything seemed to be moving beneath me, and I opened my eyes to the sharp slap of daylight.

I was lying at the bottom of the dingy, one ear plugged with water. I pushed myself onto my knees, shook my head, and everything around me exploded, like dropped glass.

'Jesus,' Rex said. 'Have you been here all night?'

I couldn't speak. Every inch of my skin was on fire.

'I've been worried sick,' he said. Even the sound of his voice seemed to cause the dingy to rock harder. We were being towed; I could hear other voices, a rumbling outboard. *Chelone*'s hull loomed over us. Then Rex was standing behind me on the swim ladder, using the entire length of his body to keep me from tumbling into the water.

'You got her?' somebody said, and Rex said, 'For God's sake, Meg, don't pass out here.'

The hot touch of his skin against mine was like iron. I forced myself to take another step, just to get away from it.

And then I was sprawled on the cockpit floor, taking sips of Gatorade from the cup Rex pressed to my lips.

I was naked in our berth, laid out like a corpse on a clean, white sheet.

I was staring into the teak-framed mirror on the bulkhead, examining a face that I didn't recognize, a face even more distorted than the one I'd stared at in the hospital, after the crash. Raspberry boils distorted my cheeks. The bridge of my nose was gone. Purple blossoms wound their way around my neck, and I closed my eyes, let Rex guide me back down onto the berth.

'What's wrong with me?' I managed to say.

'Poisonwood,' he said.

Gusts of wind spun across the intersection, and I was walking, I was running through the frost toward the site of Evan's shrine. Trash scattered everywhere. Weeds coiled like snakes. Beneath the tangle: a cracked votive candle, the dampened mush of sympathy cards, notes, a scrap of photograph. How could this have happened? How could the same people who'd erected this cross, who'd attended the funeral, who'd written those letters to the paper on our behalf, have simply driven on past, day after day, ignoring what they'd seen? How easily any one of them might have found themselves here: unconscious on a stretcher, or cursing at the sky. Attempting by sheer, brute force of will to undo what had just been done. Cindy Ann and I knelt side by side, tearing at thick fistfuls of quack grass, goldenrod, Queen Anne's lace. One by one, other women joined us, orange vests burning, a bright circle of fire.

I awoke, dressed in a long T-shirt, to the filtered light of a kerosene lamp. My skin felt strangely heavy, tight, but there wasn't any pain. I didn't know what time it was. I didn't know what day. I knew only that something terrible had eased; I felt clearheaded, calm, clean.

Outside it was raining. From somewhere far away came the mutter of thunder, deep, sustained, like the clearing of one's throat before something important is said. I slid my legs out of the berth, sat up, waiting for the dizziness to pass, and I remembered being a child, Evan's age, and awakening after a fever. Then, too, it had been night-time. Everything had seemed extraordinarily still. I'd gone down the hall to Toby's room, gotten into bed beside him, pinched the backs of his arms until he woke up, bewildered. *What?* And I'd laughed – not because I had pinched him, as he'd thought, as my parents would tell the story for years – but because I was so happy to see him, so delighted and relieved, a traveler coming home.

Rex sat at the galley table, writing in the ship's log. He looked up just as the ship's clock chimed.

Six bells. It was three o'clock in the morning.

'Feeling better?' he asked.

'Yes,' I said. 'Thank you.'

We were speaking politely, the way we did after an argument, mutually embarrassed, shamed. At his elbow sat a glass of Scotch and, beside it, a piece of notebook paper, folded into two. Coming closer, I saw my name written on it in Bernadette's graceful hand. Rex pushed the paper toward me.

'*Rubicon*'s gone,' he said. 'She weighed anchor a few hours ago.'

'Gone?'

He lifted his glass. 'Leon had another seizure, I guess. They're taking him for tests at some hospital in the States.'

'Miami Children's?' I said.

'Audrey didn't say. She and Earl stopped by to check on you.' He nodded at the note. 'They left you this.'

I opened it and read:

Dearest Meggie,

Sorry to say good-bye this way. Despite our differences, I believe you will agree when I say that, mostly, people are good at heart. I will always remember the time we've spent together at Houndfish Cay.

Godspeed.

Bernadette

I sat down at the table, closed my eyes, rested my lumpy forehead on the smooth, cool teak.

'It was Earl who found you, by the way,' Rex said, and his hand moved through my hair. 'I've never known you to drink like that, Meg. What the hell happened out there?'

It wasn't me, I started to say, but stopped. There was no way to explain. Again, I saw the roadside, the weeds, the clots of colorful trash. Evan's cross. Cindy Ann's ring. I saw my reflection in the mirror: wounded, disfigured, pestilent. Not the kind of vision I'd longed for, after Evan's death, when I'd woken each day to the insult of silence, when I'd lit votive candles, week after week, in the darkness of St Clare's church. Then again, nothing was ever the way you imagined. Nothing ever turned out the way you planned, predicted, promised yourself it would be.

'Rex,' I murmured into the teak. 'I need to go home for a while.'

'This is your home,' Rex said, but when I raised my head to look at him, he took his hand away.

'This is about Toby's wedding, isn't it?' He sat back angrily. 'I knew I should have pitched that goddamn invitation overboard.'

'What this is about,' I said, 'is that you lied to me about Arnie.'

As soon as I said it, I knew that it was true. All those solitary trips to Echo Island. The way in which I'd been manipulated, back in June. I only could hope my brother would believe I hadn't known, then, what Rex had meant to do.

'I wanted to give you a break from it, that's all,' Rex said.

'So you made the decision for me.'

'I did. And look at the result. We always knew she wasn't remorseful, but now we can prove it to a judge. This time, her life *will* be impacted. She'll be starting from scratch, three kids, no job, forty thousand left to her name.'

I swallowed hard. 'It doesn't change anything.'

'Of course it does. It means she'll think twice before she goes out and kills somebody else.'

'Let me get something straight,' I said. 'You're doing this

because you want to protect other people? Or because you want her punished, no matter what the cost?'

'It won't cost *us* anything, Meg.'

'I wasn't referring to money.'

He bent his head over the ship's log again, as if he hadn't heard.

For almost twenty years, I'd counted on our marriage the way I'd counted on my heart to beat, my lungs to take in air. Steadily. Thoughtlessly. Through the years of infertility. Through the necessary changes after Evan's birth. Through the first aching year of his loss. But over the past few months, what I felt for Rex had dulled so gradually that – like a shift in clear weather, the first purple tint in an otherwise bright sky – I'd been able to shrug it away as a trick of the light, nothing more.

Until now.

'I told Bernadette about Evan,' I said. 'Some other people, too.'

Rex passed his hand across his face. It was raining harder now, and water dripped from the corner of the overhead hatch.

'It doesn't matter,' he finally said. 'I told Eli a few weeks ago.'

'You did *what*?' I shook my head, couldn't stop shaking it. 'Jesus, Rex, is there anything else you're not telling me?'

'What's the big deal? It's not like he would have told anyone.'

'He would have told Bernadette. My God, she *knew*, Rex, she knew all along—'

'Why would he tell her? I told him in confidence.'

'Because that's their relationship.' I was shouting. 'They don't keep secrets from each other. They don't have that kind of marriage, the kind of marriage we clearly do.'

'Listen to yourself,' Rex said, and he was shouting, too. '*Their relationship*. What relationship? What do they have beyond that poor child? He'll be dead in another six months, and what will they do with themselves when that happens? What are they going to do?'

His voice broke. He was crying. The rain was gusting, hammering the cabin top.

'It's been a year, Meg, and nothing gets better. What are we going to do?'

The anniversary of Evan's death had started out like any other day. Yoga class, followed by a quick dip in the ocean. Back to the boat to tidy up, punch down the bread dough that I'd left to rise, finish the week's baking before the sun got too high. Midmorning, Bernadette had shown up in *Rubicon*'s dingy, Leon settled into an old beanbag chair, his wheelchair folded up in the bow. Wasn't it a perfect day, she called, for snorkeling at Hunter's Cay? She'd already packed a picnic lunch. All we needed were our flippers and masks.

Rex was still in his boxers, sipping coffee from a chipped china mug. 'Go ahead,' he said. 'Have a good time.'

'Come, too.'

He shook his head. 'I need to work on the bilge pump.'

I couldn't object to that. 'Okay.'

Five minutes later, I was perched beside Leon. Bernadette steered us out into the channel.

Hunter's Cay had originally been developed as a day destination for cruise ships, complete with covered gazebos, wooden boardwalks, tikki huts, outdoor grills. But the narrow passage from the ocean side was routinely treacherous. Passengers aboard the ships arrived too seasick to eat the waiting conch salads, too queasy to purchase the tropical drinks from the open-air bars. They were not in the mood to dance beneath the tents set up along the water. They certainly were not in the mood to recommend the trip to friends. Within a few years, the venture went bankrupt; the cruise ships left the area for good, abandoning everything when they went, down to the generators, the lightbulbs, the pots and pans, the woven rattan chairs. Rumor had it that the company was based out of Scandinavia. There was no chance, now, that they'd ever return to clean up the mess they'd made. Cheaper just to write everything off. Cheaper to let the rust and rot return everything, over time, to the jungle of scrub palm and poisonwood that had been there in the first place.

But Hunter's Cay, ruined though it was, was something close to paradise for Leon Hale: the cleared paths meant we could push his chair across the island to the outer beach, which was protected by a wide, curving reef. We ate our

picnic lunch beneath the shade of a grassy-thatched gazebo;
afterward, we sat at the water's edge, waiting for Bernadette's
mandatory hour to pass before we could lace Leon into his life
preserver, float him out toward the reef. Bernadette was
sketching a sea biscuit that had washed up a few yards away;
Leon sucked on a grape-flavored lollipop, which I held for
him, mopping at his chin. Just inside the reef, terns were
diving at things in the water; farther out, something large and
shiny jumped, then landed with a flat-bellied splash. The wind
must have shifted, because, precisely at that moment, a wave
of artificial grape-smell hit me –

– and I found myself thinking of Evan's bronchitis during
the weeks before his death. He'd first gotten sick after
Halloween. A cold, we'd thought, but it came with a cough
that lingered on up to the week of Thanksgiving. His
pediatrician had prescribed one antibiotic, another, another
still. 'If this one doesn't work,' she told me, 'we'll send him to
Mercy for a workup, maybe have him spend the night. So it's
really important he take every dose, all of it, on schedule.'

But this last antibiotic only came in a cherry-flavored base.
Evan *loathed* cherry. Flushed, furious, he gagged up the first
dose I forced between his teeth, shrieking as if I were trying
to make him swallow human blood. Leaving him with Rex, I'd
driven to a ma-and-pa pharmacy thirty-five miles west of Fox
Harbor, where Mallory – yes, it had been Mallory – had heard
there was a pharmacist who could disguise the taste of

anything, borrowing flavors from the old-fashioned soda counter.

The pharmacy was on Main Street, and its front window displayed an eclectic mix of items: crutches, a coffeemaker, a wedding dress. Inside, the cashier explained that the pharmacist, Doc Worthing, was out walking his dog, but if I wanted to wait at the counter, she'd make me a root beer float. How could anyone object to a root beer float? I sat down to wait for Doc. Half an hour later, he finally arrived, slightly out of breath. He was an old man, tidy in a bow tie, and he stroked his white mustaches as I told him about the length of Evan's illness, opened my coat to show him the streaks of cherry-flavored medicine I still wore.

'If I can't get him to swallow it, they'll put him in the hospital,' I said, swiping at the sudden, ridiculous tears that forced their way down my cheeks.

But Doc nodded sympathetically. 'I tink I can help,' he said. Was the accent Luxembourg? Dutch? Ten minutes later, he'd disguised the nasty cherry with a grape-flavored syrup, plus a drop of lemon oil.

'It still smell like da cherry,' he said. 'But I bet he like all da same.'

Evan, in fact, had loved it. By the next day, that terrible cough had finally begun to subside. Licking a drip from the edge of the dropper, I'd thought of grape Kool-Aid, grape Popsicles, smooth grape bubble gum, the kind that comes in fat, purple cubes and doesn't lose its flavor, no matter how long you chew it, no matter, even, if you leave it stuck, overnight, to the side of your bed. Later that night, creeping into his room, I could still smell the sweetness of his breath.

'Life is too short,' Doc Worthing had said, 'to swallow da taste of bitter medicine.'

Leon had been watching me closely; now, he pushed the sucker from his mouth with his tongue.

'Laa-laa,' he said.

It was his comfort word, equally meaningless and meaningful. I bent to him for a sticky kiss, and to my surprise, he hugged me, one skinny elbow locked behind my neck. I closed my eyes, and it was Evan who clung to me that way, smelling of shampoo and boy-sweat and grape. Evan, dead one year now. Evan, gone for good. I felt as if I'd made it all up: his birth, his infancy, the years he'd spent toddling into steady, sturdy childhood. Perhaps Rex felt the same way. Perhaps this was why the date had gone unmentioned between us.

'*December third*,' I whispered to Leon. '*Today is December third.*'

'Hour's up!' Bernadette called, cheerfully. 'Anybody ready for a swim?'

That night, aboard *Chelone*, Rex was in a foul mood. He hadn't worked on the bilge pump. Instead, he'd spent the day fishing with Eli on *Rubicon*'s dingy, a bottle of rum in the cooler. They'd managed to catch a few mutton snapper, but they were small, and the fillets had come out raggedy, unappealing. The propane grill refused to light, and then, when it did, one of the fillets slipped between the rungs, landing in the flames. Rex was jabbing at it with a fork when I stuck my head out the companionway, holding a pair of tongs.

'Here,' I said. 'Try these.' And he snapped, 'If I want your help, Meg, I'll ask for it.'

The fillets were burned, but we ate them. There was nothing else to eat. Rex poured himself a Scotch – his second drink since I'd come home, or was it already his third? I hated myself for counting. I hated myself for not calling him to task for the way he'd spoken to me. But it seemed easier just to let it go, try to forget about it. He was tired, after all, from an afternoon on the water. I was tired, too. Later that night, after supper, after the dishes had been washed and put away, I was getting ready for bed when Rex appeared at our stateroom door.

'You go ahead,' he said. 'I think I'll just sleep on the settee.'

I looked at him. 'Are we mad at each other?'

He made a funny sound, the spark of a laugh that didn't quite catch. 'The berth mattress bothers my shoulder, that's all.'

'You should start doing those exercises again,' I said.

'They didn't help.'

'You didn't give them a chance.'

'They only made things worse.'

'Then come with me to yoga class. Or the marina pool. You need to get more exercise.'

'Especially at my age,' Rex said, quoting the Bermudan doctor. Only there wasn't a trace of humor in his voice.

For a moment, neither of us said anything.

'Well,' I finally said. 'Get a good night's sleep.'

'You, too,' Rex said, and then: 'Look. I'm sorry about before. I didn't mean to be cross.'

'It's okay,' I said, and it was. It didn't seem important anymore. We even kissed good night before he turned away, and in the morning, it was as if the previous day had never happened.

But that night, again, he stayed up late, drinking. Slept on the settee.

And the night after that.

And the night after that.

Part Three | Blue Water

Chapter Nine

The Echo Island airport was roughly the size of a living room. It consisted of two rows of plastic chairs, a liquor stand, an artificial Christmas tree, and a gate shared by a half dozen airlines, none of whose names I recognized. My poison-wood rash had stopped blistering; now it was starting to peel. A man approached me, standing too close as I studied the spidery scrawl of available flights on the chalkboard.

'You burn yourself?' he asked, staring at my forehead. It was nine in the morning, but the liquor stand was open. I could smell the rum on his breath.

'Long story,' I said.

He laughed. 'I've got time. C'mon, let me buy you a drink.'

'Look,' I said, pulling at the neck of my T-shirt. There, across my collarbone, the rash had formed a necklace of scabs, the healing skin around each one like a crown of neon pink. 'It's flesh-eating bacteria, okay? Highly contagious.'

The man backed away without another word.

The only flight north I could find was aboard a single-engine plane that appeared considerably smaller than *Chelone*. It was scheduled to depart for Great Exuma Island in less than an hour. From Great Exuma, I could fly to Eleuthera, then Marsh Harbor, where – the ticket agent assured me – I could get a connecting flight to Miami within a few days. It was already the eighteenth of December; still, with a little luck, I'd arrive at my parents' town house in time to catch a ride north to the wedding.

'How much do you weigh?' the ticket agent asked.

Sneaking another glance at the plane, I inflated the figure by twenty pounds.

We took off – three passengers plus the pilot – so low to the ground that we could see inside the fuselage of another small plane that had crashed into the tidal pools just beyond the runway. I was beginning to think we might join it when my window blew open with a bang. Papers flapped around the cockpit like fierce, white birds. The pilot, cursing, turned us around and dove back toward the airport. Two of my fellow passengers were sportsmen returning from a bonefishing tour, and they cursed enthusiastically along with the pilot. The third passenger said nothing. He appeared to be asleep, although his eyes were open, fixed. The moment the plane stopped moving, he scrambled across my knees, punched open the side door, and jumped. We watched as he sprinted across the airstrip, disappeared behind two Porta Pottis into a stand of dead palms.

'Chicken shit,' the pilot said. He pointed to the backpack that the man had left behind; wordlessly, the fishermen pitched it out the open door. 'Okay, lady,' he said to me. 'Here's what you gotta do.'

Ten minutes later, we were taking off again as I sat twisted sideways in my seat, pinning the window shut with my shoulder. Just as the pilot had promised, it stayed up on its own once we reached cruising speed, which we did much more rapidly with just the four of us, the fishermen joking agreeably now, even the pilot looking pleased. Below were the teal green waters of the Gulf Stream, the pale yellow areoles around each tiny island. The dark shadows of sand sharks nosing along the shallows. The deep blue strokes of the channels. Here were the sailboats with their white-tipped peaks, and the long, streaming wakes of sport fishers. Two trawlers in tandem, rocking like turtles. A container ship, heading north toward the United States.

Home.

I closed my eyes, sleepy with the noise of the engine, the steady vibrations like a big cat's purr. At dawn, Rex had dingied me to the ferry dock, kissed me – a kiss that made me sorry to be leaving – then headed right back to Ladyslip, not waiting to wave me off. By now, he'd be aboard *Chelone*, putting a second coat of varnish on the teak. In the afternoon, he'd dig out his flippers and mask, clean the bottom of the hull. Barely a week had passed since *Rubicon*'s departure; still, he'd managed to repair the bilge pump, change the engine oil, fix the leaky hatch. He was doing his shoulder exercises. He was going for a swim every morning. He'd cut off his beard, shaved the remaining stubble down to the soft, pale skin. By the time I returned from Wisconsin, he promised, both he and *Chelone* would be shipshape, ready for another passage. Perhaps we could hop southeast through the Turks and Caicos, follow the curve of the Dominican Republic until we reached Puerto Rico. We might continue on to the Virgins, Antigua, St Lucia. Who could say we wouldn't decide to follow the northern coast of Venezuela, reserve passage through the Panama Canal, spend next summer in San Francisco Bay? If all went well, if conditions were right, we could even consider Vancouver for fall. Nights would be chilly, but we had the propane heater, and the turning leaves would be fantastic!

'I'm ready for a little cool weather,' he said as we lay on our backs, shoulder to shoulder, in our berth, looking up through the open hatch at the pale flush of stars overhead. 'A change of scene. Aren't you?'

'Vancouver,' I said. My hands were pinned beneath my thighs. The healing rash itched fiercely; I was trying not to scratch. 'How long would we stay?'

'Till the butter gets too hard to spread.' Then he laughed. 'I don't know. Not more than a week or two. That was our mistake here, Meg. We got too comfortable, stayed too long.'

He'd flushed his painkillers down the head. He'd emptied his Scotch overboard. Things were going to be different, he assured me, when I returned from Wisconsin. Thinking it over, he'd decided it wasn't such a bad idea for me to spend a few weeks in the States. I could visit our tenant, review our accounts with Lindsey Steinke, pick up more traveler's checks at the bank. I could stop by Arnie's office in Milwaukee, have a look at those photographs, sign the settlement agreement. Or, if I didn't want the hassle, Arnie would send the paperwork to Fox Harbor, or Miami, whatever was most convenient. All I had to do was ask him. All I had to do was make the call. It would be like having a tooth pulled. I'd wonder why on earth I'd ever waited.

'Well, I'm sorry to see you go,' Audrey said when I arrived on the beach for a final yoga class. 'The whole community seems to be breaking up early this year.'

We lay on our towels in corpse pose, waiting, but nobody else arrived. Carole had stopped coming. Pam, along with Marvin and their dogs, had taken off for Cuba with a group of Canadians. Bernadette was gone, of course, as was Jeanie McFadden. Some people had flown out for the holidays; others were busy preparing for visits from relatives and friends. Audrey herself seemed absentminded, unfocused, as we moved through our warm-up routine: mountain pose, staff pose, seated sage.

'Make sure you carry enough cash,' she said, startling me

from my own wandering thoughts. 'Scatter it through your bags. Twisted sage.'

We each bent our right knee, hugged it, turned slowly to the left.

'I'm bringing a backpack,' I said. 'That's it.' Packing had taken me all of five minutes: a pair of jeans, a change of shirts, sweatshirt, underwear, passport. From inside the liner of my foam berth mattress, I'd extracted my wedding ring. 'I can borrow whatever I need from my mother. And I've got winter clothes in Wisconsin, in the attic. We boxed everything up in cedar chips before we left.'

Audrey exhaled deeply; we twisted the opposite way. 'Winter,' she repeated. 'Do you know, it's been over twenty years since I've seen snow?'

I studied Audrey's back and neck, the long, lean sinews of her body. She'd recently celebrated her seventy-sixth birthday; her husband had sweet-talked her onto the beach, where we'd all surprised her with sparklers, cupcakes, funny little handmade gifts. As the plane chattered and rattled its way through the clouds, I tried to imagine myself in thirty years, still living aboard *Chelone*. Bright-eyed (I hoped) and brittle-boned (perhaps), my hair tucked up in a bun. Childless. Homeless. Destined to move from place to place, just like the nymph Chelone, carrying everything I owned upon my back. Not that I'd be alone, of course. Rex would be with me, his high cheekbones sharpened with age, his gray eyes dulled with sun. He'd refused to come with me to Wisconsin. He'd said he couldn't imagine returning to any kind of life onshore: not now, not anymore, not even for a few weeks. He advised me not to speak to Cindy Ann, to avoid eye contact should we happen to meet — which we would, of course, at Toby's wedding. Any kind of interaction could, potentially, complicate the settlement. If she spoke to me, I should keep silent. To Mallory, I might say 'Congratulations,' but it would be better to say nothing at all.

'And what,' I asked, 'do I tell to my brother when he asks if I deliberately misled him back in June?'

'Tell him,' Rex said, 'you are not at liberty to discuss any matters pertaining to the case without your attorney present.'

'Oh, please.'

'You've got to see the larger picture, here, Meg. There's no point derailing months of work with a single, offhand remark.'

In Eleuthera, I boarded another flight — a twin engine, this time, with six seats and air-conditioning — and by late afternoon, we were landing in Marsh Harbor. The ticket counters had already closed for the day, so I took a taxi into town and found a place to stay along the waterfront. There were restaurants, craft shops, an ice cream parlor, even a coffeehouse that served espresso, cappuccinos, lattes. No more than two dozen businesses in all: still, it was too much. Too many people passing on the sidewalks, some turning to stare at my raw, pink forehead and cheeks. Too many cars on the streets, too many scooters on the sidewalks. Teetering bicycles, stray cats, skittery packs of potcakes. I'd gone out looking for something to eat; now I discovered my appetite was gone. Looking in the window of the art gallery, I felt the way I had as a high school senior, when our class had taken its graduation trip to New York City. We'd stayed at a noisy Midtown hotel, four to a room hardly bigger than the beds. Outside our window, forty stories below, were the taxi-clogged streets I'd seen in movies, diligent streams of pedestrians, glittering advertisements rising like giants, like conquering gods. While the other kids trooped off to *Phantom of the Opera*, I stayed behind, claiming a stomachache that, over the course of the three-day weekend, transformed itself from fiction into fact. I didn't go shopping at Macy's. I didn't ride the subway to the Guggenheim. I didn't wait in line to take the elevators up to the top of the World Trade Center — one of those seemingly small decisions that haunts you, looking back, for the rest of your life. Instead I sat in the hotel room, flipping through the TV channels, looking for shows I recognized: reruns of *Gilligan's Island*, *All in the Family*, *M*A*S*H*.

The morning after I got back home, Toby took me out for breakfast. I told him the trip had been no big deal, that, mostly, I'd watched TV.

'You are seriously telling me,' he said, 'that you went all the way to New York City to watch television?'

'It was *my* vacation,' I said, defensively.

'Aw, Cowboy,' Toby said. 'Damn.'

We were at the Cup and Cruller. We were having the special: pancakes shaped like Mickey Mouse heads with fried-egg eyes, sausage link smiles. I felt young and stupid and foolish. I'd been looking forward to New York for months. I didn't understand what had happened.

'You should have given your reservation to someone who couldn't afford to go,' Toby said. 'Your friend Cindy Ann, for instance.'

'She's not my friend.'

'She used to be.' He studied my face. 'I don't suppose you'll ever tell me what happened between you two?'

I touched an egg with the tip of my fork; it broke, spilling warm, oily yolk across my plate. 'Her stepdad was weird,' I said.

'So that's her fault?'

I remembered the door to the crawl space. I remembered Cindy Ann's voice on the phone, the night that she'd called me from the DC. *He made me touch it.* I felt the way I had in Manhattan the few times I'd forced myself to venture out of the hotel, as if my breath were being sucked into the humming of the traffic, the shuddering of the subway, the collision of languages, sentences, shouts of people who might as well have been ghosts. I saw them all while, at the same time, seeing no one, in the same way that no one saw me. All of us were equally invisible, standing shoulder to shoulder at each curb, everybody's gaze fixed on someplace in the distance, on the sidewalk, on the flashing sign insisting DO NOT WALK.

'He did something to her,' I said. 'I mean, before he killed himself. But you can't tell anyone, okay?'

Maybe he thought you wanted him to. I would always remember the look on her face, just after I'd said it. It was a terrible thing to say. It made it seem as if I thought Cindy Ann was the one who'd done something wrong. Which wasn't what I'd been thinking at all. It was just that I'd been knocked off balance. It was just that I couldn't wrap my mind around the thing that she had said. The way I'd felt when Bernadette told me she'd forgiven Dr Matt for what he'd done.

Hasn't anyone forgiven you? Are you certain?

Perhaps Cindy Ann had forgotten what I'd said. I'd seen her at the park, shortly after Evan's birth, and I remembered, now, how happy she'd been for me, how she and her girls had crowded around us to see him. How she'd run a gentle hand over his head. How she'd held out a finger for him to grasp. For the first time, it occurred to me that Cindy Ann would remember this, too. I imagined her, again, in the detective's photographs, sitting at her kitchen counter, bringing the glass to her lips. She had not been enjoying an evening with friends; she certainly hadn't been laughing. She'd been by herself, in a darkened house. Idly, I scratched at my chest, at my arms, where the rash was still dark, the color of wine. Such a terrible itch that could not be sated. Such a terrible thirst that could not be quenched.

I bought a plate of conch fritters from a stand, walked over to the ferry dock, sat down to eat them at one of the gull-spattered benches that overlooked the harbor. Rex and I had anchored here back in August; perhaps, in another week or two, *Rubicon* might be tucked somewhere among the twinkling mast lights and bobbing hulls, stopping over on her long, slow passage to Miami. I wondered if Leon had had any more seizures. I wondered if, perhaps, I could send a note to Bernadette in care of the pediatric neurologist. Susan Martin, Audrey thought was her name, or maybe Susan Martinson? Susan, Suzette, something like that. How many pediatric neurologists at the Miami Children's could there be?

The last of the light drained into evening. The bars and restaurants filled, lines overflowing onto the streets. In the lobby of my hotel, I called my parents from a pay phone, left another message on their answering machine – the same message I'd left from the airport in Eleuthera – telling them that I was on my way. I called Toby at the fish store, spoke to that machine as well, considered calling him at his apartment over the mill, then changed my mind. What if Mallory picked up? What was I going to say? If she'd hated me before, she must despise me now, believing, as she must, that I'd deliberately lied to Toby about our plans. And yet, she and Toby had sent the invitation. There wasn't a trace of bitterness in what either of them had written. I wondered if they'd seen the photographs of Cindy Ann. I wondered if, perhaps, they'd come to feel differently about the civil suit, about our reasons for pursuing it, now that there was proof of what we'd claimed. Or perhaps Cindy Ann hadn't told them about the settlement. Perhaps she'd told no one at all. Why reawaken all the same conversations, speculations, that had shimmered for months beneath the Cup and Cruller's perpetual cigarette haze?

Back in my room, I was restless. I turned on the television, turned it off again. I touched the coffeemaker, the remote control, the light switch. I flushed the toilet. I filled the ice bucket, picked up a piece of ice and held it, aching, in my hand. All the things I'd once taken for granted: like oxygen, friendship, marriage. When Rex had told me he couldn't imagine returning to life onshore, not even for a few weeks, I'd felt something tear at the back of my mind, quietly but irreparably, like a thin, soft sheet of felt. Now, with something like relief, I considered the possibility that I, too, had been ruined for shore. Perhaps, as soon as I got to Wisconsin, I'd be ready to turn around again. Fly back to Echo Harbor. Hop aboard *Chelone*, take off without a backward glance.

The following morning, I found a seat on yet another mosquito-size plane, and by midafternoon, I'd cleared Customs and Immigration and was on my way to Ibis Lakes. I hadn't visited my parents since the Labor Day weekend before Evan's death, and as I lowered the taxi window to punch in the gate code, I remembered, abruptly, Evan's fascination with the key pad, the guard box, the wrought-iron security gate, which swung back on its black hinges like something out of Batman. The taxi passed between a series of tall fountains, following the curve of the golf course with its manicured sand traps and shallow lakes, until it reached the first grouping of town homes, each with the same cream-colored siding, the same attached garage, identical pillars standing guard on either side of the arching doors.

It is still hard for me to imagine my parents actually living in a place like Ibis Lakes – five thousand square feet under air, my father is proud to say – in a so-called planned community like this one, professional landscapers tending the hedges, a maid service passing through once a week. When I was a child, my mother collected the leftover slivers of soap from the bathrooms, saved them in a Baggie – the same clouded Baggie, year after year – until she had enough to squish them into a single, recycled bar. She used powdered milk in her coffee, watered the ketchup, the orange juice, the soup. When she wasn't at the office, she was working in the kitchen, working in the garden, wrestling the vacuum cleaner from room to room. My father himself worked sixty-hour weeks, alternating his suits until the elbows and knees turned silver; nights, he dozed on the old Sears couch beneath my mother's vast collection of framed family photos. Unlike my friends, I was given no allowance. If I needed money for a movie, I asked my mother, who kept a record of what I spent. Later, in high school, when I started working for Toby, I was expected to put a percentage of what he paid me toward that debt.

And yet, when my tuition bills came, my parents wrote the checks, no questions asked. They'd paid cash for the town house, which was easily three times the size of our split-level ranch. Now they belonged to golf clubs, went to benefit concerts and gala balls. My father had his own golf coach. My mother had a weekly appointment at a spa. The story they told — to us and to others, perhaps even to themselves — was that they'd made their fortune from the sale of Hauskindler Stone and Brick. It was Rex who'd pointed out the obvious: the company had made good money all along.

'Why else would the buyers have paid what they did?' he said. 'Your folks lived that frugally because they wanted to.'

I disagreed. 'They lived that way because they didn't know anything different.'

'Here,' I told the taxi driver, pointing to an end unit. I wouldn't have known it from the others except for my mother's collection of orchids, hanging from a low branch of a live oak tree that shaded the screened-in side yard. Walking up the driveway, my backpack slung over my shoulder, I could already tell that my parents were gone. The Christmas lights framing the windows were dark. The blinds were drawn, the porch light on. The fountain in the entryway stood silent, the empty well filled with my mother's potted plants: bromeliads, African violets, a woody stalk of thyme. Still, I rang the doorbell before letting myself in with my key, guiltily, uneasily, even though I knew I would have been welcomed. During the early years of our marriage, Rex and I had come home more than once to find my parents sitting in our living room. My mother would have done the dishes. My father would have oiled the garage door hinges, replaced a burned-out lightbulb, emptied the drip pan under the ice maker. They'd be looking at us expectantly, waiting for news about my latest pregnancy test, about the date of the next in vitro, about where we stood in adoption proceedings, hands folded, like Christmas bows, in the center of their empty laps.

The town house was immaculate, magazines spread across the coffee table, paddle ceiling fans stirring the quiet air. White leather couches. Glass end tables. A green silk sweater, neatly folded, lay draped across an embroidered parlor chair. All the kitsch and clutter of our split-level ranch had vanished. My mother's flour canisters with the porcelain chickens on the lids. My father's overshoes, which he'd always called 'rubbers', waiting on their mat beside the door. My mother's family photos watching from the quarrel of mismatched frames she'd collected at yard sales and secondhand shops, one more outrageous than the next. The photos started in the foyer, then spread across the living room, up the stairs and down the hall: baby pictures, wedding pictures, graduation pictures, family pets, everyone and anyone who'd passed, even briefly, through the sights of her Polaroid. There'd been a picture of Cindy Ann and me – along with six other fourth grade girls – dressed up as turkeys for a Thanksgiving play. There'd been another picture, taken the summer we'd been friends, of the two of us heading out to the beach, wearing matching yellow bikini tops, frayed jean shorts. One of my sixteenth birthday, opening gifts, Toby's rabbit ears above my head. A picture of Rex, red-eyed with surprise, the first time I'd brought him home. During idle family arguments over when and where something occurred, my mother would rise with the poise of a judge, pace the walls until she'd found precisely the right photograph to support her interpretation.

And yet she hadn't moved a single one of the photos to Florida. Instead, she'd parceled them into boxes, half for Toby, half for me. Mine were still up in the attic; Toby's, I guessed, were moldering in his apartment over the mill. Neither of us had wanted them. We'd never liked them. They'd embarrassed us.

'You could hang them in Florida, you know,' I'd said. 'I believe they have walls there, too.'

'I'm not moving two thousand miles,' my mother said, and there was an edge in her voice, 'to re-create the life I'm living here.'

In the cinnamon-scented kitchen, I discovered the note

she'd left for me, pinned to the stainless steel refrigerator with a magnet. She and my father had left for Wisconsin that morning. *Flown* to Wisconsin, in fact – the first flight of my mother's life. They'd made reservations at the Pfister Hotel; I should call them on my father's cell. My mother's joy at the prospect of seeing me shimmered between each line, as if she had dusted the words with glitter the way that, once, she'd dusted the notes she left for me to find after school. *Put in the pot roast at five o'clock. Preheat the oven to 325. Call me so I know you're home.*

I telephoned my father. He picked up on the first ring.

'Meg?' he said, but it was all he got to say before my mother – I could *see* it happening – snatched the phone out of his hand.

'We got your message yesterday,' she said, her tone no different than if she'd just seen me a few hours earlier. 'I tried to book a flight for you, too, but everything's full. We were thinking, though, that maybe you could drive up in my car, it's got all-weather tires—'

'Mom,' I said. '*Mom*.'

She waited.

'I can't believe you actually got on an airplane,' I said.

'Me, neither.'

'So, how was it?'

I could hear my father in the background, laughing, guessing what I'd just asked.

'Let me put it this way,' my mother said. 'If you do end up

driving to Wisconsin, you'll have a companion on the way back.'

It was decided, on the spot, that this was what I'd do. If I left in the morning, taking my time, I'd arrive at the Pfister on the twenty-third, the day before Christmas Eve. Plenty of time before the wedding. Plenty of time, in case it snowed.

'Have you seen Toby yet?' I asked.

There was a slight pause before my mother spoke. 'We were hoping to get together for dinner, but he had to back out. He's been busy with – things.'

'Does he know I'm coming?'

'Oh, yes. He's happy you're going to be there.'

He isn't upset about the settlement? It was on the tip of my tongue. But I didn't want to make my mother feel as if I were trying to drag her into it. Besides, it seemed more and more likely to me that she didn't know a single thing about it.

'I suppose he'll be spending Christmas Day at Cindy Ann's,' I said. 'With her kids and everything.' I was proud of how steadily, how reasonably, I spoke. Again, I heard my mother pause.

'He hasn't really told us his plans. But I went ahead and got four tickets to *A Christmas Carol* at the Pabst. I can donate them back, I suppose, if we don't use them. Remember how we always used to take you kids?'

'I do,' I said, though what I remembered was going on school field trips, lining up with the other kids for weekday matinees. Back at the Cove, the boat kids had been planning their own version of the play. Scrooge was to be a joyless ship's captain, Cratchit a good-hearted mate. Leon, assisted by Eli, had been designing the sets. Would Rex go to the performance, I wondered, or would he stay aboard *Chelone,* alone? What was he going to do for Christmas — grease pumps? Strip teak?

'That's okay, then?' my mother said, and I said, 'What?'

'The tickets. For Christmas Eve?'

'Fine. Sorry, it's been a long day.'

'I'll let you go, then. We'll talk when you get here. Have a good night's sleep.'

'Tell her to sleep in,' I could hear my father prompting. 'Tell her there's no rush.'

'No rush,' I agreed, but just a few hours later — too unsettled to close my eyes — I found a leather travel bag and packed a few of my mother's sweaters, a cream-colored cashmere coat, a pair of wool pants from the cedar-lined closet. Her shoes, unfortunately, were no warmer than mine, and half a size smaller besides; I resigned myself to wearing my boat shoes until I could stop by our house for my boots. Then I carried everything down to the garage, along with my battered backpack. A sensor cued the overhead light; I froze, blinking, like a burglar. The air smelled gassy, moist and still. I put the travel bag into the trunk of my mother's Mercedes, opened the garage door, backed out into the drive, and I was just about to close the door again when I noticed something in the storage alcove, covered with a quilted sheet.

Leaving the Mercedes idling, I got out, returned to the garage. There it was: the child-size, spring green, motorized VW bug my parents had bought for Evan, the Christmas after he'd turned three. He'd been so excited that he'd stumbled getting in, falling against the frame. Later, when we managed to coax him out, we discovered that he'd given himself a bloody lip. No matter. Every day, for the rest of our visit – and for every visit after that – he'd practically lived in that car, my father and mother walking beside him as he drove it up and down the street, one hundred times, two hundred times. Meanwhile, Rex and I sat beside the pool, shaking our heads, repeating words like *excess*, *overindulgence*. Children around the world were starving. What had my parents *spent* on that damn thing?

I pulled back the sheet, peered in the window. In the passenger's seat sat a small, stuffed zebra that Evan had named – for reasons unknown – Louise. *Jeez, Louise*, Rex had called her. I touched Louise's plush, soft fur, but I did not pick her up. Instead I tugged the sheet back into place, exactly as it had been. I'd always assumed that my mother, in her systematic pragmatism, would have given the VW away: to a church, to a children's charity, to Goodwill.

That she hadn't, affected me more, comforted me more, than anything she'd ever said.

The language we speak shapes the world we see. In college, fulfilling the same humanities requirement that had sentenced me, earlier, to a semester with the Greeks, I'd rediscovered a quotation I'd first learned as a senior at Harbor High. 'It has been documented by linguists,' Mr Grumbach told us – had, indeed, told generations of honors students – 'that the Eskimo, in his native tongue, has a thousand names for snow.'

Mr Grumbach paused for us to take that in as we doodled, bored, in our notebooks. Outside our window, it was overcast, cloudy. Gray. Foggy. Thick as pea soup. Later it would sleet, an icy, stinging rain that would cover the roads and trees, the same rain that seemed to be falling in Madison when, several years later, I learned that Mr Grumbach's thousand words had been something of an exaggeration. 'Dozens of words,' my professor explained. She'd lived among the Inuit in the 1950s; the language of her particular hosts was spoken, she said, not written. Still, she wrote the words as best she could, phonetically, on the board. One of them meant something like *hard-crust-top-wet-below*. Seeing it written down that way, I could hear how it had squeaked beneath my short, pink boots on the day that Toby, then seventeen, had walked me out to the snow fence at the edge of our long driveway. I was seven years old, my breath sweet with hot chocolate. We spent the afternoon tunneling into the five-foot drifts like moles. By the end of the day, we'd hollowed out a series of rooms, connected by a single, narrow tunnel, through which Toby chased me, back and forth, growling like a bear. When we crawled back out, it was already dark. The moon was out. It was snowing again, small, precise flakes that clung to the sleeves of our coats without melting as we trudged back up the driveway toward the warmth and light of the house.

Emerging from a Holiday Express in Ohio, my ankle aching from the unaccustomed cold, I stared out at the flat, frozen fields and remembered, again, the different kinds of snow: dry, wet, packable, powdery, drifting, blowing, biting. The layering of clothing. The plastic bags I slipped over Evan's socks to ease his foot into its boot and, later, to keep his foot dry when the seams soaked through. The icicles hanging down from the roof. Stalactites – or was it stalagmites? *Teeth!* Evan shouted, pointing at the ragged line above our porch, and Rex lifted him up, helped him snap one off to suck. Walking along the lakefront, looking at the crystalline formations of ice. Driving around after dark to see the Christmas lights, inflatable Santas and snowmen, stars perched high upon silo tops. Reindeer constructed from bales of hay, glo-stick horns, white cloth tails. In the morning, wild turkeys like blackened stumps, scattered in clumps at the edge of the road. Afternoons, they waited for us to appear with leftover toast scraps, vegetable trimmings, handfuls of birdseed meant for the feeder.

'We could shoot them,' Evan said one day, and I'd turned to him, astonished.

'What?'

'Shoot them,' he'd explained, patiently. 'With a gun.'

He was five at the time, and I riffled through a mental Rolodex of friends, acquaintances, influences. 'Who has been talking about shooting things?' I said, and he said, in his clear, boyish soprano, '*Mom*. You have to shoot things to eat them.'

He was staring at me. Challenging me. We kept no guns in the house, not even toys. I said, 'I guess I just prefer that other people shoot them for me, that's all.'

He smiled then, eager, relieved. '*I'll* shoot them for you,' he said.

The highway sliding beneath me. The land lying down, scrolling past. I'd come nearly two thousand miles, alone. Passage-making. Single-handing. Taking advantage of the good weather window: ice blue skies, starry nights. Field after field, wave after wave, dividing itself, repeating itself. Hickory trees, chestnut trees, rough-coated birch with their ice-laden boughs. On a service road, a gorilla-size snowman smiling toward the horizon. At a gas station, a dreamy-eyed child, chewing on one mittened thumb. The mittens I'd crocheted for Evan, connected by a chain-stitched string. *Sissy mittens*, Rex had called them. *Sorry, hon, but it's true.*

'Are they really sissy mittens?' I'd asked Evan, and he'd said, kindly, generously, 'It's okay, Mom. You didn't know.'

Homemade decorations at a truck stop diner: egg crate sections and yogurt tops, pipe cleaners, candy canes, glue. Stringing long chains of cranberries, popcorn, looping tinsel over the tree. Painting wooden clothespins into red-vested soldiers, topped by a tuft of cotton-wool hair. Mom, look at this one. Mom, look at me. *The language we speak shapes the world we see.* Words like cut geodes, crystals of memory, spark and flame. How many names, the professor had asked, do *we* have for cold weather? How many names for sunshine? For automobiles? For a redwood tree? How many names for abstractions such as sorrow, fortitude, hope? What does this tell us as a culture, as a people, about what we value most?

Six hours to Milwaukee. Four hours. Three. It is early afternoon. It's the day before Christmas Eve. And yet, when I finally reach the downtown, I find myself passing exit after exit, accelerating north to Fox Harbor. Flying along I-43 until city gives way to suburb, until suburb gives way to farmland, the pale glimmer of the lake to the east like a clear, benevolent eye. I am no longer driving so much as being driven, every muscle in my body leaning, longing. Old Dixie exit to County C. West on C toward the Point Road. In the distance, the husk of the one-room schoolhouse, the blinking yellow light above the intersection. But as I pull up onto the shoulder, what I find is absolutely unlike what I'd dreamed. Pain shoots through my ankle as I step down into the gulley, slipping and sliding in my thin boat shoes, closing the last fifty feet between my body and the spot where, I'm beginning to understand, my life will always be tethered, connected, no matter how long the leash I might choose, no matter how far I might go. Strange to think that this should be a comfort. Strange to think that Evan's body sleeps behind St Clare's, while it's here that I sense his presence, feel him to this day.

He was with us. He was real.

I kneel on the frozen ground.

His cross stands proud and straight as a heron. Clusters of plastic flowers faded, yes, but neatly arranged. Of course, the parents of Evan's friends would have tended it, passing it each day, pulling over for a minute or two after dropping the kids off at school. Of course, what I'd seen that night, on the path, was a manifestation of my own guilt: for surviving the accident, yes, but even more so, for surviving my own grief. Even now, at the back of my mind, a dark voice still whispers it is wrong of me to laugh, to love, to step, even briefly, from shadow into light. What kind of mother outlives her child? What kind of mother wouldn't die, too? Sometimes, I still wonder if things might have been easier, had I found myself marked permanently, been physically changed in some way. So that each time I looked in a mirror, each time I reached for the crutch or the cane, there'd be an alignment between what I felt within, the way I appeared without.

A car approaches on the Point Road, slows, vanishes into the thickening gloom, and I stand up again, my ankle grown stiff, batting frost from the hem of my mother's coat. I am ready, now, to fall into her arms, to let my father treat me to a good dinner and wine. I am ready for a night at the Pfister

Hotel, the oversize chairs, the plush feather beds. I am ready to permit myself, at last, the possibility of comfort and care. My child is dead. My husband is adrift. My home is occupied by a stranger, whose permission I must ask in order to retrieve my clothes. My brother is getting married to a woman who, frankly, I knew best as the sunny-eyed child she was that long-ago summer, chattering in Dan Kolb's lap as Cindy Ann and I washed and waxed and scrubbed, trying to remove a stain that had already marked us, claimed us, would never quite come clean.

'You should have told me about Dan Kolb,' Toby had said at the Cup and Cruller that morning, and he'd said it again, a few days later, aboard the *Michigan Jack*. It was the end of April, and the smelt were still running. The decks were covered in fish slime, and I was hosing them down, readying the *Jack* for its next charter trip in an hour.

'She made me promise,' I said, spraying the mess toward the scuppers.

'I could have done something to help.'

'What, shoot him?'

'Not funny.'

'I wasn't trying to be funny.' I had to raise my voice to be heard above the water.

'Did you talk to her about it? After he died, I mean?'

I shrugged. In fact, I had tried, and more than once, but each time, Cindy Ann had overpowered me with small talk.

One night, a month or so after Dan Kolb's funeral, I'd gone down to the DC at closing time, ordered fries and a Coke. Cindy Ann was working, of course. She was always working.

'What are you doing afterward?' I said, nibbling on a fry.

'Going home, I guess.'

'Want to walk down to the lake?'

She laughed. 'Meggie. It's fucking freezing out.'

'So?'

'Besides, I have to get home. But thanks.'

'How's your mom?' I asked.

'She's fine. How's yours? Your mom and dad, I mean.'

'Fine,' I said. 'Listen—'

'How's *Toby*?' she said, landing hard on his name. To my surprise, I saw her neck flush dark against the mustard-colored uniform.

The deck of the *Jack* was glistening, clean. I shut off the hose, drained it, coiled it up for next time.

'I asked her out once, you know,' Toby said. 'Right after the two of you stopped hanging out.'

'You asked Cindy Ann *out*?' I said. 'Like, on a date?'

He was counting life jackets, stuffing them into a large, mesh bag. 'Why not?' He cinched the bag, stuffed it into the gap above the cabin rafters. 'That night, on your birthday, where she drove you home? We had a great conversation. Just talking, you know, in her mother's car.'

'What did you talk about?'

'Politics,' he said, dumping ice from the coolers. 'Travel. Places we wanted to go.'

'So what did she say?' I said. 'I mean, when you asked her.'

Toby stepped up onto the dock. 'She said that I disgusted her, if you really want to know.' He laughed, but it was an angry sound, resonant with hurt. 'She actually called me a pervert.'

'She probably thought I'd told you,' I said. 'She probably thought that was why you'd asked.'

Toby froze. 'That's sick,' he said.

I stepped up beside him without saying anything. At that moment, we both understood that it was true. And I thought, Everything she does, everywhere she goes, this is how she will look at the world. This is the lens through which she'll see. This is what she'll struggle against, always.

How many words do we have for *regret*? How many words for *failure*? How many words for the dark gap between what might have been, what almost was, what happened in the end?

'What did you say to me?' Cindy Ann said.

Carlton unlocked the van. 'I asked if you were feeling okay. You've been looking a bit under the weather.'

'I'm fine.'

Cindy Ann stepped up onto the running board, climbed all the way to the back. The others piled in after her, kicking the salt from their boots, breath forming curlicues in the cold,

December air. A few of the women looked at her, cutting their eyes toward the driver's seat, but Cindy Ann just shrugged, stared out the window at the flat, gray shape of the public works building. For almost eleven months, she'd been sitting up front with Carlton, the two of them talking quietly while, behind them, the others bantered, talked, teased. Most recently, Joey Schlegel was their target: a handsome high school senior, the only male on Community since September. Joey had stolen a car and left it parked on the railroad tracks, though, of course, he claimed it was one of his friends, it wasn't his fault, he'd been totally screwed. By now, Cindy Ann knew the whole story, the way she knew the stories of all the others, what they'd done. Falsifying documents, passing bad checks, vandalism, child neglect, animal abuse. People came and people went, some for a few months, some for just a weekend. She was the only one who'd been there almost a year, the only one among them who had actually killed somebody. 'Road Rage', they called her, behind her back, then not behind her back, which was how she'd ended up riding in front with Carlton in the first place.

But she couldn't risk Carlton smelling her breath, not now, not with only a few more weeks of this bullshit to go. Besides, what had seemed like kindness – the way he'd say hello to her, after Sunday mass; the way he always remembered to ask about Mum; the way that, lately, he'd held the van when she found herself running a few minutes late – was probably just the usual stuff. He'd heard things about her, figured he could fuck her. He'd turn out to be a pervert, just like the rest. Why else hadn't he married again, his wife dead ten years, his own kids already off on their own? Cindy Ann lowered herself in the seat. *Pervert*, she thought to herself. *Skank. Reprobate.* The same names that the girls called each other at home, in seriousness or jest, she never really knew.

What she did know was that she could not have imagined calling her own sisters by those names. No, she'd always looked out for Becca and Mallory, gotten them fed and dressed for school, bought them books and clothing out of the money she earned at DC. Even now, her own life going to shit, she gave Becca cash whenever she asked – no questions, no IOUs. Even now, she was trying her best to protect Mallory from Toby Hauskindler, calling her, e-mailing her, even showing up at Mallory's apartment over the mill, the way she'd done last night.

'Oh, Cee, don't do this, *please*,' Mallory said, before Cindy Ann had had a chance to say a thing. Sitting at the back of the public works van, Cindy Ann closed her eyes. She could see Mallory as she'd stood in the doorway, shivering in a pair of worn slippers, a flannel shirt, paint-spattered jeans. In the background, she heard a man's sleepy voice – it had been a little later than she'd realized – and then Mallory had turned her head, spoken into the sudden, angry glare of the kitchen light:

She isn't like this, not really.

'Pervert!' Cindy Ann had shouted, enraged, into the center of that brightness. After the wedding, as soon as the bank foreclosed, she and the girls would be moving into Toby's old apartment across the landing, Toby's suggestion, he was even paying the rent to hold the place for them. Trying to get his hands on the girls, did he think Cindy Ann couldn't see it? Why else would he be doing this? Besides, wasn't it his fault she'd let down her guard, let the Van Dorns' detective catch her drinking in the first place? Giving them shelter was the least he could do for them, under the circumstances. She wasn't beholden to him, or to anyone. She didn't owe him a goddamn thing.

'You'll regret this!' Cindy Ann had screamed, and Mallory had said, 'Just let us take you home, okay?'

They were all perverts, Cindy Ann thought as the van pulled off the highway onto the shoulder, bouncing hard over the frost heaves until it shuddered to a stop at the edge of the fields. Toby, Carlton, the repo men who seemed to be arriving every day, even Joey Schlegel with his baby-faced grin, his tangle of curls which Pamela Ulrich (shoplifting, petty theft) had just finished braiding into two, neat pigtails.

'You a virgin, still, Joey?' Pamela asked as Carlton opened the sliding door, and Joey said, without missing a beat, 'You bet I am, Pammie. Just like you.'

Shouts of laughter as they stepped down into the cold, lemon-colored light tinting the gloom. Cindy Ann took an orange work vest from the pile, a trash sack, a grab-stick, turning away from Carlton before he had a chance to speak. The men passing in their cars were perverts, too, slowing to ogle them as they spread into rows, the hoarfrost making the grass feel like cardboard beneath their feet. A feeling that was not quite hunger burned just below Cindy Ann's breastbone, and she thought about a story she'd heard on the news, some woman posing as a hitchhiker, riding around the country. Whenever a pervert stopped to pick her up, she stabbed him, robbed him, left him by the road. Reaching the stick toward a plastic bag, Cindy Ann thought about that woman, now on death row, and wondered if she ever regretted what she'd done. Maybe, after the girls were grown, Cindy Ann would do the same thing. Or maybe she'd just drive out to her mother's farm one afternoon, take a walk back to the old veal pens, shoot herself just like Dan had done.

A plastic lid. A paper cup. A half-frozen can of beer. Crows rose from a hawthorn bush, a black, beating cloud of wings, and Pamela jumped and said, 'God *damn*, them fuckers give me the creeps.' Across the intersection stood the husk of the one-room schoolhouse, crumbling walls of yellow brick, and Cindy Ann glanced at it, noted it, and then stopped, realizing where they were. Just over a year had passed since the accident. Alone, she always drove the other way into town; the few times she'd passed by with Carlton and the crew, she'd kept her gaze fixed on her hands. *Life goes on*, Mum always said. She still said it now when Cindy Ann stopped by to wash her hair, to sit with her in the Garden Room, to have lunch in the cafeteria. Or else she'd say, *The love of my life.* These days, there was little else she said. She had no idea that Cindy Ann hadn't paid her resident fees in months, that Cindy Ann had lapsed on her mortgage payments, that creditors were calling Cindy Ann around the clock. She hadn't a clue that, by the end of the year, they'd be moving her over to the county facility, while Cindy Ann and the girls would be moving to the mill. There was no money left for Mrs Railsbeck. No money for the girls' music lessons. No money for Laurel's braces, for Amy's college tuition. No money, even, for the gym membership, though, at least, that was paid through the year.

A child's flip-flop. Another beer can. Beyond the blinking light, a little blue car, no larger than a mouse, made its way down the Point Road, exhaust trailing behind it like a lengthening tail. To the east, on County C, a second car, also blue, was picking up speed as well. Catty-corner across the intersection, poised on the edge of the gulley, Cindy Ann could just see the small, white cross, half-buried in the weeds. Remarkable, really, how frequently the crew would encounter little shrines like these. Most of them long overgrown, the bones of each cross like an old skeleton, crumbling into dust. Others were more recent, dates still visible on the paint, bunches of artificial flowers tangled at the base. Carlton didn't mind if someone wanted to stop, put things right, digging the crosses back into the ground, rearranging flowers, pulling weeds. Sometimes, in fact, he even helped, pulling out his pocketknife, returning to the truck for a piece of string. For a while, there'd been a young woman named Cecilia who'd wept, each time, kneeling down to pray. For a while, there'd been a woman named Jo-Lynne who'd made sure to call out to Cindy Ann, 'Hey, Road Rage – this one yours? How many points you get?'

A hand on her sleeve. She shook it away. The first car, the second car, each heading toward the other as if drawn by some terrible knowledge, forbidden, absolute.

Carlton's voice. 'You sure you're okay? You want to go back to the truck?'

The yellow light, blinking time, indifferent as a wrist-watch. Cindy Ann couldn't speak, could only point as the wet screech of brakes cut the air, the first car shooting through the intersection even as the second car swerved toward them, popped off the road, churning up gravel, clots of frozen earth, before righting itself, passing them by, the driver – a woman – white-faced, shaking her head. The first car was gone. It had never even slowed. Everything had happened in what seemed like an instant.

'Jesus,' Carlton said, and then he called to the crew, his voice uncharacteristically harsh. 'We cross the road together, hear me? We follow protocol. We—'

But Cindy Ann was running now, up the embankment,

down the edge of the highway, darting across the intersection toward Evan Van Dorn's shrine. Trash everywhere. Faded plastic flowers. One arm of the cross propped against the ground, the other reaching skyward, as if drowning, begging for help. *Life goes on.* All those pious teachers who'd erected this cross, who'd gone to the funeral, who'd sent their cards of mourning; all those parents who'd shown up for the candlelight vigil, who had written those terrible letters to the paper, demanding Cindy Ann's head on a platter – where were these people now? *She* was the one pulling up fat, frosted fistfuls of quack grass, snapping off stalks of dead goldenrod. The others caught up, knelt down beside her, orange vests burning like a ring of fire. And then, Carlton was kneeling, too.

'He was six years old,' she said.

'I'm walking you back to the truck,' he said.

'The love of my life,' she said, but the cross broke apart in her hands.

More hands, now, patting her back, rubbing her shoulders, stroking her hair: Carlton's, Pamela's, even Joey Schlegel's. Trying to help, to heal. Her last clear thought, she'd tell me, later, would go something like this: *Oh, they wouldn't touch me that way, if they knew how much it hurt.*

Chapter Ten

Amy Kreisler opened the door to find a barrel-chested man in an orange work vest, a white van idling behind him in the driveway. She didn't ask questions, just cocked her hip, waiting for him to get to the point. The doorbell had been ringing a lot these days: repo men, the sheriff's deputy, a Realtor from the bank. By January first, it wouldn't matter anymore. Mum and the little girls would have moved into Toby's old place at the mill. As for Amy, she'd be staying with her best friend, Kristen, and her family at their house on Nelson Heights. Mum was crazy if she thought, for a minute, that Amy would be living in some freezing-cold dump, no hot water except what you heated on the stove, I mean, *please*. No wonder Toby had moved across the landing to Aunt Mal's efficiency, where, at least, she had *tried* to fix things up. It wasn't that he was trying to help them out, as people said. It wasn't that he was going to be supporting Mum, financially. And if he was, well, he was a sucker, there wasn't any need for that. That was the thing about Mum. She always had more money tucked away. She'd say she didn't, but then, if she really wanted something, she'd go ahead and buy it anyway.

'You must be Amy,' the man said, stepping forward as if he planned to come in. Amy glanced into the kitchen, but there was only the leftover clutter of boxes and bubble wrap, newspapers, wadded-up balls of packing tape. Ever since Mrs Railsbeck stopped coming, Mum had been increasingly careless. Last night, Amy had arrived home from work to find empty wine bottles, a broken glass, lasagna fixings strewn across the countertop. The oven was preheating. The refrigerator door stood open. It was as if Mum had been abducted by aliens in the middle of making supper. 'Mum?' Amy called, but there'd been no answer. No note. Nothing. The girls – thank God – were asleep in their beds. It had been after midnight when Aunt Mal had brought Mum home, Toby following in the Suburban.

'Call if you need anything,' he'd said, pressing the keys into Amy's hand, but Amy hadn't thanked him, merely slipped them into the pocket of her robe without looking at him. It wasn't that she disliked Toby, the way Mum did, it was just that there was the matter of his sister, who hated them, who was trying to sue them, who actually thought they'd run into her car on purpose. Sometimes Amy would forget about this, usually when she and Toby were talking about the future of the fish store – Amy planned to major in business administration, and she had lots of ideas about potential online venues – but then, all of a sudden, she'd remember, and, after that, she wouldn't know what to say. That was the one good thing about the foreclosure, the auction, the bankruptcy. As Aunt Mal liked to say, by the time the Van Dorns quit dickering over the settlement, there wouldn't be two nickels left for them to rub together.

But if that were the case, then maybe it *was* true, what people said about Toby having to support them. When he and Aunt Mal first got engaged, they were planning to buy a little cottage on the lake; they'd even driven her and the little girls out to see it one sunny afternoon, while Mum was on Community. But then, all of a sudden, they'd changed their minds. They'd moved into Mal's efficiency. They were pretending that Toby still lived at his place so the crazy old landlord, Mr Dickens, wouldn't try to raise the rent. All of this made Amy very uncomfortable when she thought about it, especially since she was giving Mum less than half of what she earned at the Dairy Castle. The rest she was using to buy stocks online: technology, mostly, a few bio techs, a couple of blue chips for stability. Analysts were saying the NASDAQ might actually hit 5,000 by next year. No way was she going to miss out on something like that.

The barrel-chested man seemed to be waiting for her to say something.

'Yes?' Amy said, impatiently.

'Your mother,' he began, then stopped.

'What did she do now?' Amy said, but the man seemed surprised by this, even a little offended.

'Nothing,' he said. 'But she's real upset. I thought that maybe if I brought her home . . .'

His voice trailed off as he nodded toward the van, and Amy suddenly recognized him: Mum's supervisor. The one who sometimes said hello to them at church. The one who drove Mum and the other convicts to their various Community assignments. *For God's sake, stop calling us convicts*, Mum would say, and Amy would say, *What should I call you, then? Volunteers?* By now, the little girls were at the door, too, Laurel gnawing on a cold slice of pizza, Monica carrying her Princess doll.

'Wait here,' Amy told them, grabbing her coat from the floor where the mahogany coat stand once had stood, and she followed the man out into the driveway. She could just see her mother's head, tipped forward, as if her chin were on her chest. Drunk, Amy thought, but when the man opened the door, she saw that this was wrong. Mum's eyes were open, her face peculiarly white. She did not look at either of them. The wind toyed with a strand of her long, blond hair.

'Is there somebody you could call?' the man said.

A single tear ran down the side of Mum's face, but it wasn't as if Mum herself were crying, because anyone could see that Mum simply wasn't there.

'Just a minute,' Amy said, and she ran back toward the

house, ducked through the still-open door where the girls were waiting, watching.

'What's the matter?' Monica said.

'Shut up,' Amy said, and she picked up the phone, dialed Aunt Mal at the mill. No answer. She dialed the fish store, only half-listening as Laurel complained about the pizza, something about green peppers, too many, not enough, her turn, her share. 'Shut up!' Amy said again, just as Toby picked up, and there was the man in the doorway again, half-carrying Mum, his face beet red with strain.

'Everything okay?' Toby said, and Amy could hear customers in the background, the rattle of plastic bags. In an hour, Amy herself would have to be at work. That night, she and Kristen were supposed to go to a movie with Kristen's boyfriend, Al, and a friend Al thought would be perfect for Amy. Besides, Amy had calculus to study for. She had a paper on the New Deal.

'I think you should come over,' Amy said.

'Okay,' he said. 'As soon as I can.'

The man was in the family room now, looking for some-place to put Mum down, but the comfy old couch and chair were already at Toby's place. All the living-room furniture had gone back to Ethan Allen. The dining room set had vanished, too. The man dragged Mum back into the kitchen and dropped her, with a grunt, into one of the kitchen chairs.

'Mommy?' Monica said.

'Hello?' Toby said.

'No,' Amy said, and her voice was trembling. 'I think you should come now.'

There was a beat of silence.

'I'm on my way,' Toby said.

Rex and I had spent our wedding night at the Pfister Hotel. The following day, we'd flown out of O'Hare for a honeymoon week in Tuscany. We rented a villa in an olive grove, just south of Florence, overlooking a quiet lake. It was November, unseasonably cold – though warmer than Wisconsin – and we'd hiked, every morning, along an old donkey trail until we'd reached the little town of Caprese Michelangelo. There, we'd eaten our breakfast of white beans drizzled with oil before prowling the local markets for vegetables, fish, cheese. Afternoons, we drove too fast along narrow, curving roads, the mountains standing over us like broad-shouldered angels. Rex said, more than once, 'We are lucky, so very lucky,' and though I agreed, something within me winced, longing to shush him, hush him, hide us both away. Old gods, it seemed to me, were sleeping everywhere. It wouldn't take much to awaken them: a glimmer of hubris, the least suggestion of good fortune. Each time the road dropped out beneath us, I white-knuckled the door handle, held my breath. Blindly, we plunged into valley after valley, rising and falling as if in flight, the trees a blur of color as we passed.

Awakening at the Pfister on the morning of Christmas Eve, I found myself missing Rex terribly. The troubles we'd been having seemed like nothing from where I lay, alone in a king-size bed as extravagant as any wedding cake: canopied, frosted, fringed. Beyond the heavy damask curtains, I could see the same gunmetal gray Milwaukee sky that had, on the first day of our marriage, appeared unexpectedly silver. Reaching my hand beneath my pillow, I'd discovered Rex's hand, slipped my fingers into his, then realized – with a small, startled shriek – it wasn't his hand but my own, numb from the weight of my shoulder.

Slow kisses. Pins and needles. Desire awakening, sharpening.

I would have settled, now, for simply hearing his voice. He still hadn't called in on my father's cell phone, the way we had arranged, though we'd gotten a brief, cryptic e-mail: *Hard 2 phone. Everything fine. Hope yr same.* Perhaps, he'd been too busy with *Chelone* to make it to Echo Island. Or perhaps the ferry had stopped running, as it did from time to time, due to weather, to mechanical problems, to the whims of the family that owned it. More likely, he'd been trying to call but kept getting disconnected. Last night, from the steakhouse where we'd all gone out to dinner, my father had checked for messages on my parents' Florida machine.

Nothing.

'Now you know how we've felt all these months,' my

mother said.

A rap at the door: *shave-and-a-haircut*. My mother's signature knock. I got up, grateful for the distraction, and slipped into a plush, hotel robe. On top of the TV sat the FedEx package Arnie's secretary had sent, per my instructions, care of the hotel. The package was still unopened. I flipped it over, so the address wouldn't show, before letting my mother in.

'It's eighteen degrees outside,' she announced, indignantly, stepping into the room. She was neatly dressed in a wool pantsuit, balancing two hotel mugs filled with coffee. I felt like a teenager, caught sleeping late, complete with a raging case of bed head. Not to mention the remains of my poisonwood rash, which was looking more and more like a bad case of acne. 'You know what the temperature is in Miami today?'

I took the mug she offered me, shook my head. Sipped. The coffee was sweet, nearly white with cream.

'Eighty-two.' She glared around the room, as if she were looking for someone to blame. I'd forgotten how *personally* my parents took cold weather, as if it were something that had been engineered, specifically, to torment them. 'Are you hungry? There's plenty to eat in our room. I just came back from the buffet.'

From the pocket of her tailored jacket, she removed two hard-boiled eggs. I started to laugh, I couldn't help it. Here was something else I'd forgotten. At the steakhouse, my father had ordered the New York strip, while my mother, demurely, chose the salad bar. After eating what he wanted, my father handed his plate to my mother who, in turn, passed him her salad bar leavings: baked beans, macaroni, Jell-O salad. I glanced around, hoping the waiter hadn't seen, but my father just laughed.

'As if he cares,' he said.

'As if any one person could eat six dollars' worth of salad,' my mother said.

'Six ninety-five,' my father said.

'And these steaks are just too big for one person!'

'So ask for a second plate,' I said, but my father shook his head vigorously.

'Bastards charge you a plate fee.'

'At least the bread is free,' my mother said, giving the bulge in her purse a little pat.

How they'd driven Toby nuts, when he'd still lived at home, with all their little shortcuts, coupons, early bird specials. Those mashed-together slivers of soap that broke apart in your hands. Toby. I'd called him after getting in from dinner, this time at his apartment, but a child had answered – had his number changed? *I'm not supposed to talk on the phone, okay?* she'd said, and then hung up. He hadn't been at the fish store, either, which wasn't surprising, considering the time. Still, in the past, it wouldn't have been unusual for Toby to be there, working late, perhaps even spending the night stretched out on the hospital cot he kept beside his breeding tanks. I reminded myself that his life would be different, now that he was engaged. He'd be spending time with Mallory, after work, on weekends. In fact, with the wedding just a few days away, he might not have time to see me. Perhaps, after what Rex had done, Toby didn't *want* to see me. Perhaps he'd sent the invitation for the sake of his conscience alone, expecting it wouldn't reach me, that I wouldn't come from so far away.

'So what's on your agenda for today?' my mother asked, sitting down with her mug at the glass-topped table.

I settled myself across from her. 'Depends on Toby,' I said. 'By the way, did his home phone change or something?'

'Who knows?'

My mother cracked one of the eggs, began to pick at the shell. I'd been surprised to learn that she and my father still hadn't seen him – or Mallory either, for that matter. In fact, they'd only spoken with Toby twice. He was busy, he was sorry, he would make it up to them. There'd been talk of a prewedding dinner (where? with whom?), but that seemed to have fallen through. 'Ah, the pressures of prenuptials,' my father had said, grinning, but this didn't make any sense to me. It wasn't that type of wedding, after all. How many details could there be, arranging for a justice of the peace to spend fifteen shivering minutes aboard the *Michigan Jack*?

'It's just so strange,' I said to my mother, now. 'I can see where he might not want to see me, but he can't spare half an hour to say hello to you?'

'I don't think you ought to take it personally,' my mother said. 'I think something's wrong.'

'Like what?'

'Well, he and Mallory had a contract on a two-bedroom cottage – did I tell you this? No? Well, a few weeks ago, they backed out of it. No warning. Lost their deposit and everything. And I just talked with Anna Schultz – she says hello, by the way – and she's heard they're staying on at the mill. Keeping both apartments.'

'Maybe they're not getting along,' I said, and it was hard to filter the eagerness out of my voice.

But my mother shook her head. 'Anna thinks it's some kind of financial trouble. Evie Haldiger heard the same thing. You went to school with one of the Haldigers, didn't you?' She cocked her head, thinking. 'Vivian? Or was it Beatrice?'

I couldn't have cared less about the Haldigers just then. 'What expenses could he have, Mom?' I said. 'The fish store's up and down a bit, but he makes good money on those charters. Besides, you and dad would help him out, if he needed it. And Mallory works, too.'

'Actually, we offered to buy that cottage for them. A wedding gift.' My mother held out the peeled egg. 'Anything to get him out of that hellhole.'

'I'm not hungry.'

'You aren't getting enough protein, I can tell.'

I took the egg; it was rubbery, cool. 'So why did they break their contract?'

'I don't know. But *you* should know that Toby refused our help with it.'

'Why?'

'Because he felt – well, he and Mal were concerned that it might cause problems with you and Rex.'

'They can't think we'd be jealous of the money,' I said, flushing at the casual way my mother shortened Mallory's name.

'They think,' my mother said pointedly, 'you'd object to us doing something for him that would also benefit her. And I must admit, I had qualms about it myself. For Evan's sake.'

I ate the egg. I didn't know what to say. Had Rex come back from Echo with the news – *Christ, your parents even bought them a place to live!* – of course, I would have felt betrayed. And yet, I realized, I sincerely wanted Toby to have a home. I wanted him to be happy. He and Mallory were remarkably right for each other, despite the difference in their ages, their lifestyles, their assorted idiosyncrasies. The times they'd babysat for Evan, Rex and I had returned home, late, to find them playing Scrabble at the kitchen table, classical music on the radio, sipping tea made from herbs that Mallory had gathered, wild, along the railroad tracks. *Profligate* intersecting with *claxon*; *civisms* running up against *elision*. Toby was smart, even brilliant, but he'd barely graduated high school. Mallory had dropped out at sixteen, yet the camper she traveled around in every summer, selling jewelry at festivals and craft fairs, was crammed with paperback classics: Tolstoy, Austen, Camus. Where else would Toby find someone with his level of education, coupled with his own intellectual intensity? Where else would he find somebody who practiced what she preached about the virtues of inner beauty? Beneath the wool cap and the oversize shirts, Mallory was attractive, vibrant. Beside her, Toby both reflected that beauty and, somehow, absorbed it, too.

A few months prior to Evan's death, Mallory had invited us all to dinner at her efficiency apartment over the mill. 'Will we all fit?' I'd asked Toby, who'd said, 'Why don't you come and see?' Rex had begged off, claiming work, but when Evan and I arrived, we discovered a lovely meal laid out on the floor, spread across an Indian print: spinach lasagna, home-made bread, apple pie for dessert. The apartment itself, like Toby's, was a festival of code violations: taped-over outlets, that bathtub still in the kitchen, the toilet – so I discovered – in a sink-less cell so low that you had to duck your head. But the boarded-up window overlooking the parking lot had been painted with a beaming, golden sun king, and the cracked plaster walls were concealed beneath the long, thriving arms of hanging ivy. A cast-iron dog, nearly three feet tall, kept the warped closet door from opening. A salvaged carousel horse pranced, midair, from its pole; it actually seemed to be bracing up the ceiling.

Evan, of course, had been delighted with it all. He suggested that we abandon our own dining table as soon as we got back home. He liked the futon couch, which doubled as a bed. He especially liked getting to choose his own tea mug from the mismatched assortment that hung, in a descending row, from hooks pushed into the wall.

'You found these in the *trash*?' he said, his voice scaling upward with admiration and awe.

'It's amazing what people throw away,' Mallory said. 'Pretty much everything in this room is something I found at the curb.'

'Including me,' Toby said, only he was laughing as he said it.

'That's right,' Mallory said. 'Dusted you off, changed your diet—'

'Now, if you could just get him to trim that beard a little bit,' I said, trying to join in, but it was wrong.

'I like your brother's beard,' Mallory said, meeting my gaze.

I said nothing.

'Total acceptance,' Toby said, jumping in to fill the silence. 'What more could any man ask for?'

When we got back home, Evan raced up the stairs to the

crow's nest, eager to tell Rex that we ought to get rid of our table so we, too, could eat on the floor. I put away our coats, cleaned up the remnants of Rex's solitary supper – he was good about putting dishes away, but never noticed crumbs on the counter – then sat at the table, sorting through the mail, thinking about the way Mallory had looked at me when I'd commented on Toby's beard. The way I would have looked at anybody, any woman, who'd made a similar remark about Rex. I would never like Mallory Donaldson, I decided. I'd never be fully comfortable in her presence. But I could see how, over time, I might come to like her – even love her – for Toby's sake.

For her goodness to him. For her protectiveness.

'So what did she serve you?' Rex asked, coming down the stairs. 'Weeds and seeds?'

'Lasagna,' Evan said, trooping after him, wearing his spaceship pajamas.

'Everything was homemade,' I said, determined to be positive. 'And no white flour. No sugar. The apple pie was sweetened with dates. Did you brush your teeth?' I asked Evan, who arched his back and clung to the banister, echoing, 'Brush, brush, brush!'

'Did he brush his teeth?' I asked Rex.

'Not yet,' Rex said, and he was laughing. 'I'm sorry, I just can't imagine Toby eating that way.' He picked Evan up, turned him upside down, carried him down the stairs by the knees. 'Do you know what your uncle used to eat for breakfast every day?'

'Eggs!' Evan shouted. His head swung a mere inch from each step; I had to look away.

'A Snickers bar and a Coke.'

'Diet Coke,' I said. 'Be fair.'

'And there he is, poor bastard—'

'Rex.'

'Poor chap, eating tofu three times a day.'

He dropped Evan into my lap, right side up, and Evan said, with sudden seriousness: 'Mallory doesn't eat anything that has eyes, Dad.'

'You mean,' Rex said, lowering his voice in exaggerated horror, 'she only eats things that are *blind*?'

For a split second, Evan's expression mirrored Rex's, albeit sincerely. Then – *zing*. He got it. He shrieked with delight. We all were laughing together, now: uncontrollably, deliciously, cruelly. The laughter of people who belong to something, in the presence of someone who doesn't.

Now I sat with my mother in silence, swallowing the last, dry mouthfuls of egg. Voices passed outside the door, a family heading toward the elevators, the mother's voice low, but carrying: *Don't run.*

'Anna told me something else,' my mother said. 'About Cindy Ann. If you want to know.'

I waited.

267

'She's not going to be at the wedding. She's checked herself into some kind of hospital. For people who have been, you know, abused. Sexually, I mean. It's somewhere north of Madison.' My mother tapped her finger against the glass tabletop. 'I never heard anything about her being abused before, did you? Though the stepfather, what was his name—'

'Dan Kolb.' Suddenly cold, I tucked my bare feet under my robe. At least, I thought, I won't have to see her. At least, she won't have to see me.

'Anything's possible, I suppose,' my mother continued. 'But it seems like something an attorney would suggest, doesn't it? To make her situation seem more sympathetic? Though I guess that wouldn't matter, now that you've dropped the suit. And I have to say, I'm glad you did.'

I glanced at her, sharply, but no. She did not suspect the truth. Had there been so much as a whisper afloat, she'd have had the whole story from Evie Haldiger.

'I couldn't care less about *her*, you understand,' my mother continued. 'But I always hoped she'd pull herself together, for the sake of those girls. And Mal is a decent person, a good person. You can see how hard she tries. She sent us a sympathy card, did I tell you that? On Evan's anniversary?'

'We didn't drop the suit,' I said.

My mother looked stunned. 'But – of course, you did. Before you bought the boat.'

I got up, walked over to the TV, picked up the FedEx package. 'I thought we did,' I said. 'But it turns out that Rex didn't. He and Arnie got a detective to follow Cindy Ann around, taking pictures.'

'Pictures of what?' my mother asked.

I dropped the package between us on the table. 'Pictures that document the fact that she's still drinking. She's been drinking all along, Mom. Rex always thought that she was.'

'And driving?'

'I suppose it's safe to assume,' I said, 'that if there's one, there's probably the other.'

'I don't believe it,' my mother said. 'I just can't believe she'd be so *stupid*!'

'Here's proof,' I said, nodding at the package. 'And a settlement offer, too. Supposedly, she's already signed it. Rex, too – or, at least, Arnie signed on his behalf. All I have to do is write my name on the dotted line.'

My mother was studying my face. 'But you don't want to do it?'

'If I don't, I think it will be difficult for Rex and me to live together again.'

Suddenly, I felt so unbelievably sad that I had to close my eyes. For God's sake, I thought. It's Christmas Eve. It will be our second Christmas without him. And I just stood there for a moment, missing him so overwhelmingly: his body, his physical presence in the world.

'I imagine,' my mother said, gently, 'that it's difficult for two people to live on a boat during the best of times.'

'It's more than that. We're not getting over this. We seem better, at least on the surface, but we're not. We're just as furious and helpless and—'

My mother put her hand on mine.

'I can't even talk about it,' I said, 'because it just goes around and around in my head. Maybe Rex is right and this won't ever be resolved unless there's some kind of concrete restitution. God.' I stood up, but I didn't move away from that anchoring hand. 'I don't know what I'm doing here. I probably shouldn't have come back. I wish sometimes that a big wave would come and just – take us. End things. Once and for all.'

For a long time, my mother didn't speak. Then she said, 'You would know, from experience, how I'd feel if that happened.'

I squeezed her hand, sat down again. 'I know. I don't mean it,' I managed to say, although, at that moment, I did. 'I guess I ought to look at the photographs, anyway.'

'May I see them, too?'

I shrugged. 'Go ahead. It's just pictures of her sitting around, drinking.'

But when my mother opened the package, dozens of page proofs slid out onto the table, black-and-white glimpses of Cindy Ann's life, moment by moment, day after day. Unloading groceries, checking her mail, taking out the trash.

Standing in front of the bank with Amy; exiting the Cup and Cruller with Monica. At the upscale gym on Lakewood. Sitting on the curb after a run. A separate sleeve of photos had been taken at night, the telescopic lens aimed toward the lighted windows. There was Cindy Ann with Laurel, the two of them watching TV. The four of them eating dinner together. Cindy Ann and Monica playing with one of the cats. And I suddenly saw not only these photos, but also the ones that hadn't been taken, thousands of intimate snapshots that the detective had glimpsed during that week of her life. Cindy Ann undressing for bed, lamplight pouring down over her body. Passing, bare-shouldered, before the bedroom window, wet-headed from the shower. Dashing out, half-dressed, for the morning paper. He'd been diligent, the detective. Of course, he would have seen everything there was to see.

It was moments just like these Dan Kolb had stolen thirty years ago, biding his time. Private moments of quiet concentration. Casual clothes, careless limbs. A glimpse of a breast, a pale slice of skin.

Maybe he thought you wanted him to.

At the bottom of the pile was a manila envelope with a Post-it note stuck to the back. *Jackpot*, Arnie had written. Inside, I found enlargements of the most condemning photographs: Cindy Ann at Discount Liquors. Cindy Ann carrying the empty bottles out with the recycling. Sitting at the kitchen counter alone, another bottle in front of her, a half-empty glass. That same glass in her hand. That same glass at her mouth. Her expression like the pale, lost face of a ghost. Lines on either side of her mouth, purplish shadows under her eyes. Flesh thickening, slightly, around her upper arms. A body that might have been my own.

I guessed that Arnie had sent all the photos on purpose, in order that I might see for myself what, once, had galled me, enraged me. The semblance of normalcy in Cindy Ann's life. The trips to the store, to the bank, to the gym. The meals with her daughters, the bedtime routines. But the longer I looked at each picture, the more obvious it became to me that nothing had been normal in Cindy Ann Kreisler's life for a very long time. Still, her signature on the settlement agreement looked exactly as I remembered it – swollen with looping circles, curlicues, that dangling, girlish *y*.

Putting down the pictures, sliding them back into the envelope, I felt as if I was putting away the dark weight of my anger. Again, that unalloyed sadness overwhelmed me: heart to stomach, muscle to bone. How it *hurt*, and there was nothing to distract me, protect me. I would have to stand and take it on my own.

'Will she go to jail?' my mother asked, and I knew she was seeing what I had seen, because her voice sounded small and sad.

'She could. She isn't supposed to be drinking.' I touched the fat settlement agreement. 'But this is a financial settlement. Basically, she'd be paying us to keep these photos out of court.'

'With what? Evie says her trust money's gone. The bank's foreclosing on her house. Her oldest daughter has moved in with friends. From the sound of things, she's ruined herself completely.'

I waited to feel something: vindication, satisfaction. Instead, what I felt was concern. I remembered Amy in that Dairy Castle uniform, moving toward me like a ghost. Thinking to myself, how strange it was, that she'd have to work the same, terrible job her mother had held. Had hated. Cindy Ann had never said so, but I knew.

A thought occurred to me, then. 'Have you heard where the younger girls are staying?' I asked. 'While Cindy Ann's at this hospital, I mean?'

'Who knows? Her mother certainly can't take them. I suppose they're with her other sister, you know, that Jehovah's Witness.'

But I was up out of my chair, pacing around the room. *I'm not supposed to talk on the phone*, that clear little voice had said. The voice of a girl, roughly eight years old.

The voice of Cindy Ann's youngest daughter.

'I know why Toby is avoiding us,' I said. 'He and Mallory are taking care of those kids.'

'In that hellhole?' my mother said. 'Good god, I hope not. For everybody's sake.'

But I was already making plans. I needed to shower and dress. I needed to phone Lindsey Steinke, set up a time to go over our financials. I needed to stop by our house, check on our tenant, pick out a couple of sweaters, mittens, proper boots. After that, however, I'd be free to do some detective work of my own.

'I'm going to find out,' I said.

The potholes scattered through the mill parking lot had been spackled by thick, yellow slabs of ice. Slowly, cautiously, I pulled around back and parked beside the exterior set of stairs leading up to Toby's apartment. The shades were drawn, but behind them, lights – all the lights, it seemed – were burning gold, the excess spilling out into the gloom. It was barely afternoon and yet, already, there was that sense of impending twilight that seems to linger even on the finest winter days. Clouds lay heavily at the edges of the fields, and the air held the faint, metallic tang that promises below-zero cold. I got out of my mother's car and nudged my backpack onto the floor, fat with the cedar-smelling socks and pull-overs I'd taken from the attic. There was no sign of Toby's truck or Mallory's weather-beaten Nova. Still, I could see dark shadows drifting, fishlike, behind the living-room shades. Suddenly, I wished I'd waited for my parents, who'd promised to arrive later on in the afternoon. They were probably sitting down to lunch in the Schultzes's warm kitchen just about now: Anna's roast chicken, her pineapple upside-down cake.

'Join us,' my mother had said. 'Whatever's going on at the mill will keep for another few hours.'

Instead, I'd called our tenant, Chester Logan. Chester was from Chicago, a twenty-something Internet entrepreneur. He had 'checked out of real life' – or so he'd explained, six months earlier – in order to write a technological thriller, something quick and snappy. It was going to sell a million copies, Chester was absolutely certain; Rex and I had listened to the entire plot, sitting at our kitchen table, wishing Chester would just sign the lease and go. Now, Chester was just as certain this novel was going nowhere. He was spending more and more time in Chicago, getting back into the technology game. What would I say if he found a subletter? Or, perhaps Rex and I were getting tired of life at sea? In which case, all I had to do was give him a few days' notice. All I had to do was say the word.

'Let's talk about this face-to-face,' I said.

Standing in the entryway of the home where I'd lived for nearly twenty years, I struggled not to burst into tears. The floor tiles were crusted with road salt and grit, the living-room carpet hopelessly stained. Dried-out pizza boxes littered the kitchen counters, and a pyramid of empty Budweiser cans decorated the antique buffet. Worst of all was the smell of mildew, the dark spot on the ceiling over the dining-room light fixture. Had there been some kind of leak? Chester looked pained.

'Sorry. I was filling the Jacuzzi tub, and, I don't know, I kind of fell asleep.'

I told Chester I'd get back to him, after Christmas, about the lease, after I'd had time to think things through. After I'd had a chance to talk with Rex – though, already, I knew what Rex would say.

Put the house on the market.

It was what he'd originally wanted to do.

The landing between Toby's apartment and Mallory's looked exactly as I'd remembered it: abandoned. The wooden railings were rotting, riddled with holes left by carpenter bees. Dead leaves scattered in crackling ribbons, re-arranging themselves with each gust of wind. But a homemade wreath hung from Toby's door – the kind made out of pinecones, Styrofoam, glitter – and I recognized the same art project I'd been forced to do, forty years earlier, at school. Behind it, two young voices were arguing, rising and falling in a complicated counterpoint that resolved itself, abruptly, in silence. Putting my ear to the door, I could hear a television sitcom: canned laughter, tinny bursts of applause.

'Cut it out!' someone shrieked, and there was a crash, followed by the sort of scream that means business. I tried the door, but it was locked; since when had Toby ever locked the door? The doorbell, of course, was broken. I knocked, then hammered with my fists.

'Is everyone okay in there?' I called.

Instantly, the wailing stopped. Someone turned off the TV. I could hear rapid footsteps, a single bleat of dismay, then nothing.

'Is anybody bleeding?' I called. 'Just tell me that.'

Another pause. Then:

'Yes.'

'A lot of blood or a little?'

The wailing began again. The first voice said, a bit impatiently, 'She's okay. She's always hurting herself.'

Toby had always kept a spare key – heaven knows why – at the top of the doorframe. Feeling around in the grit with my fingertips, I dislodged it. It fell with a Christmas-y chime.

'I'm letting myself in,' I said.

'We're not supposed to let *anyone* in,' the first voice said.

'Is that Laurel?' I asked, opening the door.

The last thing I expected was the weight of an opposing body, thrown hard against the back of the door, a reverse battering ram. The door slammed on my shoulder, bounced back; I swore, caught the kick plate against my foot, then nudged my knee through the gap. By the time I wriggled inside, both girls were running, screaming, darting around either side of a large, toppled Christmas tree, which stretched the full length of the living room. A cat – one of Cindy Ann's

Angoras — flashed past, round as a puffer fish, every hair standing on end. I could only hope that Mr Dickens was as deaf as he'd always pretended to be whenever Toby cornered him about apartment repairs.

'It's okay, it's okay,' I kept saying. But whose apartment was this? All of the junk and clutter was gone. Not only could you see the floor — aside from the tree, filling the room with its good, green smell — but it was carpeted, and the walls were a bright collage of artwork, prints, dozens and dozens of photographs. My mother's photographs, in fact; Toby's share of the framed snapshots that had always embarrassed us so. There he sat, a fat, happy baby. There he was again, holding me in his lap. There was the seemingly endless succession of family pets: the fish and rabbits, the cats and dogs, the terrible lovebird that shrieked and bit us all. Beneath this display was a fat, floral couch, a matching chair and end table. Bookshelves filled with books. Magazines in a basket. The bedroom door closed with a slam, but, before it did, I glimpsed tidy bunk beds, a pink and green rug, the second cat perched on the window ledge. I also saw a little girl, slightly older than Evan would have been, her forehead glossy with blood so red, so brilliant, it looked fake.

Shit.

'Does Toby keep a first-aid kit?' I called, stepping into the bathroom. Here, too, everything was tidy. Scoured tiles.

Clean towels hanging from the racks. Scented soap in a dish. The only thing I recognized about this place was the cold; I could see my breath with each exhalation.

'I have a gun,' came Laurel's voice. 'You better not try anything.'

For all I knew, this was probably true, but my shoulder hurt and I was starting to lose patience.

'For Pete's sake, use your head,' I said. 'Would I be looking for a first-aid kit if I were trying to *hurt* you?' I found cotton gauze, some iodine. 'Now, come out of there so I can look at Monica's forehead.'

'Who are you? How do you know our names?'

'I'm your aunt. Or, at least, I will be as soon as *your* aunt marries my brother. Are you going to open that door, or do I need to call the Cup and Cruller?'

The bedroom door opened. Blessedly, there wasn't any sign of a gun. Just Laurel, standing with folded arms, one hip jutting out. Unlike her sisters, her mother, she was plain: heavyset, fierce as a little bull terrier. Beside her, Monica peered at me impishly, blinking at the blood in her eyes. Both girls wore ski vests over their sweaters. Their noses were running. Their hair needed washing.

'Mal's not working today,' Laurel said.

'Where is she?'

'What happened to your face?'

How tired I was of that question. The flesh-eating bacteria

story had worked so well I considered trotting it out again. But I didn't have the energy.

'It's a rash,' I said.

'Oh. I thought that maybe, like, ugly faces just ran in your family or something.'

She was alluding to Toby's birthmark; it took every ounce of self-possession to keep my expression steady. 'Actually, this looked much worse a week ago. Now, would one of you tell me what happened?'

To my surprise, Monica skipped forward, hurled herself into my arms. Too late, I remembered my mother's pale coat, but already, it was streaked like a candy cane. Evan had died without losing a single drop of blood; at the wake, he'd truly looked like he was sleeping. And now, here was Monica, this living, talking, *furious* child, bleeding as if she'd slit her jugular.

'She *pushed* me,' she sobbed. 'I was up on the chair——'

'I didn't push you,' Laurel said, bored. 'You fell. Like I said you would.'

'Did she hit the wall?' I asked. 'The end table?'

'She wasn't supposed to touch the tree, okay? We're supposed to decorate it tonight and, I don't know, sing campfire songs.'

'Christmas carols,' Monica howled.

'Mum's in a psycho ward and you're gonna sit around singing Christmas carols? Sweet.'

Abruptly, Monica stopped crying. 'Life goes on,' she said. She sounded like a very old woman when she said it.

'Hold still,' I said, and I parted the wet, sticky mass of her hair. There it was, a half-inch cut, just above the hairline. It didn't seem too bad; in fact, the bleeding had nearly stopped. I pressed a clean, white square of gauze against the cut. An odd, animal look came over Laurel's face, part fascination, part loathing. 'What are you doing here, anyway?' she said. 'Aren't you supposed to hate us?'

I decided not to risk any answer. 'Go to the kitchen,' I told her, instead, 'and get me some wet paper towels.'

Instead, she turned and disappeared into the bedroom. Fine. The second cat, still on the window ledge, blinked its golden eyes.

'You're okay to walk, right?' I asked Monica, who nodded with her whole head – another good sign, I thought. In the kitchen, I had her hold the gauze while I mopped her face, blotted her hair as best I could. She studied me closely as I worked, her gaze moving over me, feature by feature.

'You're the lady from the accident,' she said.

'Yes,' I said. 'I'm going to make you an ice pack, okay?'

'I don't remember it.'

'The accident?' I was digging around in the freezer. 'It happened very fast.'

'No,' she said. 'I mean, I don't remember *any* of it.'

There were only a few cubes of ice. I wrapped them in a

dishcloth printed with roses, settled it onto her head. My shoulder still tingled from the impact of the door; I rubbed it, thinking of Rex. 'There are parts I don't remember, either,' I said, ignoring Rex's voice in my ear: *don't discuss the accident, don't reveal anything*. What would he say, I wondered, if he knew where I was right now?

'But *she* doesn't remember anything for, like, two weeks.' Laurel had reappeared, holding the first cat, draped over her shoulders like a stole. 'And she wets the bed. What a nut case.'

'Shut up.'

'She's going to end up in a psycho ward, too.' She lowered her voice to a criminal's hiss. 'In a straitjacket. In a room with padded walls.'

If there really had been a gun in that apartment, I would have been a dead woman. 'Where's your aunt today?' I murmured to Monica.

'Helping Grandma move somewhere else.'

'To another nursing home,' Laurel said. 'Igor's helping, too.'

Monica's pale eyes flashed. 'His name is Toby,' she said. For a moment, I could actually see that they were sisters. Half-sisters.

'*Eee*-gore,' Laurel moaned, dropping the cat with a thud. It rocketed back to the girls' room, shot beneath the bunk beds. I glanced at the kitchen clock. 1.15. I doubted my parents would arrive before two.

'Have you girls had lunch?' I asked.

'We're not hungry.'

'*I'm* hungry,' Monica said.

In the refrigerator, I found only soy milk, carrot juice, a few slices of veggie cheese. 'It doesn't work,' Laurel said. 'Not like we need a *refrigerator* in here.'

Funny girl. There was brown rice in the cupboard, along with dried beans, lentils, a braid of garlic hanging on the wall.

'What if we order a pizza?' I said, but at that moment, there was a noise on the landing. Footsteps. The door swung open and Toby appeared, plastic bags of groceries dangling from each fist. When he saw me, his birthmark flushed dark, the way it did, blanching the other side of his face. 'What the hell?' he began, but then he saw Monica, her blood-stained sweatshirt, her matted hair. In a flash, she was crying hysterically, as hard – if not harder – than when she'd first fallen. He dropped the groceries, vaulted the tree, scooped her up into his arms.

'What happened?' he said, glancing between Laurel and me. 'What the hell did you do?'

The question could have been aimed at either one of us. A crafty look passed across Laurel's face, but before she could open her mouth to blame me, Monica was sobbing out the whole story: how she'd made a special decoration, how she'd tried to put it on the tree, how Laurel had pushed her and then the tree—

'The bleeding's stopped,' I told Toby, trying not to feel hurt that he'd suspect me, even fleetingly, of hurting this child. 'I don't think she's going to need stitches. And the cut's up in her hairline where it isn't going to show.'

'You know what happens when you get stitches?' Laurel said.

'Laurel,' Toby said, wearily.

'They take this huge needle and they stick it in you. *Jah!*'

'Can we still have pizza?' Monica asked, sniffling.

'We were about to order one,' I explained, picking up the groceries, setting them on the counter, 'but I can make something else, if you want. Burritos?'

I held up the box.

'Those suck,' Laurel said. 'They're vegetarian.'

'Pizza,' Monica said, nodding.

I waited for Toby to agree, but instead he sank onto the couch, still holding Monica in his arms. She tucked herself tightly against him; he rested his chin on the top of her head. It struck me, then. He loved this child. For all I knew, he loved them both.

'What are you doing here?' he asked.

'I came for the wedding,' I said.

'We invited you to join us aboard the *Jack*, not in our home.'

'Toby.'

'Considering the sort of litigation going on, *contrary* to what you told me in June—'

'I only told you what Rex told me. I thought I was telling the truth.'

'Funny, but your name's on the settlement, too.'

'Which I haven't signed.'

'So sign it. Get it over with. Anything's better than having it hanging over our heads like this.'

'I suppose you've seen the photographs,' I said.

He did not look away. 'If you want me to admit that you told me so, okay. You told me so. You and Rex both said that she was still——'

Then he glanced down at Monica, who was staring up at him; suddenly, I felt ashamed.

'I'm sorry,' I said. 'This isn't what I'm here for. I'm going to order that pizza, okay? Besides, Mom and Dad will be here any minute.'

'*What?*'

'We just want to help, that's all,' I said. 'We figured out why you were hiding from us.'

Toby closed his eyes, defeated. 'You don't know the half of it, believe me.'

'So fill me in.'

He made a slight, negative motion with his head.

'He can't talk in front of the *baby*,' Laurel said. 'And, besides, you're *not* here to help. You're here to spy on us. You might fool him, but you can't fool me.'

'Should I call Pizza Haven?' I asked Toby, ignoring her, as if she were a tantrum-ing two-year-old, kicking and screaming in the candy aisle.

'Out of business. There's Pizza Hut.'

'You're a spy,' Laurel shouted, 'and he's a pervert!'

'Pizza Hut it is,' I said, sliding the phone book out from underneath the phone. 'Can I order something with meat?'

Toby and Monica said, together, 'No meat.'

Laurel kicked the Christmas tree. 'Nobody ever listens to me! Maybe I should just run away!'

'Well, stick around for one more day, if you can stand it,' Toby said, calmly. 'Your mother's coming home.'

In her astonishment, Laurel looked, abruptly, like the child she was. Monica, on the other hand, was suspicious.

'When?' she asked.

'Tonight, actually.'

'Is she better?'

Toby bit his lip. 'We'll have to see.' He looked at me. 'She just called Mal from the hospital. We don't have all the details, but the long and the short of it is, the insurance denied the claim. The hospital's kicking her out. They won't even let her spend the night.'

'But it's Christmas Eve,' I said.

'And Mal's got her hands full, getting her mother settled – did I mention they think Lena might have had a minor stroke? – which means I've got to drive to Twin Lakes to pick up Cindy Ann myself. That's three hours round-trip, and the truck doesn't have any heat right now and the guy I hired to fill in at the store hasn't shown up for the past week. Oh, yeah, and Mal and I are getting married in forty-eight hours.'

'*And* the Christmas tree fell down,' Monica whispered, as if, once again, she might start to cry.

'Are you ever going to call for that pizza?' Laurel said.

I looked at her as if she were an alien. Then again, I was hungry, too. 'Sure,' I said. 'Why not?'

I called from the phone in the kitchen. When I returned to the living room, Toby was hauling the tree upright, and Laurel and Monica were settling down to watch a video. 'It'll be thirty minutes,' I said, steadying the upper branches while he adjusted the stand.

'I still can't believe you're here,' he said.

'I can't quite believe it myself. I only got the invitation last week.'

'You said on your message. Actually, I'm surprised that it found you at all.'

We looked at each other.

'I really didn't know about the suit,' I said. 'I've been sick about this, Toby, truly.'

He nodded toward the kitchen, and I followed him there, leaving the girls glued to the screen. I braced myself for his questions, his anger, but as soon as we were out of their sight, he merely knelt before the oven, lit the pilot, left the door open like a gaping mouth. The first faint breaths of warmth stirred the air; I put out my hands, rubbed them together. Even the oven racks, I noticed, had been cleaned.

'This is how we heat the place,' Toby said, leaning back against the counter. 'But we can't let the girls light the pilot unless one of us is here, and we just aren't prepared – we're simply not equipped—'

'It will be easier,' I said, 'once Cindy Ann is back again.'

But Toby shook his head. 'I can't believe they're sending her home,' he said. 'She was practically catatonic, Meg. Her therapist told us about this place, it's for women who have survived some kind of—' He glanced toward the living room. 'Trauma.'

I nodded. 'I know. Mom told me.'

'How does Mom know about any of this?'

'We're in Fox Harbor, remember?'

He smiled, but only with his mouth. 'The thing is,' he said, 'Cindy Ann liked it there. She thought it was helping. I thought it was helping. I actually had a conversation with her, and she apologized for calling me – well, the things she calls me whenever she's been drinking.'

'Things like what?' I said.

Once again, he closed his eyes. I realized, with a start, that he was fighting tears. In all the years I'd known him, I'd never seen him cry, aside from Evan's funeral. And then, again, six months later, when Rex and I told him good-bye.

'Toby,' I said. 'Jesus. How can I help?'

A full minute passed before he spoke. 'You could open the fish store for a few hours. Check the stock, do feedings. There's instructions on the fridge. If Mom and Dad are coming anyway, maybe they'd keep an eye on the girls so I don't have to drag them up to Twin Lakes. Especially since I don't know what Cindy Ann's state of mind's going to be when I get there.'

But I had a better idea. 'You go to the store,' I said. 'I'll stay with the girls until Mom and Dad come, and then—'

'Mom and Dad can't drive to Twin Lakes. It's a long way, Meg, and it's going to be late—'

'I know,' I said. 'What I'm saying is, I'll do it. I'll pick up Cindy Ann.'

Chapter Eleven

It was dark by the time I arrived at Twin Lakes. The town itself was little more than a crossroads, extended by a strip mall, a minimart, a farm dealership. A single sign pointed me toward the hospital, which stood at the edge of a windswept field, light pouring out of every window as if a small, steady fire burned within. Perhaps, in summer, it could have been called pretty, with its fieldstone facade, all those shining panes of glass. Willow trees lined the long, winding drive that led to the parking lot. But now, in winter, the black sky wiped of stars, it looked exactly like what it was: a place for people who'd exhausted every other possibility. As I followed the salted walk toward the lobby, I could see the stripped-down furnishings of each second-story room: twin beds, open shelves, a desk, a chair, a lamp.

No pictures on the walls. No television. No personal effects.

The doors leading into the lobby were locked. I rang the after-hours bell, grateful for the warmth and weight of my own boots. The cold seemed to be rising from the ground.

Inside the waiting area, women in green scrubs were setting up folding cots, spreading them with sheets, their movements like a slow, choreographed dance. None of them looked up. I rang the bell again. Vinyl chairs were stacked against the thick, glass windows, and in one of those chairs, pulled away from the others, a woman sat in street clothes, a small, flowered suitcase beside her, staring out at the darkness. I walked over so I was standing in front of her; still, she didn't blink, didn't move. We were so close I might have touched her. I knocked, tentatively, on the glass.

The woman started. It was Cindy Ann Kreisler. Her features were swollen, as if shaped out of dough. For a moment, it seemed that she still didn't see me, but then she stood up, leaned forward. We studied each other's faces through the reflections of our own until, at last, we heard the rattle of keys, and I turned to greet the nurse who was unlocking the front door.

'You're late,' she said, not looking at me. She was young, thin, her cheeks pocked with old acne scars. 'We close at six. Administration is waiting to see you.'

As soon as I'd stepped through the door, she locked it again, checked it twice.

The women setting up the beds had finally stopped what they were doing. They were, I realized, patients. One woman stepped toward me, smiling, but the young nurse put her body between us, motioning me forward.

'This way,' she said.

I glanced at Cindy Ann, but she'd settled back into the chair, resumed her contemplation of the darkness.

'Why are they sleeping in the lobby?' I said, following the nurse down a brightly lit hall. The walls seemed to reflect that brightness, as if they'd been coated with high-gloss paint. 'Don't you have enough beds?'

'Suicide watch,' she said, and she stopped walking, knocked on a door. 'Administration will assist you.'

'With what?' I said.

'Paperwork.'

She knocked again, then glanced at me, her gaze sweeping upward from the floor to my face. 'What happened to you?' she said.

I was getting awfully tired of that question. 'It's a rash. It's getting better.'

'No,' she said. 'Your coat.'

'My coat?' I repeated, staring down at myself. My mother, upon arriving at Toby's, had attempted to spot-clean Monica's blood from the cream-colored cashmere, but she'd merely succeeded in making it worse. Beneath the forgiving lamplight of Toby's living room, it hadn't seemed so bad; here, it looked as if I'd been involved in the sacrifice of a small animal. My mind leapt, unbidden, to Laurel, whose parting words to me had been, 'Don't get in an accident or anything.'

'Christmas punch,' I said.

The nurse narrowed her eyes, but then the door opened, and she turned away, hurrying into the blinding brilliance of the hall, as if she were afraid. Yet who or what was there to fear? Certainly not the plump, pretty woman who stood before me, smiling.

'Come in,' this woman said, pleasantly, and I stepped into the carpeted office, my eyes welcoming the potted plants, the gentle light, the framed landscapes. 'Have a seat.' She gestured to one of two leather chairs across from a wide, modern desk. As I sat, I heard a strange, gurgling noise, like an old-fashioned percolator boiling on a stove. 'I'm Joanna. I'm in charge of patient accounts.'

I glanced under the desk and saw a little white dog, slightly larger than a hand grenade, bristling on a nest of wooly blankets.

'That's Trixie. She won't hurt you,' Joanna said, laughing agreeably, but I tucked my feet under my chair. Now that I was sitting here, there was something about this office – indeed, something about Joanna herself – that put me on my guard. I thought of the nurse, how she'd scuttled away, a field mouse sensing the hawk.

'I was told that I needed to sign some paperwork,' I said.

Joanna turned to her desktop, tapped in a password. 'Let's just print up a hard copy, shall we?'

I was expecting some kind of release form. Instead, what Joanna handed me was a bill for nearly thirty thousand dollars.

I stared at it, shocked into silence, my gaze moving over the various charges: room, board, group therapy sessions, individual psychiatric consultations. Charges for toothpaste, hand cream, shampoo. Linen charges. Processing fees.

'I need you to sign here,' Joanna said, 'and initial here and here.'

'But this says that I agree to take responsibility for this bill.'

Joanna nodded calmly, reasonably. 'Our policy does not permit the discharge of a resident before appropriate financial arrangements have been made.'

'So make appropriate financial arrangements with Cindy Ann,' I said. 'I'm just here to pick her up.'

'Unfortunately,' Joanna said, smiling sympathetically, 'Ms Kreisler's state of mind does not allow us to discuss this with her in a rational manner.'

'If that's the case,' I said, 'perhaps you shouldn't be releasing her.'

Joanna's smile remained unchanged. 'She is being discharged at her own request.'

'That isn't my understanding.'

Joanna raised an eyebrow. 'People in these situations can be – less than reliable.'

I leaned forward in my chair. 'First, you kick her out without so much as twenty-four hours' notice. Now, you try to bully me into signing for a bill that isn't mine. Are you crazy?'

From underneath the desk came that low, percolating growl. Joanna looked at me mournfully. 'Here at Twin Lakes,' she said, 'we try to be sensitive about the way in which we use that particular word.'

I started to laugh, I couldn't help it. Trixie's growls erupted into a battery of short, shrill yaps.

'Now, Trixie.' Joanna directed that same sad expression toward her knees. 'Excuse me,' she murmured, and then she bent forward, lifted the trembling white fur ball into her lap. 'Animals,' she said, conversationally, 'are remarkably tuned to human emotion.'

'I'm not paying you thirty thousand dollars,' I said. 'I'm not signing anything. Now, if there's nothing else—'

Another paroxysm of barks, like a spasm. 'Trixie, baby, *hush*,' Joanna said, then to me: 'One moment, if you will.'

Already, I was at the door, my hand on the knob; it wouldn't turn. For the first time, I noticed the security panel beside it, the card swipe, the blinking infrared eye. Joanna had let me into this room. Could it be that she'd have to let me out, too? She waited, with a hunter's patience, letting me draw my own conclusions.

'Under the circumstances,' she said, 'we might consider alternative arrangements.'

'Meaning what?' I said, leaning back against the door.

'In special cases, the hospital will agree to accept a ten

percent deposit on the balance. That way, we can proceed with a legally compliant discharge.'

'But it isn't my debt.'

'We accept all major credit cards, plus American Express.'

I opened my mouth to tell her where she could stick those credit cards, one by one, but then I remembered the card swipe beside me. The locked door at the front of the lobby. The frightened young nurse. My father had given me his cell phone to carry – perhaps I should call my brother? An attorney? But what, practically speaking, could Toby do? And Arnie would advise me to book a room as soon as I'd explained what I was doing there. Joanna was smiling pleasantly, the same pleasant smile she'd worn as I'd come in, and I realized she would sit here all night without hunger, without thirst, without so much as a wince of irritability or embarrassment. This was, indeed, crazy, in every sense of that word, and as I tried to imagine what Rex would advise, suddenly I knew.

'My wallet is outside,' I said. This, in fact, was true. It was in my backpack, still on the floor of the car.

'Very well,' Joanna said, and, taking Trixie into her arms, she followed me out into the extraordinary yellow light of the corridor. As we approached the lobby, I could hear a series of muffled thuds, and I imagined some kind of therapeutic pillow fight, a soft exchange of blows. But, rounding the corner, I saw only the cots, each with its folded blanket, its obedient pillow, small and still. Women were sitting beside one another, lying on their backs, talking. A few were sitting apart from the others, writing in identical spiral-bound notebooks. When they saw us, the quiet conversation gave way to expectant silence. Again, the same woman rose, came forward, smiling, as if she would speak; again, the young nurse stepped between us, hurrying over from the nurse's station. Joanna was still smiling her own unrelenting smile, though I noticed, perhaps, the slightest hesitation when she saw Cindy Ann — who was no longer sitting, alone, in her chair, but standing in front of the lobby doors — swinging her suitcase, hard, against the glass.

Whump.

Again, she took aim.

Whump.

The other women watched expectantly. Without turning her head, Joanna called, 'Key?' but the nurse already had them in hand. Cindy Ann, without actually seeming to notice her, stepped aside so she could fumble it, nervously, into the lock.

'Ms Kreisler,' Joanna said, placing one manicured hand on the nurse's sleeve, 'will remain here, where it's warm and dry and comfortable, while her companion retrieves her purse.'

The nurse glanced at Cindy Ann skeptically. 'You hear that?' she said. 'You *wait* for your friend. Right here.'

At the word *friend*, Cindy Ann lifted her head. Our gazes met. Held. I remembered the night of my sixteenth birthday, the Styrofoam cup in my hand. I remembered watching, as if from far away, the madness taking place all around us. *This is fucked*, Cindy Ann had said. And so it was. I cut my eyes at the door, mouthed one word.

Run.

We didn't run. But the moment the door swung open, we ploughed through both Joanna and the nurse like a team of yoked oxen, intent on our purpose. With my shoulder, I steered Cindy Ann in the direction of my mother's car, the remote standing ready in my hand. Headlights flashed, doors unlocked. The engine purred to life. We tossed the suitcase into the back and peeled out of the parking lot without having heard so much as a cry from the shadows still standing in the entryway, dark arms waving like the arms of survivors emerging from an apocalyptic blaze.

'Put your seat belt on,' I said automatically, and as Cindy Ann turned to look at me, I realized what I had said. How ludicrous it was, the two of us, together, pulling onto the icy highway. Cindy Ann laughed, a rusty little sound; I started to laugh, too, then tried to disguise it as a cough. But now Cindy was laughing again, a deep belly laugh that went on and on until I realized that it wasn't laughter after all. She was crying. I was crying, too. At the Twin Lakes minimart, I turned off the road, and there was nothing I could do, nothing I could say. I forgot all about Cindy Ann. I forgot all about Joanna and Trixie, Toby and Mallory, my parents and the girls. I forgot about Rex and all he might have said if he'd ever, in his wildest imaginings, suspected that I might wind up here: alone in a car with this woman whom I simply couldn't hate any longer, with this grief that I still didn't know how to face. Time passed. The heater hummed. A few cars pulled up beside the minimart; a few others pulled away. Eventually, I realized that Cindy Ann was silent, that the pressure against my knuckle was a plastic-coated tissue pack.

'At the beginning of every group session,' she said, 'they'd distribute these from a basket. One pack per person. I never imagined they'd be *charging* us.'

The tissues felt as if they'd been made from recycled newspaper. 'Six dollars,' I said, recalling the outrageous figures. 'Fifty cents more than they charged you for toilet paper.'

'You saw the bill, then.'

'Joanna wanted me to pay it.'

'She's a psychopath, truly. Her and that dog. Everybody calls them Dr Trixie and Mr Hyde.'

I blew my nose, wiped my eyes. 'How the hell did you end up in a place like that?'

When Cindy Ann didn't answer, I backed out of the parking space, crawled through the mess of slush and ice. The signal clicked, flashed green, and then we were back onto the highway.

'It was like I couldn't move anymore,' Cindy Ann said. 'I

couldn't *think*. The counselor I've been seeing recommended this place. Dr Cantreau. The insurance was supposed to pay for six weeks.'

'So what happened?'

Cindy Ann shook her head. 'I don't know. I guess they just changed their minds.'

'You paid the premium on time?'

'Of course, I did. I did! Mal gave me the money to do it.' Suddenly, Cindy Ann's voice reminded me of Monica's, stretched thin and high with urgency. 'Oh, God, she probably thinks I spent it on, on – booze, or—'

'Nobody's saying that,' I said, quickly.

'But that's what she's thinking. Toby, too. Who can blame them? I keep screwing up. I just screw everything up. Look at this place. I mean, it was helping. Some of it was weird, sure, the part you saw, but the counselors were great, the people, you know? And then, this morning, the day nurse comes and says there's a problem, I have to speak to Joanna. Thirty thousand dollars! Everything I've touched, everything I've tasted – toothpaste, bottled water, those fucking scrubs we had to wear – there it all is, like a grocery bill. And I thought these people *cared* about me.'

Silently, I returned the package of tissues.

'It should have been me that got killed in that accident. It's true. All of us know it. And it would have been such a *mercy*.'

For no reason, for every reason, I started to cry again. 'I

have to stop doing this,' I said. 'Whoever said that crying makes you feel better was—'

'—so absolutely full of shit. I know.'

We were approaching the interstate. I slowed, waiting it out, like an unexpected squall. It could have been a few minutes. It could have been an hour.

'What are you doing here?' Cindy Ann finally said, only now her voice sounded flat, far away. 'I signed the settlement, in case you didn't hear. There isn't much left, but you'll get something, at least.'

Glancing at her, I recognized the look I'd seen on her face at the grocery store. I'd mistaken it, then, for indifference. Now, I saw it for what it was. There would be no making this right, and she knew it. She was waiting, without resistance, for whatever it was I might say. I could hurt her, now, perhaps even kill her, with a single, well-chosen word.

I followed the ramp onto the interstate, my burning eyes fixed on the broken, white lines, until I was ready, after so many months, after so many years, to answer her question. 'I wanted to tell you I'm sorry for what I said. When you told me about Dan Kolb.'

Her hands worked against each other, hard, in the core of her lap.

'I was upset,' I said. 'I wasn't thinking straight. I always wanted to tell you that.'

After a while, she said, 'I always wondered.'

Then she said: 'Oh, Meggie.' And we drove for what seemed like hundreds of miles, the darkness like a thick bandage over a wound.

'I am,' she said, 'so sorry. So unspeakably sorry. Too.'

At the mill, Toby's truck and Mallory's Nova were nosed into the hay bales along the south wall. I crowded the Mercedes beside them, trying to get as much protection as I could. According to the dashboard thermostat, it was three below zero – ten degrees colder than it had been when I'd first set out for Twin Lakes – and as I got out of the car, I imagined Rex, perched on *Chelone*'s bow in his shirtsleeves. Looking up at the same night sky. Listening to the tinkle of Christmas carols floating across the Cove. Every year, the marina held a Christmas dance, ending with a Candlelight Promenade: drunken couples stumbling toward the beach, howling carols at the moon. Eli had regaled us with the stories. From the beach, the party would migrate over to Island Girls. More dancing. More drinking. An annual adult talent show that Ladyslip regulars spoke about in whispers and guffaws.

How strange, how foreign, it all seemed to me now, as I helped Cindy Ann across the icy parking lot. The medications she'd been taking made her dizzy, she said, especially after she'd been sitting for a while. Her face and hands were swollen, bloated. Her hair was falling out. She walked with the stiffness of a very old woman, staring at the ground. Surely, I thought, as we started up the steps, if Rex could be here, if he could actually see—

My father's cell phone started to ring. It startled us both; the jolt rippled between us. I suppose we were imagining Joanna, swooping out of the darkness on her broom. 'It's just my mother checking up on us,' I said, searching for the sound inside the deep pocket of her coat. At last, I found it, flipped it open, pressed its icy cheek against my ear.

'You've caught us on the landing,' I said, breathless from the cold. 'Come out and let us in.'

'You're where?' Rex said, his voice as clear, as warm, as if he'd materialized beside me. I stopped where I stood – Cindy Ann stopped, too – and my cold cheeks flushed with heat. I felt as if I'd been caught doing something shameful. Sexual.

'Where are you?' I said, turning away from Cindy Ann.

'Nantucket,' he said, then laughed.

'*What?*'

'Okay, a Beneteau fifty-seven called *Nantucket*. Hey, listen, you want the good news or the bad news?'

My heart seized. 'Bad news.'

'Of course you do.' He laughed again. '*Chelone* needs a new compressor for the refrigerator.'

'Oh,' I said.

'Now for the good news. *Nantucket* has a used one we think is going to work. I'm talking on her world phone – it's this cell phone you can use almost anywhere. Isn't it amazing? We need to look into getting one of these!'

The door to Toby's apartment opened. Mallory stepped out.

'Are the girls still up?' Cindy Ann called. She climbed the last few steps alone; Mallory embraced her.

'Toby's parents took them out to see *A Christmas Carol*. They had these tickets—'

I'd forgotten about the tickets. Rex was still talking. 'Just a minute,' I said, because now Toby was on the landing, too.

'I'll be right in,' I said, raising my voice to be heard above the wind, and then I turned, walked back down the stairs into the cold. A little alcove stood just beneath the stairs; I ducked into it, pressed against the cinder block walls.

'What's going on?' Rex said. 'Who's there?'

'My family.'

'What are they doing up so late? Waiting for the animals to speak?'

'Something like that,' I said. For years, Evan had believed – as I had, as my parents had, as my German grandparents had, long ago – that on Christmas Eve, at midnight, all animals everywhere could speak with human tongues. It seemed wrong of Rex to joke about it now. Quickly, to change the subject, I said, 'So how's *Chelone*? Aside from the compressor, I mean.'

As Rex told me about the test sail he'd taken, the stress

fractures he'd discovered in the whisker poles – *whisker poles?* – I could hear music, voices, laughter. I could also hear, in Rex's watery tones, the faintest lisp, which meant he'd been drinking.

'You've really been working on the boat?' I said, interrupting him, and he said, 'Of course I've been working on the boat, haven't you been listening?'

But my chilblained ear was absorbing the lyrics to '*No Woman No Cry*,' courtesy of the world phone's excellent reception.

'Sounds like quite a party.'

'For Pete's sake, Meg. It's Christmas Eve. I came aboard to look at the compressor, and Jack invited me to stay.'

'I'm sorry,' I said. 'It's just – everything *will* be ready to make passage, won't it? As soon as I get there?'

'As soon as we get the new whisker poles installed. I just ordered a set through a rigger in Miami. You'll have to pick them up, okay?'

'A real blue water passage,' I said. 'Away from everything.'

'*Nantucket* spent some time in Tobago a few years back—'

'Tobago,' I said. 'That's perfect.'

'—Jack and Nancy. I think you'd really like them. And they're giving us a great deal on this compressor, if I can figure out how to get the damn thing through the forward hatch. Solves a problem for them as well.'

Wind beat around the corner of the mill, roared into the alcove, doubled back. The gust tore Rex's words from my ear, scattering them like grain.

'What?'

'I said, Have you talked to Arnie yet?'

'No,' I said. 'But I saw the photographs.'

'And?'

'They're very upsetting,' I said. 'In every possible way.'

For a minute, neither of us said anything.

'Hello?' Rex said.

'Do you love me?' I said.

His laugh was abrupt, broken by static. Even the world phone's connection, it seemed, was doomed to the uncertainties of distance. 'Meg.'

'I need to be certain. I need to know what I'm coming back to.'

'You're coming back to me,' Rex said, and now the sounds of the party seemed to fade. 'To us.'

I waited, not breathing, willing the connection between us to hold.

'I love you. More than ever.' There was no pause, no slur. 'I don't know how I'd live with myself if I thought you didn't believe that.'

'So if I don't sign the paperwork—' I began.

'—how brave you are, going to the wedding, looking Cindy Ann and her sisters in the face. I've been wanting to—'

He hadn't heard. Now there was a humming, like the drone of a distant plane.

'Rex, I have to tell you this. I've made up my mind not to sign.'

'—things haven't been right between us. I know I haven't . . . all that I should—'

'I missed that, honey,' I said.

'What?'

'This is so very difficult,' I said.

I would wait to tell him, I decided, until I'd returned to *Chelone*. Perhaps until we were back on blue water, en route to a place like Tobago, the chart kits unfurled in our laps. Slow waves rising and falling all around us. Nothing but time to work things through. Again, I lost the sound of his voice, and it was as if he'd been swept away from me by an unforeseen gust of wind. I remembered that first squall, when he'd been knocked from the cabin top. I remembered the lightning strike, the smell of ozone like an ache behind my eyes. Now, clinging to the phone, I repeated, '*Are you there? Are you there?*' An incantation. A prayer. And then, suddenly, I could hear him again.

'—*Rubicon*,' he was saying. 'At least, that's what she told Audrey . . . could . . . back to North Carolina after all, but—'

He was talking about Bernadette. 'Did you say they made Miami?'

'—haven't heard, so I guess—'

Static like the sound of rising water.

'I'm losing you,' I said. 'Can you try calling back?'

'—home?'

I took a guess. 'After New Year's. After I pick up the whisker poles. Do you have a street address?'

The phone chirped sweetly. The call had ended. I waited for another minute or two, in case it might ring again. Then another blast of wind sent me scurrying up the stairs and into the relative warmth of Toby's apartment.

Mallory had made a late supper for us all – lentils and rice, homemade naan, a creamy yogurt sauce to go with it – and we crowded around the small kitchen table, breathing in the smell of jasmine, curry, the pungent sandalwood incense Mallory set to burn on the counter. 'Purifying,' she explained. And, indeed, as we ate, it seemed as if something unpleasant were being siphoned from the air, making it easier to breathe, to speak.

Pass the bread, please.

Pass the salt.

The girls, it turned out, would be spending the night at the Pfister; my mother had already tucked them into my canopied bed, wrinkled and red from sitting too long in the deep Jacuzzi bath. I could sleep on the couch, Toby assured me, or in one of the girls' beds. Or – if I preferred – I could have Mal's place, where they now lived, across the hall.

'It doesn't matter,' I said. I was utterly exhausted. Numb. Grateful to know I wouldn't have to drive all the way back to Milwaukee.

This is delicious.

Thanks. Want more?

I can't believe how great this place looks.

One by one, the cats appeared, butting their heads against our ankles, blinking their strange, gold eyes. Abruptly, Mallory said to me, 'Thanks for your help today,' and Cindy Ann said – I could see how hard she was trying – 'I'd still be sitting in the lobby. Me, Nurse Ratched and her little dog, Toto.'

'What was it like there?' Toby said.

We looked at each other, Cindy Ann and I.

'It was nuts,' I said. 'It was like *The Twilight Zone*.'

Mallory flushed, started to object, but Cindy Ann stopped her.

'It's true,' she said. 'But there were good parts, too. Being with the other people, women just like me. Who have experienced things—' Her face colored as she spoke, but then she continued. 'I mean, like what Dan did to me.'

I glanced at Mal's face; of course, she knew. Perhaps Toby had told her. Perhaps she'd always known.

Cindy Ann pushed a limp strand of hair from her face. 'Most were alcoholics. Or drug addicts. Some were cutting themselves, starving themselves. It's the first time I haven't felt like a freak.'

'Nobody thinks you're a freak,' Mallory said.

'My girls do,' Cindy Ann said. She was directing her words to the arrangement of dried milkweed pods at the center of the table. 'They knew I was coming home tonight, right?'

'Of course,' Mallory said.

'That's why they stayed at the hotel.'

'You shouldn't take it that way,' Mallory said, and Toby said, 'It's just that they were exhausted. And we thought it would give you a chance to get settled in, you know, get some rest.'

Cindy Ann pushed the lentils around on her plate. 'I want to see them,' she said. 'I want a chance to explain. Things are going to be different now. I want everyone to know that.'

'You can tell them tomorrow,' Mallory said.

'Is Amy coming, too?'

'For Christmas dinner.'

'And Mum?'

'Actually,' Mallory said, getting up, 'Mum's not doing so great.'

She excused herself, then disappeared into the kitchen, averting her shining eyes. Toby pressed his thumb to a stray grain of rice. I felt that I should do something, say something, but I didn't know what. On the kitchen counter, the last smoky wisp of sandalwood rose like a pale offering, and as I watched, it seemed that my life began to split, like the blossoming of a flower, until it contained not only the present moment, but others, each growing out of the next, an arrangement of separate petals connected by a single, golden core. I was sitting on a trawler on Hunter's Cay, nursing a deliberate shot of Scotch. I was driving down a highway, Cindy Ann by my side. I was dressed in green scrubs, smiling, lying down for the night in a brightly lit room. Each of those moments, each of those lives, existed simultaneously. I didn't know which to believe in. I didn't know where I actually stood.

Abruptly, the kitchen clock chimed. A cat launched itself into Cindy Ann's lap. Deep, rolling purrs flooded the room with such force that even Mallory smiled, reappearing with dishes of green tea ice cream.

'What a sound,' she said.

'Because of midnight,' I said, and Toby said, 'You're right. I almost forgot.'

'Forgot what?' Cindy Ann said.

'Listen,' I said, and another petal opened to the light. Rousing Evan from his bed that last Christmas – the same way that, once, my mother had roused me. Breathing in his sleep-smell. Feeling the weight of his still-limp body, the damp flush of his skin. Helping him into his snowsuit and boots as, downstairs, Rex waited with the flashlight, the thermos. The three of us hurrying down the road toward the Haldigers' chicken coop, where Evie kept some guinea fowl, a nanny goat, and an ancient piebald pony.

'Is it time?' Evan kept saying. He was awake now, eager, pulling at our hands.

Only the pure of heart could hear the animals speak on Christmas Eve. This was why little children could hear them, while grown-up people could not. *What are they saying?* my mother would ask as I breathed the warm air of the Schultzes' cow barn: manure and silage, sweet grain and dust. Otto Schultz always came out to meet us, give the cows a little extra feed — *something to talk about*, he'd say. As he moved among the stanchions, I waited for the sounds of all those moving jaws to congeal. Straining to make language out of what I heard. Worrying I wasn't good enough, pure. Because the truth was that I never heard anything. Year after year, as my parents and Toby listened, too serious, I would make something up.

Cup, I'd said. *Christmas. Hop along. Velvet.*

'They're saying that they want more bread,' Evan told us. 'The guinea hens. And they want to keep their babies this time.'

'Babies?' Rex said.

'The goat,' Evan continued somberly, 'would like a radio.'

'And what about Poppy?' I asked. Poppy was the pony, gluey-eyed, stiff.

'Poppy's going to heaven soon,' Evan said. 'He says he has everything he wants.'

Had Evan really said this? Was it possible Rex and I had

laughed? Now, sitting at Mallory's table, the taste of the ice cream soured on my tongue. I got up, circled past the Christmas tree, went into the girls' room – but, no. This was worse. Maybe I should drive back to Milwaukee after all, find another room at another hotel. Or maybe I should try and get to the airport, book a morning flight to Miami, spend the night stretched across a row of plastic chairs. One thing was suddenly clear to me: I couldn't stay. Not here. I stepped back and bumped into Toby. Somehow, I thought it might be Rex. I wanted it to be Rex.

'What—?' Toby began, and I blurted out, 'I never heard them, you know. The animals. I just pretended to.'

'Everyone pretends,' Toby said.

'I think that Evan really heard them. I'm pretty sure he did.'

'I wouldn't be surprised.'

'But I'll never get to ask him, later. When he's older.'

'You're tired,' Toby said.

'I mean, think of all the things I'll never know. Big things. Important things. Why should this one even matter?'

'Why don't you try to sleep?' Toby said. 'I'll sit with you, if you like.'

'Because I'm *not* tired,' I said, but then my face split into an enormous yawn. For some reason, this made me laugh, and I was laughing still as Toby eased me onto the bed, pulled off my boots, pinched each big toe lightly the way he'd done when I was small. To my relief, the pillow beneath my head didn't smell like anything in particular. Fabric softener. Perhaps the slightest trace of shampoo. Evan's pillow, his sheets, his room in the morning, had always smelled like tapioca. It wasn't just me who thought so; Rex often commented on it, too. You could wash all his bedding, dump him in the tub, and the next morning: sweet tapioca.

'Don't tell me this is Laurel's bed,' I said.

'It's Monica's. It's okay.'

'Laurel said she had a gun in here.'

'Do you think Mal would let any one of us keep a gun?' Toby covered me with the blankets, a quilt, and then he spread a sleeping bag from the closet over the top. 'Sorry it's so cold,' he said.

'I'm sorry for the girls,' I said.

'They usually sleep together,' Toby said. 'They're actually good friends when there's no one around to see.' He sat down on the edge of the bed. 'They've been through a lot. The rest of us, too. You wouldn't believe what Cindy Ann can be like. When she's drinking, I mean.'

'She says things are going to be different.'

Toby made a face. 'Do you know how many times we've heard her say the same thing?'

'Maybe this time it will be true.'

'Maybe,' he said, and then he sighed. 'I keep remembering what she was like, that summer you two were friends.

Whenever she's really angry, abusive, that's the person I try to keep inside my head. The way she was with her brother. The way she looked after her sisters. Working so hard all the time, like she did.'

'I know.'

'I think I was in love with her, a little.'

'Me, too.'

He pulled the covers up to my chin.

I said, 'Why did all this have to happen?'

'I don't know.'

'What is the point of it?'

'Try to sleep.'

Something struck the bed, then, as if a piece of the ceiling had fallen. I started. 'What was that?'

'Just a cat,' Toby said, and there it was, kneading the mattress beside me. I touched its fur, lightly, and it put its beautiful face close to mine. Blinked, clear-eyed as any god. And, like any god, it did not speak.

Chapter Twelve

The day of the wedding dawned bright and clear, but just before noon, great clouds rolled in, and by the time we stepped aboard the *Michigan Jack* – my parents, Cindy Ann with all three of her girls, Becca with her own boy – it was hard to keep our teeth from chattering. My parents stared balefully up at the sky, hands jammed into their pockets, scarves doubled twice around their necks. 'This goddamn weather,' my father muttered, and my mother said, 'How people *live* this way.' Still, the *Jack* looked beautiful, her sleek lines sparkling with white lights and garlands. And then there was the harbor itself: winter-proofed boats and weathered pilings, curious gulls like whitecapped spectators. Toby's bare hands shook as he worked the surprisingly delicate ring onto Mallory's finger, from nervousness or cold, I could not say.

Afterward, I kissed him, congratulated Mallory, exchanged a few, quiet words with Cindy Ann. 'I thought it was going to be awful out here,' she said, her breath escaping in round, white puffs. 'But, really, it was pretty.'

'If you don't mind the frostbite,' Laurel said.

My parents, who were listening, started to laugh. Laurel looked startled, but pleased. Amy, wrapped in her mother's old beauty, turned away from us all. 'I'm *hungry*,' she said, and Mallory said, 'I bet everybody's hungry, right?' She had her arm around Becca's Harvey; Monica clung to her hips.

Mallory Hauskindler. To everyone's astonishment, she'd taken Toby's name. Her dark head was covered by a blue stocking cap, and when Toby tugged, lightly, on the pom-pom at the end, she smiled up at him, radiant, expecting his proud kiss. How I wanted to feel again, for Rex, what I knew she must be feeling. How willing I was, at that moment, to do whatever it would take. As much as we'd lost, Rex and I, what we had still amounted to more. I would learn to love our life aboard *Chelone*, to call that life my home. Rex would learn to accept my decision to give my brother this blessing.

I'd already excused myself from the wedding lunch, and while the others turned left off the dock, cutting through the marina parking lot, I followed the wooden boardwalk that ran along the edge of the harbor. At the end stood the Shanty restaurant; inside, I spotted Lindsey before she noticed me. She was at the same table where the two of us had sat the last time we'd met. I watched her eating popcorn from the complimentary bowl, gazing out the window at the scruffy-looking mallards picking their way across the yellowed ice. In that gray, puffy jacket and piano keyboard scarf, she looked exactly as she might have looked two years earlier, five years, ten. How grateful I was, how comforted, that Lindsey, at least, hadn't changed! Twenty years from now, she'd be sitting here still, laughing over Bart's latest golfing escapade, tunneling through the pockets of her purse, looking for her wallet, a pencil, her keys.

She saw me, then. Stood up. Surprised me by taking me into her arms, holding me tighter, tight.

'Hey,' I said, smelling that scarf, a season's worth of residual shampoo, moisturizing lotions, perfume. Suddenly, sharply, I thought of Bernadette, the smell of her sunblock, her warm, freckled skin. Certainly *Rubicon* would have made Miami by now. Perhaps Leon was already scheduled for tests, sitting in a room somewhere, waiting to be seen. Or perhaps he'd already been admitted. Perhaps they'd found something fixable, concrete: an infection, a chemical imbalance, a small, harmless blip of the brain.

'I wanted you to hear it from me,' Lindsey was saying, and I thought that, perhaps, I'd misheard her, though her lips had been pressed to my ear.

'What?'

'Barton and I have separated.'

She'd already seated herself without looking at me, spreading a thin, paper napkin over her knees. Shame kept me silent; I'd never even considered the possibility that something in Lindsey's life might go wrong. A waitress arrived to fill our coffee cups. She was young, heavyset, unsuspectingly pretty. 'How are you ladies today?' she asked, as if she really meant it.

'He's in love with someone else,' Lindsey said, after the girl had gone. 'Apparently it's been going on for years. Everybody knew.'

I opened a laminated menu. 'I didn't.'

'I'd walk right out of here if I thought you did.'

I met her gaze. 'I wouldn't blame you.'

The waitress was standing over us again.

'Fish fry,' I said. 'With coleslaw.'

'The same,' Lindsey said, and then, to me: 'Sorry.' In a swift, nervous gesture, she plucked my menu out of my hand, tucked it back into place behind the condiment stand. 'We're putting the house on the market. We're selling everything, dividing what we get. No lawyers. We're trying to keep things civilized. Because it was, you know, a mostly good marriage. I know that sounds strange, considering—'

'It doesn't sound strange,' I said. 'Lindsey. It's me. You don't have to explain.'

She had opened another napkin, smoothed over the first. 'I'm moving to Arizona. Tucson. My sister loves it out there. Fred Pringle's going to be taking over your account until you can make other arrangements.'

'God, Fred. I haven't thought of him in ages.'

'He's an ass, I know. I'm leaving you in the lurch.'

'No, you're not,' I said, but Lindsey was rooting around in that bottomless purse, lifting flaps, unzipping pockets.

'Speaking of asses,' she said, removing a fat, manila file. 'I suppose you've already spoken with Chester?'

'He wants to break the lease,' I said.

'He's broken it.' Lindsey handed me a letter. 'He'll be gone, as of New Year's Day. You'll need to find someone to watch the place, especially during this kind of weather. It could be awhile before you find another tenant.'

'My brother can do it,' I began, then stopped. Toby didn't have time to look after his own life, much less mine. 'Look, I'll figure something out. I'm sorry, Linds; I'm still in shock. What will you do in Tucson?'

She shrugged. 'Work. Maybe put out my own shingle.'

'Or retire?'

Her laugh was short and swift as a slap. 'With what? I've got to think about the future.'

'You've got savings,' I said. 'Equity. It's not like you'll be starting from scratch.'

'I've got to find a place to live. Buy furniture. A car. Pots and pans, all the rest of that crap. And what if, tomorrow, there's a lump in my breast? What if I break my back?'

'You have your sister. And friends. And—'

'It isn't the same. Think about it, Meg. Think about how it would be if you couldn't depend on Rex.'

For a moment, I was silent. 'I know,' I said.

The food came, along with fresh coffee. We moved things around on our plates.

'I think you should talk to a lawyer,' I said. 'Not to make things adversarial. But why should you have to worry about money when Bart's the one who—'

'I told you, no lawyers,' she said, interrupting. 'I remember how those lawsuits changed you. That's not going to happen to me.'

'What changed me,' I said, deliberately, 'was losing a child.'

She bit into a piece of fish. 'Losing a child,' she said, 'wasn't what you talked about. It was litigation. Getting even. *Justice*. And, believe me, I understand because I'm so upset right now, I'm so angry—' She paused, swallowed, took a deep, visible breath. 'I know that if I sat down with an attorney, I'd walk away hell-bent on punishing Barton for every wrong thing he's done since the moment he was born.'

'You have to admit,' I said, 'that this particular wrong thing is a bad one.'

'It is.' Her voice was small, and I felt ashamed. She dropped her face into her hands. 'What if I can't forgive him for this? Thirty-two years. All that history between us. What if I end up hating him? And I do hate him, sometimes. I really, truly do.'

The waitress appeared again. 'Everything okay?' she asked, then froze, her mouth a plump, pink O, when Lindsey lifted her tear-streaked face.

After we'd paid, we walked down to the beach, following the path behind the water treatment plant, the same path that Cindy Ann and I had taken so many years ago. By now, the clouds had passed out over the water. The lake was vibrant with ice and sun. Lindsey unwound her piano scarf, let it hang over her shoulders like a priest's fat stole.

'I've always hated this thing,' she said.

'Why wear it then?'

She shrugged. 'There's nothing wrong with it. It's a perfectly good scarf.'

I peeled it away from her, balled it up, chucked it out onto the ice. 'You're starting over with everything else. You might as well buy a scarf.'

The scarf skittered for a yard or two, then snagged on a rough spot, unfurled like a monochromatic flag. 'Barton gave me that scarf.'

'Screw him,' I said. 'Look, I admire you for not wanting to be mad at him, but *I* can be mad, all right?'

Lindsey sighed. She said, 'You know, I don't even play the piano. What the hell was he thinking?'

We had come to the end of the beach. At the edge of the bluff, the water had frozen into abstract sculptures, some of them nearly as high as the junipers wedged between ridges of granite, pink quartz. I remembered the green smell of those junipers, their dusty blue berries, hard as pearls. How Cindy Ann pointed them out to me as we'd scaled our way down from the upper bluff park, following trails cut by erosion, until we arrived at the moon-washed beach. Sitting on our slab of sandstone, humming with residual warmth from the sun. Cindy Ann talking about becoming a botanist, a plant geneticist – we'd just finished studying Mendel, his blue-eyed alleles, his wrinkly peas – and I'd envied her, then, because there were so many things she wanted to do, while I myself, imagining the future, saw nothing but white space, a terrible blank page. So I lay down on my back, not speaking, just looking up at the sky. Cindy Ann stretched out beside me. Her shoulder just touched mine. She said, 'Have you ever walked on the moon?'

Now I asked Lindsey, 'Did I really change so much?'

'I shouldn't have said that.'

'It's okay.'

'No, it isn't.'

'I'd like to know what you think.'

She kicked at a beach pebble trapped beneath a cracked, shining circle of ice. 'I think you made the right decision, buying that boat,' she said. 'Leaving town.'

'You're avoiding the question.'

'Yes and no. I guess, at the time, I really didn't understand. I thought you should see a therapist, remember?'

'I got mad at you for saying so.'

'It was bad advice. I saw a therapist myself, right after Barton left me.'

'What did he say?'

'She.'

'Sorry.'

'She told me to get an attorney.'

I laughed, and so did Lindsey. It was the first time I felt like I knew her again, and perhaps she felt the same way about me. On the way back to the car, she suddenly took my hand, swung it as if we were sweethearts. 'How was the wedding, by the way? I meant to ask.'

'Sincere.'

'At least Cindy Ann wasn't there. I hear she's in some kind of mental hospital.'

'Actually, she was released.'

'She didn't come to the wedding, though.'

'No, she was there.'

Lindsey stopped walking. 'You're taking this awfully well.'

'It's – an acquired state of mind.'

'That's the one thing I can't imagine,' she said. 'Finding myself face-to-face with Stanley. Or, worse, running into the two of them somewhere. Not that I'm equating—'

'Stanley?' I said. 'Who's Stanley?'

'Bart's golf partner.' She looked at me. 'Didn't I tell you that part?'

I shook my head.

'He said he tried for years. To bury that part of himself. He says he still loves me in the best way he can.'

We were walking again, approaching the parking lot. I'd just been thinking I would make it through the day without crying; I reminded myself it wasn't the first time I'd been wrong. Helplessly, hopelessly, I swiped at the cold tears stiffening my cheeks, but Lindsey didn't notice. She'd dropped my hand to dig in her purse, rattling handfuls of change.

'I suppose,' she said as we stepped up onto the asphalt, 'I should do the right thing and tell them about your house. They're looking for something together.'

'It's okay,' I said. 'Besides, I've got someone else in mind.'

'*Ha.*' She'd found her keys. It was a small triumph, but enough to make both of us smile. 'I like to think of you out on that sailboat,' she said.

'I like to think of you in the desert.'

She nodded, dreamily. 'Dry heat. All that sky.'

'With a big canteen.'

'With a life jacket.'

We laughed, but this time, it was more to please each other than ourselves. As she drove away, I realized that I hadn't asked for her sister's address, for an e-mail address outside of Lakeview, for any contact information whatsoever. But there'd be no point, really, in trying to keep in touch. A year from now, she'd be living in the desert; Rex and I might be anywhere in the world. He'd been right about selling the house, I decided as I got into my mother's car. It was simply too difficult, finding a steady tenant, managing things long-distance. And this would be another concession I could offer when he learned that I hadn't signed the settlement, that I'd actually taken steps toward a relationship – for what else could I call it? – with Cindy Ann Kreisler.

Don't worry, I told Evan. *Everything's going to work out.* Since arriving in Wisconsin, I'd been catching myself talking to him, explaining things, listening for his answers. Whenever this happened, I felt quieted, as if a dull, steady hunger had been appeased. And yet I understood myself. It wasn't as if I truly believed that he was there.

That night, back at the Pfister, I phoned Cindy Ann at the mill. She didn't seem surprised to hear from me. In fact, she sounded happy I'd called. Amy had taken the girls to a movie. Toby and Mal were off for their honeymoon night in Eau Claire. Cindy Ann herself had just gotten in from a meeting.

'Me and the other town drunks,' she said.

'How do you feel?'

'Right now, okay. That's as far ahead as I'm allowed to think.'

'One day at a time.'

'More like ten minutes. God, it's freezing in here.' I heard water running in the sink, then the splash of liquid in a glass. 'That's the one advantage about this place. You don't need to wait for the water to get cold.'

'What if I said I'd found a better place for you all to stay?'

At that moment, it seemed easy, even effortless. My backpack stood, packed and waiting, by the door. In the morning, my mother and I would drive back to Miami. Rex had sent an e-mail with the address of the rigger; as soon as I picked up the whisker poles, I'd return to the Bahamas, weigh anchor, set sail.

'It would make a lot of sense, if you think about it,' I said. 'I'd get someone to look after our house. You'd get heat and hot water. But you'd have to do some serious cleaning. The tenant hasn't taken good care of the place.'

'I just worry,' Cindy Ann said, 'that he wouldn't want us living there.'

I thought, at first, that she meant Chester. Then Rex. Then I understood.

'Evan wasn't like that,' I said.

'Have you seen him?' she asked. 'Since the accident, I mean? Like, in a dream, or—'

I felt myself tense. 'No.'

'I haven't either.'

'Why would you?' I said, trying to keep the irritation from my voice.

'Because I was the one who did this to him,' she said. 'I'm the one took his life.'

I was suddenly, wildly angry. *You took all of our lives*, I wanted to say. I had to hold the words in, literally, my own hand pressed against my mouth.

'I guess you're right,' I finally said. 'It would be too hard on everyone.'

'I'll find you somebody else,' she said, quickly. 'I'll ask around at tomorrow's meeting. You've done so much for me, for us—'

'I've done nothing,' I said, and when I hung up the phone, I felt happy to think we'd spoken for the last time. But, in fact, I called her three times more before leaving Florida: from the lanai at the back of my parents' town house; after picking up the whisker poles at the rigger's; after spending the day at Miami Children's, talking with receptionists, chattering groups of technicians, anyone who might recall a brain-injured boy, in a handmade wheelchair, who'd been living aboard a sailboat. Scanning directory after directory, I couldn't find a single pediatric neurologist – or pediatric anything – whose name remotely matched the one that Audrey had remembered. The Coast Guard had no record of *Rubicon* clearing back into the States.

Over the next few months, the letters I'd send to the New Bern PO Box would be returned to my parents' address, each of them red-stamped.

Chapter Thirteen

The whisker poles were not long and straight, as I'd
imagined. They were two heavy coils of stainless steel,
roughly the size of Hula Hoops. For three solid days of travel,
throughout one random delay after the next, I'd worn them
around my neck like a yoke: slogging between airports,
waiting for ferries, checking in at damp-sheeted hotels. By
the time I boarded the ferry to Hunter's Cove, it felt as if a
permanent groove had been worn into the tops of my
shoulders. No matter. Approaching the dock, I saw *Chelone,*
anchored across the bay. Even at a distance, her rub rails and
hatch covers shone like polished gold. Stretched across the
cabin top – where in the world had he found it? – Rex had
hung a glittery banner that spelled out the words WELCOME
HOME.

The moment he caught sight of me, waving from the
stern, he was over the safety lines and into the dingy, jerking
at the starter cord: once, twice. And even before I'd wrestled
the poles to the edge of the pier, he was buzzing across the

quiet harbor, rocking the other boats with his wake. 'I've had that banner up for the last two weeks,' he called, cutting the engine, gliding up against the pier. 'People around here are calling you my imaginary wife.'

When he tossed me the line, I missed it. Handing the poles down into the dingy, I nearly toppled us both. 'Got to get your sea legs back, I see,' he said, helping me onto the bench seat. 'You're so pale!'

'You're so tan!'

'And your poisonwood's gone!'

'At least where it shows.'

'Let's see.' He was tugging, tickling at my T-shirt.

'Come here,' I said, and kissed him.

He was clean-shaven, clear-eyed, fit. His hair, close-cropped, felt like velvet beneath my hand. The taste of him, the smell of his skin – familiar, yet unexpected – made me immune to the whistles and cheers from the half-dozen men standing around the dockside bar. They wore identical yellow T-shirts, dark blue shorts, and baseball caps. I glanced back at them as we pulled away. 'A baseball team?' I asked.

Rex laughed. 'The Men's Historical, Cultural and Sociological Expedition Society.'

'Are they from some university?'

'Nope. They just meet here to party once a year. They offered me and Jack an honorary membership, but Nancy wouldn't let us join. Said she would speak on your behalf until you could defend your own territory.' He grinned, then nodded at the streamlined Beneteau anchored fifty yards from *Chelone*. 'There's *Nantucket*.' On the forward deck, a handsome, swimsuited couple were hard at work on the stainless steel. 'We've been talking about buddy-boating to Tobago – I mean, if we all agree. It would be good to have some company, in case anything goes wrong. And then, when we get there, they could show us around.'

It wasn't what I'd imagined – traveling within sight and sound of another boat – but it was certainly safer, more practical. And blue water was blue water. One little speck on the horizon wouldn't make us feel any less independent of land. 'When's the next weather window?'

'The rest of this week doesn't look good, but we've got to install these poles anyway. And I was thinking it wouldn't hurt to have *Chelone* checked out by a professional rigger. By the time we get that done, we should be due for a good high pressure system.'

We'd reached *Chelone*, and as Rex tied up the dingy, I marveled at all the work he'd done during the weeks I'd been gone. Her hull was freshly waxed, her sails neatly flaked, even her lines exactingly coiled. She looked as new, as energized, as Rex appeared himself, and as I turned toward him, his mouth met mine, and we half-stumbled, half-crawled down the companionway into the salon. There I lay back on the spotless settee, let him tug off my jeans. Closed my eyes to better feel the good weight of his body. The fit of his hip against my own. The curve of his neck. His firm, freckled shoulders. 'Too many clothes,' he said, sitting back to strip away his shorts and T-shirt. Both of us naked in the afternoon light, new lovers, suddenly shy. My upper chest still bore plum-colored markings from places where the poisonwood rash had burned deepest: a painted necklace, a faded tattoo.

'Souvenirs,' Rex murmured, tracing them with his fingers. Then he bent down to kiss me again, his warm breath melting away the weeks of dark, Wisconsin cold.

Afterward, we let the fading sunlight lap the heat from our skins, and when Rex got up to pour us each a glass of wine, I noted it, but did not object. A glass of wine at five in the afternoon was not a double shot of Scotch. Besides, it was red wine. Good for the heart. Certainly, it was good for the disposition. Rex did not ask about Toby's wedding. He did not ask about the settlement. The hard knot of caution in my stomach uncoiled. Once again, we were floating, disconnected, from the dream that had been our lives onshore.

'You ought to see *Nantucket*'s wine cellar,' Rex said, sitting back down beside me. 'Another good reason to buddy-boat.'

'They have a wine cellar?'

'They have everything. World phone. E-mail. Bread maker. I'm serious! They've even got a washing machine. Okay, so it barely holds three pairs of jeans. But, still.' He balanced his cool, plastic cup on my bare thigh. 'They don't own a single thing anywhere else in the world. Nothing to worry about except what's in front of them. Nothing to tie them down, hold them back.'

'No tenants,' I said. 'Did you get my e-mail about Chester?'

'I did.'

'You were right about the house,' I said. 'I think we should go ahead and sell it.'

'You serious?' He jumped to his feet, began to pace the narrow salon. 'God, what a relief it will be, getting out from under that thing! And with the money we can—' He paused, and both of us listened. A dingy had been approaching; now it idled off our stern. 'Probably Jack and Nancy. I'd already invited them for dinner. Are you up for it?'

'Sure,' I said, and I ducked into our stateroom to change into shorts and a fresh T-shirt. Overhead, I could hear the exchange of voices; after a moment, *Chelone* rocked with the weight of additional bodies coming on board. There'd be plenty of time to catch up, I figured, when Rex and I were on our way to Tobago. There'd be more than enough opportunities, then, to answer all the questions he still hadn't asked.

Rex was laughing as I stepped up into the cockpit to shake hands, first with Nancy, then with Jack, who stood with his foot propped on a large, thumping cooler.

'Show Meg,' Rex said.

'Sure,' Jack said, and he lifted his foot. 'Can't hurt to have a second opinion. We caught this little sweetie off Scotland Point. I was just asking Rex if he thinks we ought to eat it.'

'Dare you,' Rex said.

'I can't even look at that thing,' Nancy said.

All of them were watching me now. Jack cracked the lid; I peeked inside. 'Good god. What *is* it?'

'Beats me,' Jack said.

It looked like a snake, only thicker. With fins. Fierce bristles jutted from its gills. It smelled unpleasantly of its own oily skin, and I watched for a moment as it writhed and snapped. Beneath it, under a layer of ice, three wide-eyed grouper lay gulping, astonished.

Nancy said, 'Have you ever seen anything like it?'

We hadn't. It wasn't even pictured in our field guide. Perhaps it was something old and undiscovered. Perhaps it was something mutant and new. We flipped it back over the side, where it lay, briefly, on the surface. Then it dove with a furious splash and disappeared.

For dinner, we grilled the grouper, along with plantains and zucchini Rex had bought from a local garden, fresh coconut he'd picked up along the trails. Jack opened the special bottle of wine he'd been saving, he said, for my return, and we ate in the cockpit, plates balanced on our knees, talking as if we'd all known one another for years. I had to keep reminding myself, in fact, that we'd just met.

'How long have you been cruising?' I asked.

'Five years,' Nancy said. 'Our kids think we've lost our minds.'

'They're worse than parents,' Jack said, rolling his eyes. 'Always worrying. Always trying to tell you what you should and should not do.'

After drawing a bucket of salt water, Nancy and I put the dishes to soak and climbed up onto the cabin top, leaving Rex and Jack exchanging war stories: rough crossings, knock-downs, lightning storms. For a while, she and I talked about places we'd lived, jobs we'd held, people we'd known. I was tired from the travel, from the unaccustomed wine. I was find-ing it difficult to concentrate. Everything shimmered with an odd déjà vu: the easy intimacy, the sounds of the cove, the men opening another bottle of red wine. Every now and then, we'd be treated to the voices of the Men's Historical, Cultural and Sociological Expedition Society, still going strong at the dockside bar, bellowing rounds of 'Row, Row, Row Your Boat'.

'At first, we went back to Rhode Island twice a year,' Nancy said, 'but now it's been – what? Three years, at least.'

'You must miss your children.'

'Actually, Jack's daughter was just here. She stayed with us a week.' Nancy laughed. 'She says she couldn't live anywhere that doesn't have a Starbucks.'

'She wouldn't like Fox Harbor either,' I said. 'Though I suppose they're going to have one, too, eventually.'

'Did you have a good visit? Rex said your brother got married *outside*. It must have been absolutely freezing.'

'On a boat, no less. Did he tell you that part?'

'So it runs in the family, I see.'

'Actually,' I said, 'if you'd told me, even two years ago, that I'd be living on a boat someday—' I shook my head.

'Your husband's idea? It was the same with Jack and me.'

'We'd talked about it now and then, but more in a daydreaming kind of way. But then, after our son was killed, we decided we wanted a change.'

Was it my imagination, or did the twilight murmurings of the cove suddenly sharpen into dozens of harsh, individual sounds? Idling engines, slapping waves. The chime of loose sheets blown against *Chelone*'s rigging. The quarrel of parrots, roosting in the palm trees along the shoreline. I glanced at Rex. He and Jack had switched to rum, and the sweet smell hung in the air. For a moment, I was confused, thinking it was Eli Hale who'd been calling, *Mayday! Mayday!* – the punch line of some joke – but then I remembered Nancy, saw the look on her face, distressed, uncertain, and I realized what I'd done. Of course, Rex would not have said anything about Evan. I'd forgotten myself, forgotten who I was, who I was supposed to be.

'I'm so sorry,' Nancy said. 'I didn't know. Rex never said anything about it.'

'It's hard to talk about,' I said.

'How did he die?'

The question surprised me. In Fox Harbor, of course, everybody knew. 'In a car accident. I was driving him to school.'

'And you don't have any more children?'

By now, I would have done anything to take my own words back. 'We had him late in life.'

'You could adopt, you know. I have this friend, she's forty-eight? She just got a beautiful little girl from China.'

I must have stared at her. I simply couldn't speak.

'Well, you should think about it, that's all I'm saying,' Nancy said, and now she was talking too rapidly, too eagerly. 'I could give you her e-mail address, if you wanted it. What?' Abruptly, she turned her face, her entire body, toward the men, and I saw that they were looking at us, waiting for an answer to their question.

'The beach,' Rex said, and Jack said, 'How about it? Great night for a swim.'

Nancy was already on her feet. 'Sounds good to me,' she said. 'Meg?' But she didn't look at me, never looked at me again, tripping lightly down from the cabin top.

'I'm beat,' I said. 'I think I'll stay in. But you all go ahead.'

'You sure?' Rex studied me curiously. 'Okay, then. Get some sleep.'

His good-bye kiss was brief, bitter with rum.

* * *

After everyone had gone, I unpacked my backpack, took a bucket bath, fixed myself a cup of tea in the thick, clear plastic glass that Rex had liked to use for Scotch. By now, the sun was setting, so I lit the kerosene lamps, fitted the screens across the hatches to keep out the mosquitoes and night-flying beetles. Then I found the swollen paperback I'd started back in December, but after a few minutes, I put it down again, carried my tea up onto the cabin top, and sat there in the darkness, swatting bugs. Wavering bursts of torchlight carried from the dock, where the Men's Historical, Cultural and Sociological Expedition Society had started in on military cadences: *I know-a-girl named Bet-ty Sue!* My body felt sticky with salt residue. Wisps of hair clung to my temples. Making love had left me sore, and I wished that I could take a proper bath, soak for a while beneath a thick quilt of bubbles, before climbing into a wide, clean bed.

I couldn't be friends with Nancy now, any more than she could be friends with me. Buddy-boating was out of the question. Already, I could feel Rex's disappointment.

The cloud cover pulled into soft, cotton pieces. A half moon filled the air with its milky light.

That fish was weird, Evan said.

I should have taken a picture, I said.

That lady's kind of weird, too.

I nodded. *Foot-in-mouth disease.*

What's that?

It's when you just keep going on with something, making things worse and worse. It's when you can't just admit that you were wrong.

It was midnight by the time Rex returned to *Chelone*, cutting the dingy motor and rowing in, out of courtesy, assuming I was asleep. Climbing into the cockpit, he literally jumped when he saw me, then staggered back, laughing at himself. 'I didn't think you'd be up,' he said.

'Me neither.'

Rex sat down beside me, picked up my empty cup. 'Found the scotch, I see,' he said.

'It was peppermint tea,' I said. 'I thought you got rid of the scotch.'

'Just a little social lubrication,' he said. 'Nothing wrong with that, Meg. Looks like you could have used some yourself tonight.' He was studying my face. 'You and Nancy got awfully quiet all of a sudden.'

Somewhere in the cove, a heron croaked.

'I told her about Evan.'

He sighed. 'I figured it was something like that.'

'I've spent the past month with people who know. I'm not used to keeping secrets.'

'That's not exactly true, now, is it?'

'What do you mean?'

'When, exactly, were you planning to tell me you didn't sign the settlement?'

I glanced at him sharply, then looked away. Of course, Rex

would have spoken to Arnie at least once, courtesy of Jack's world phone.

'She's already declared bankruptcy,' I said. 'She's lost the house. Lost pretty much everything, in fact. I just don't see the point—'

'People like that,' Rex said, 'always want you to believe they are on the brink of ruin. She's got cash squirreled away, you can bet on it.'

'I don't think so,' I said. 'I talked with her about it.'

'You shouldn't have done that.'

Again, the heron croaked, coughed. Something splashed in the water, and I thought of that terrible unnamed fish, circling beneath us.

'Everything seemed different, once I was actually there,' I said. 'Once I was interacting with people. It's hard to see someone the way that you do when you're staring at a piece of paper. Or looking at a photograph. Or even just imagining things inside your head.'

To my surprise, Rex took my hand. 'I know,' he said. His voice was unexpectedly gentle, and, for a moment, I thought he understood. But then he said, 'Let's just put the question aside again, okay? Nothing has to be decided now. The statute of limitations gives us plenty of time—'

'Listen to me.' I spoke slowly, deliberately, each word a step that could not be retraced. 'I saw Cindy Ann repeatedly. I've talked with her on the phone. She's apologized, Rex, she's sorry, and she really has stopped drinking—'

'Don't fall for it,' he said, and now there was nothing of gentleness left, as if somewhere inside him a plug had been pulled, allowing everything soft, yielding, beloved, to drain away. 'Her attorney's been coaching her, that's all. You're losing sight of the facts, Meg, and that facts are that she killed our child, and there is nothing on this earth that she or anybody else can do or say—'

'I know,' I said. 'I know. That's why I had to forgive her.'

He leapt to his feet with surprising grace, stood towering over me like an animal. By the light of that half-shadowed moon, I could see how much he wanted to hit me, *hurt* me, a look I recognized instantly, though I'd never seen it before. In the slow eternity of that moment, I listened to the last, stubborn survivors of the Men's Historical, Cultural and Sociological Expedition Society fighting their way through a school bus round of 'Ninety-nine Bottles of Beer on the Wall'. Then, without warning, he spun away, stepped down onto the port side deck, dove overboard into the cove. I watched the sleek, dark shine of his head, moving toward the dock, until I couldn't see anything more. My face, when I touched it, burned as if he'd struck me.

That night, sleeping in the cockpit – I could not bring myself to lie down in our berth – I dreamed that Cindy Ann and I were stepping, once again, through the doors at Twin Lakes. Only this time, we were forced to plunge, headfirst, through solid glass. I woke up. It was just past dawn; Rex had not returned. I wanted to tell him about the dream, but then I remembered that, of course, I could not. I sat up, my entire body slick with morning damp, and I thought about all the secrets I'd have to keep. Even if Rex did let the suit go, I could never reveal what I'd begun to feel for Cindy Ann, a connection as irrevocable, as inexplicable, as kinship. I would have to sacrifice the very thing that would enable me, finally, fully, to survive.

Looking back, I see I could not have stayed married to my anger any longer than I did. And yet, for the next three days, I tried. Rex, in his way, tried as well. He returned to *Chelone* the following afternoon as if nothing out of the ordinary had happened. Together, we worked on the whisker poles. We checked through-hulls, plotted a course to Tobago, reviewed lists of provisions, supplies. Twice, we even made love, without speaking; afterward, we held each other as if we might physically find a way to reconnect our lives. But each night, after supper, when he dingied over to *Nantucket* for a drink, we both pretended it wasn't a relief to everyone that I chose to stay behind. And when, at last, a weather window opened, and *Chelone* followed *Nantucket* out of the cove, Rex pulled up alongside the ferry dock – never quite stopping – so that I could step ashore.

I suppose I still believed, watching the two boats raise their sails, that, eventually, Rex would grow tired of it. I suppose I still was telling myself that, sooner or later, he'd be ready to come home. Even now, there is a part of me that still waits for him, expects him to return, in the same way I keep expecting Evan.

Last fall, shortly after the divorce was finalized, I sold the house and moved to Florida, where I bought a condo in Coral Gables, found work at a local accounting firm, set about starting life over again at the age of fifty-two. Just before the move, I spoke to Rex for the last time. He'd called – as he still did once in awhile – to let me know where he was, how he was doing. This time, he'd made it as far as Panama. He was on a lengthy wait-list to pass through the canal. I told him about my plans, and he said, 'I just can't picture you in Florida,' and I said, 'I can't really picture you in Panama, either,' and then neither one of us knew what to say. Our attempts at conversation usually ended just this way. I didn't really want details about his life and who else might be sharing it. Nor did he want to hear about my life and its inevitable intersections: Toby and Mallory, Cindy Ann and her girls.

It isn't that I don't get angry anymore, sad anymore, because I do. I work at forgiveness every day, in the same way that Cindy Ann works at her sobriety. Stretches of time pass, and it's effortless, easy, until – without warning – it isn't.

The only person who truly understands this, I think, is Cindy Ann.

The night after Toby phoned to tell me about Mal's pregnancy, I woke up from a dream in which I'd climbed into their baby's crib and disassembled her as cleanly, as neatly, as Evan once took apart his Mr Potato Head. One by one, I fed each piece to the snake fish writhing beneath my feet. For days, the dream stayed with me, clung like sour air. And yet, when Sadie was finally born – dark-haired and violet-eyed – I was on a plane within twenty-four hours, my mother sitting beside me, her grip nearly breaking my fingers as the plane touched down in Milwaukee.

We found Cindy Ann at the hospital with Mallory; Toby, exhausted, had gone home to sleep. Mal had labored twenty hours before agreeing to the C-section. She tried to turn the baby for us to see, then grimaced, shook her head. It was Cindy Ann who finally lifted Sadie from her sister's bed, extended her toward my mother and me, trembling, not knowing which one of us was going to step forward first.